TROUBLE IN HARLON COUNTY

TROUBLE IN HARLON COUNTY

BOOK ONE
THE PURSUERS

Charles Paul Reed Jr.

Storybook Adventures LLC

This novel is dedicated to my friend Bobbie Lee Huff, who I jokingly accused of being a Civil War Veteran, and with whom I spent many hours solving the world's problems, and to whom I read this book before his passing.
Cover Art by Bryant Hastie with all rights to Charles Paul Reed Jr. Storybook Adventures LLC

Cover design by Pepper Reed

I very much appreciate the assistance of the following individuals who read and provided valuable input for every aspect of this novel.
(in alphabetical order)
Gary Buscombe
Mark Church
Martha Weatherl

Also, by Charles Paul Reed Jr.
Mission in Harlon County – Second Novel in the *Pursuers Series.*
Justice in Harlon County – Third Novel in the *Pursuers Series*
Tracks to Harlon County-*Twenty-one Tales of Life and Adventure,* The Pursuers Series
The Long Caper, A time-travel novel to 1865 Harlon County.

1

Northern Alabama April 1865. The artillery battery arrived a day late, and apparently, they were in a hurry to get fired up. That was a good thing because the Rebels upstream had been reinforced, and the additional men might have turned the tide as they advanced along the creek bottom, throwing lead at anything that moved.

A Union private stood ten yards in front of the cannon, waving the last men into camp with shouts to hurry up. Coming up on the man, Corporal Robert Gracey felt too tired even to growl for him to keep his shirt on as he carried his human burden out of the creek bottom past the wheeled guns. After standing in place a moment to catch his breath, he headed toward the medical tent. Corporal Gracey, known as Preacher by his friends, was an ordained minister of the Baptist Church. Slip-sliding as he stumbled along, he had carried Lieutenant Adams on his shoulders across the algae-covered river rock for over a mile. The young officer was gut shot and near death with half of his knee blown away.

Private Bronco Brumley was not far behind, with Sergeant Madison Jones holding on to his coat-tail. Sarge had been blinded by rock shrapnel when a Rebel's round struck a boulder and threw particles of quartz into his eyes. The two men had scarcely passed the impatient artillerymen when the first volleys of grapeshot from the guns ripped through the thickets that filled the creek bed, shredding foliage and any persistent Rebel soldiers alike. After a few volleys from the cannon, the Rebels ceased to return fire. Bronco led the blinded sergeant into their campsite, and he and Sarge sprawled to the ground. Their immediate concern was washing the sharp particles from Sarge's eyes before even taking time to catch their breath.

While Bronco and Sarge collapsed to the ground behind him, Preacher reached the medical tent and deposited the young lieutenant on the ground for a medical orderly to look over. Looking down at his friend, the corporal didn't hold much hope. Preacher's thick, powerful legs were bloodied and bruised from dozens of spills while carrying the young man. He set his big jaw stoically and waited. He was of a modest height with big hands, a stout, muscular body, and a sizeable square-cornered head covered with light brown hair under his Union cap. His was a big, gap-tooth smile, but his features now were grim while he waited. The orderly confirmed his worst fears. The Corporal leaned over and rubbed his knees as he looked at the young man for the last time. The Lieutenant looked pale and defenseless in death, and Preacher felt almost as bad.

There was nothing for him to do but go back to camp and report to his friends that Lieutenant Adams was lost. With the final determination of the lieutenant's condition, Preacher's concern turned to Sarge's eyes. There was a good chance that his injuries would be permanent.

As far as he could tell, young Private Bronco Brumley seemed to be the least injured of the three. The young private had joined them just as two mini balls found the young lieutenant. For a moment, Preacher considered the timing, as the loss of one young man had coincided with the arrival of another. Preacher often found ties between events that eluded others. He found purpose, whereas others found coincidence. One thing was sure. Based on his performance this day, the private was the best shot with a rifle that Preacher had ever seen.

Preacher stood for a few moments outside the medical tent and tried to push aside the death and pray his thanks for another day's survival. Then he raised his bowed head to observe the rapid arrival of a courier headed for the Company Headquarters' tent. Like others nearby, Preacher followed in that direction. The courier would have a report of the latest news after his delivery to the company commander.

Preacher was moving slowly in deference to his sore knees as the rider jumped from the saddle and entered the tent with saddlebag in tow. A commotion seemed to follow the courier's entry, for the guard stuck his head inside through the flaps. Then the man quickly withdrew before the captain stepped outside. The rider and other officers followed. Preacher saw the senior officer look to the heavens. The sun was coming out as he raised his arms overhead and shook them in jubilation. Something was afoot. Preacher increased his pace until almost within hearing range, and a soldier closer to the action passed back the news. Preacher moved forward until he had the gist of it, then headed back to his campsite as rapidly as his sore legs permitted. He arrived at his camp, physically beaten, his heart heavy over the death, yet euphoric with his news. The words seemed to echo in his head through fatigue and pain. He found Sarge and Bronco.

"Well, boys, the war's over."

"What?" Men within hearing range sprang to their feet and gathered around him.

"The war's over." Preacher addressed the groups of men who had been crouched around fires drying out. There was almost a stampede as an audience rapidly coalesced around him. The words were so beautiful that he repeated them. "The war is over. I was over at the medical tent with Lieutenant Adams. A courier just blew in. Lee surrendered at Appomattox a week ago!"

The men went crazy. Preacher turned away from the celebration and dropped down on an ammo box next to Sarge. "Lieutenant Adams didn't make it. He never even got looked at by the sawbones." Preacher appraised Sarge's injuries. "How are the eyes?"

"Well, I can see you, but they still sting like the dickens." Sarge picked up a stick and twirled it absently in his fingers. He squinted at Bronco through bloodshot eyes. "I guess you didn't know him, but he was a good man and officer." The tall sergeant nodded, "Well, you know, even if he didn't bleed to death first, the sawbones could have killed him taking off that leg. And if he survived the surgery, an infection could have finished him off. What makes me sick is that he is probably one of the last Union men to die in a damn war that was already over. For what?"

Preacher stared off in the distance. "I guess it was his time. We all have our time." He said no more. Sometimes words were an inadequate tool for acknowledging, let alone understanding, the plans of the Almighty.

"Where was he from?" Bronco was torn between the jubilation that the war was over and sad regard for the loss just suffered by his two companions.

"West Virginia," Sarge said. "His family was part of the underground railroad, helping slaves escape the south for several years."

"I never did ask him how he ended up in this outfit. Most of the boys here are from further west," Preacher said.

"He was in a military school in Indiana when the war broke out." Sarge took out his bandana, wiped his forehead, and squinted his injured eyes. "I'm whipped."

Bronco watched the older men work their way through their loss. He could see they had little room for joy on the day they had lost a friend. Many of the men around the nearby fires were clapping each other on the back. A group of three were hugging. One man raised his weapon as if to fire in the air, but a junior officer motioned him to put it away.

"Dang!" Bronco sprang to his feet. "I haven't been in the army for a full year yet, and now the war is over! When that horse buyer came by old Mister Jacob's place back in Ashville, Ohio, right after the old man passed away, he said the army needed wranglers. So, I went with him and the horses. Then, after I joined up, they said, since I already had my Henry rifle, they'd put me in this infantry company because I was ready to fight."

"Welcome to the army," Sarge said with a flicker of a smile.

"Do you know what happens now?" Bronco looked at Preacher.

"I don't know a lot, but I understand that some regiments got the news a week ahead of us. They're disbanding right and left by now." Preacher rubbed his sore legs. "They say we can head home once we draw our pay."

Bronco looked off into the distance. He wondered where his home was now? Ohio seemed far away. His grandparents were gone, and since Sam Jacobs, his old boss, had passed away, there didn't seem to be a point in going back there. Bronco looked at the two men and felt a sense of kinship though he had known them only for a few hours. He had decisions to make.

2

The news that the war was over left the camp elated but unsettled. They would be paid and receive their discharge documents. In the meantime, the men attended to their amusements. Several impatient soldiers picked up and walked off without their papers or pay. Others resorted to playing cards for hours on end.

"Hey, Sarge!" Bronco waved at the older man and motioned him over.

Sarge approached the group of men crowded around a wide board lying across two logs. As he got closer, he saw a little man wearing a bowler hat, moving his hands around the table in circular and figure-eight patterns. When he raised his hands, Sarge could see three identical objects that looked like large thimbles lying in a row. A short Irishman pointed at one of the thimbles. The "shell man" lifted it. There was nothing underneath, and the crowd groaned again. The "shell man" smiled, raised another of the thimbles to show the pea underneath, and picked up a couple of dimes.

They could see a stir among the men. Those who lost their wagers moved away from the table so that new betters could take their places. It was evident that the new players, after observing the play, were confident that they had the scheme worked out. New dimes dropped to the end of the board. Once again, the man lifted a thimble to show the location of the pebble. Once again, the thimbles quickly moved in their circular route before stopping with a grand flourish. A finger pointed. Then the thimble lifted to expose the bare board. A groan came from the crowd.

"I've already lost my dime," Bronco admitted to Sarge with a grin. He didn't seem to mind too much. "How does he do it?"

Sarge watched more dimes drop at the end of the board. "I don't know for sure, but sleight-of-hand is involved. A lot can happen while the thimbles are out of sight."

Bronco nodded. "He is good, isn't he?"

Sarge smiled. "I expect he'll leave camp with quite a bit more money than the rest of us." He looked around at the half-abandoned campsites.

Preacher joined them and watched for several more rounds. But, standing on the sidelines, none of the three could correctly locate the pea. "I've heard of sleight of hand, but this is ridiculous," Preacher said. "I think a wild-assed guess is as good as trying to follow the shells."

After eight days of restless waiting, the separation day the soldiers had been waiting for finally arrived. Preacher tucked his wad of greenbacks and the discharge documents into his coat's front inner pocket and joined Sarge, who was no longer sporting a bandage on his cheek. Miraculously the injured man reported that his eyesight was back to normal. Bronco hefted his pack. Sarge and Preacher wore most of their uniforms, combined with some civilian clothes. Preacher had spent over an hour washing the congealed blood out of his coat and pants. He threw ragged uniform parts into the fire. Anything they didn't wear, they would have to carry. That thought was in everyone's mind. The smell of burning wool was strong in the breeze.

Bronco walked up, counting his wages. He wore his full uniform. It was newer than Sarge and Preacher's, and he had no civilian clothes available. All three still wore their Union caps. He regarded the older men. He had no idea what to do next. He thought a lot about the long walk to Ohio and was aching to go somewhere else, but he hadn't nailed anyplace down. Job-wise, he knew he could do what he did best just about anywhere there were wild horses. The short supply of horses after the war suggested going west. He had heard stirring stories of western cow towns. San Francisco was already famous, but it was on the far side of the country and was even more remote than Ohio for a man on foot.

Because casualties were heavy in Bronco's squad, as in many others, the units had combined on the fly during the last skirmish. Bronco learned that Sarge and Preacher had done some heavy fighting over their two years together. Now, that chapter was closed. With their departure imminent, the question loomed more critical than ever. Bronco edged closer to the older men. "Where you headed next, Sarge?"

The tall, dark-haired man with intense eyes looked different in his partial civilian outfit. His wrinkled civilian coat had been fashionable four years before.

"Right off, I'm thinking of New Orleans." Sarge looked over from tying the straps on his pack.

"Why New Orleans?" Bronco leaned closer.

"Well, it is the first stop going west." Sarge shrugged. "Before the war, New Orleans was one of the three most prosperous cities in the country. I'm considering that I'd like to try out a passage on a Mississippi riverboat. But, when you get right down to it, I guess I want to be a step away from this." He motioned to the rapidly emptying camp around him.

Preacher leaned toward Sarge. "You still planning on that little side trip we talked about?" He glanced around at some departing men. The tone of his voice hinted at a conspiracy.

Bronco was cleaning his Henry rifle. He glanced from one man to the other. He had picked up on the remark.

Sarge saw Bronco's interest and motioned the two men closer. They both leaned in. "Here's how it stands, Bronco. We are only eighty miles from my family farm over in Georgia. Like a lot of people, my father had little trust in banks. So whenever he came into some gold, he planted it under fenceposts around the farm. So I figure that with a little educated searching, we will be able to scrounge up more than a little stake money toward expenses heading west."

"Gold?" Where did he get gold? The only gold Bronco had heard about was west rather than east. The young soldier was mystified.

Sarge glanced around to be sure no one else was in hearing range. "Well, we had a gold rush in our part of Georgia for a short time. It mainly was placer gold. They tried to mine it, but the mines played out pretty quickly. My father was an industrious man. He never invested much time in gold prospecting, but the opportunity was right outside his back door. He considered himself a farmer, not a prospector. His discoveries added up over the years as he never converted the nuggets he accumulated into cash. He showed me where he buried several pokes, and I'm planning on digging it up to pay for the trip west. It's my inheritance. I just didn't get around to collecting it until now."

"Sounds like kind of a treasure hunt." Bronco's voice rose. "That's interesting! Reckon I could go?"

Sarge smiled. He liked this skinny kid with curly hair and dead aim with a Henry rifle. Sarge gingerly touched his fingers to the area where the fragments of quartz had abraded his cheeks. In truth, he felt more than a bit indebted. His eyes were still a little bloodshot, but the swelling had subsided after more than a week since he had come in holding Bronco's coattails. "Might as well. Something tells me you'd be a good man to have along." He eyed the rifle in Bronco's lap.

Preacher nodded in agreement. The war was over, but the friction that had escalated the country into war had not disappeared. There were still gangs on the loose looking for booty. He knew that as Union soldiers traveling through the South, they could always be targets.

That evening, they participated in the jokes and funny stories of people met, and close calls survived, balanced with battles fought and comrades lost. They joined the other men in packing their gear and leaving camp the following day. Many of the men were from the same communities and were traveling home together, knowing they'd have to make heartbreaking reports to their friends' families. Even though hundreds of letters had already made that journey before them to break the sad news, families would want to know more details. Perhaps the most heartbreaking story of all was that too often, after significant battles, the dead filled mass graves, and their remains might never be recovered and identified. Somehow for many of the men, there was not so much glory in surviving as resignation.

"I sure wish I had a good horse." Bronco lamented. He watched as a passing horse kicked up its heels in reaction to the excitement it sensed around it.

"They are in short supply and may be for a while," said Preacher.

"I'd even ride a mule." Bronco grinned. "I never thought I'd say that."

Preacher smiled, "Mules are pretty dependable. They need less water, eat less, and can pack more. You just have to get used to their gait. It's true that there can be a lot of starting and stopping. They require patience, but they are good for the long haul."

"I'm still trying to get used to my own gait. I'm mighty glad to be out of the infantry for all the good it does me." Bronco slapped a muscular thigh. Just then, a man walked by with crutches and a wrapped stump. His leg was missing at the knee. The three men exchanged silent glances.

"Some of us are blessed with better scripts than others," Preacher said, seeing Bronco's expression. "All we can do is be thankful for what we have."

"Preacher," Bronco looked at the powerful older man with a candid philosophical outlook. "Are you really a Preacher?"

Preacher grimaced, then hefted his pack. "That is a long story best told around a campfire. Ask me again sometime."

The three men queued up for their sacks of food items, mostly hardtack and dried meat, and a small sack of green coffee beans at the supply wagon. The army had tried issuing ground coffee but found that the intermediaries along the supply line took advantage of the opportunity to dilute the product. It was not unusual for sawdust and other fillers to find their way into the ground coffee. So, the army changed tactics and issued green coffee beans, leaving the men to devise their own ways to utilize them. Each man filled two canteens. By eight o: clock, they were ready to travel.

3

At first, the three men headed due east before taking a road southeast toward their destination. Only a few of those leaving camp took the same route initially. Most headed north to Illinois, Indiana, and Ohio. Depending on what awaited them, some of the men exhibited good spirits. Others trudged ahead as if their destination spelled doom. There were lots of Rebels traveling through from the north and west. Only a few rode horses. Of the latter, both riders and mounts appeared to be done-in. The negroes traveling in groups of two or three usually headed north. Most of the blacks were men, but sometimes they traveled in families with children of all ages. They were a rag-tag lot. As enslaved people, most had enjoyed few personal possessions. In many respects, the condition of their apparel mirrored the state of the uniforms of white Confederate soldiers heading in the other direction.

How many men had died, Bronco wondered? Since his first days, there had been rumors that hundreds of thousands had died during the years of war. How could there be that many men in the world, let alone that many dead? Bronco had never seen a large town until he traveled through Columbus with the horse trader to an enlistment station. Growing up in a remote Ohio community, he had never seen a black man until he entered more metropolitan regions. While standing on a Columbus, Ohio street, he observed black people hurrying about their business. He remembered staring at the first black child sitting on a bench with its mother. The boy seemed so small and fragile. The child wanted something that its mother refused. The little boy kept wanting it until the mother grabbed him and walked away. How was that exchange different from similar interactions he often saw between white children and parents? He heard a drunk in a store once spouting off about negroes being inferior and not even human. Yet what he had just observed belied that claim. What he had observed proved to him that they were only people. It spoke forcefully in support of common humanness.

That night the men hunkered down around a small campfire. Preacher took out his pouch of green coffee beans and portioned some into cups extended by Bronco and Sarge and finally his own. He placed his cup of beans on some embers to roast. The others did the same. From time to time, they turned them until they were brown all around. Then each man used the blunt end of his bayonet to hammer them into as fine a grit as time and patience would allow. Although they were a reasonable distance off the main road, Sarge knew the fire could draw both friends and foes. As the highest-ranking man, he felt responsible for his friends even though his official duties were over. Once they were through fragmenting their coffee beans, they poured in hot water. Soon they were nursing their coffee. Unless they counted their beans and obtained the same mix and size of granules, every cup tasted slightly different.

Bronco turned toward the lean, broad-shouldered man whose face sometimes seemed to scowl at inner reflections. "How did you end up in the army, Sarge? You mentioned that you have a farm?"

"Well, my family had a farm, and I had a good reason for leaving. It may be a longer story than you want to hear. I was the third generation on that property, and I didn't take leaving it lightly. My grandfather got his land from the Creek Indians, who once owned most of Georgia. There had been a series of treaties made and broken mostly by white men, and finally, a Creek chief named MacIntosh signed off on a final treaty for his land in our part of the state."

"Sounds like they forced him to give up his land?" Bronco scowled. He had met a Shawnee Indian once in Ohio.

"I think Chief MacIntosh saw the end coming for his people in Georgia one way or another. There was a lot of squabbling among the Creeks. Some chiefs were ready to continue fighting for their land to the death. Those in the north Indian lands refused to participate in more treaties with white governments. They threatened to kill any other chiefs who agreed to sign treaties in the future. I think Chief MacIntosh saw that he would likely lose any future battles, and any resistance would result in more of his tribe dying. Maybe he thought he could negotiate a better deal at that point than he could after losing another war. In any event, he did sign a new treaty ceding a lot of territory to whites. Some of the Creek chiefs in the north put a death sentence on his head, which resulted in two northern Creeks attacking and killing him."

"So, the tribes were at war with each other," Bronco said.

"Well, their tribal squabbles intensified into killing from time to time, so I guess that qualifies as war. And from what I've read, conflicts among the tribes continue further out west where they migrated by force of arms."

"So, your grandfather got the land...." Bronco's voice trailed off.

"So, my grandfather got the land. He was already in his fifties. He got his small house built. He started growing hay and got a few cows. Timber was and is still the most important industry in that part of the state. He planted a little cotton. Then he got yellow fever and died within a week."

"Then your father got the property." Bronco guessed out loud.

"Yes, my father was the only surviving son. He expanded the farm to twice the size he inherited, and I lived there until I was pretty much grown. He built the big house that I hope is still there today. There were two boys and three girls. All three girls died before they were five years old. My brother, Tom, is four years older than me. When we got older, we worked with my father to harvest lumber, start a sawmill, build up the herd, and put in more cotton acres. Tom is a big man. He is over six feet tall, like my father. Tom is almost as strong as Preacher and was always the best worker in the county. My father sometimes loaned us, boys, out to neighboring farmers for short periods when we got caught up." Bronco kept probing.

"Then, you upped and joined the Union Army?"

"Well, not exactly. I was seventeen when my father died. He left the farm to my older brother. Naturally, I would have preferred that he pass down part of it to me." Sarge's face showed pain for a moment, then he continued. "There is an old English common law called primogeniture that requires land be left automatically to the oldest son. Primogeniture was abolished in Georgia in 1777 with the state constitution. But even so, there is still support for the principle of leaving the homestead land to the oldest son. The purpose of the old law was to limit breaking up properties into smaller units with each generation."

"Okay," Bronco said. He could see that despite his light tone, Sarge was uncomfortable with the subject. He was ready to let it drop.

Sarge continued, unbidden. "In the absence of primogeniture, my father still left the farm to Tom in his will. He left me the caches of gold we are going to recover. Tom has always been very sure of himself and reluctant to accept advice. Once my father was gone, he became even more hardheaded and difficult. It seemed to me that the authority of ownership went to his head. We were constantly at odds. The last straw for me was when Tom decided to sell a slave we called Brownie. He and I were the same age, and the evening before, Tom was supposed to hand him over to a traveling slave trader, Brownie, and I secretly saddled up and headed north. It was such a spur-of-the-moment move that we didn't take anything. All we had were the clothes on our backs and the little money in our pockets. We got away okay, but when we ran out of money, I joined the army out of desperation. Brownie, of course, couldn't join because he was black. Going separate ways was the hardest thing I've ever done. As far as I know, he kept going north. We haven't seen or heard from each other since. That was four years before the war started."

"So, Brownie was one of your slaves."

Sarge shook his head. "Well.... yes." He smiled at Bronco's expression. "When I was young, my father bought a black boy about my age from a neighboring farmer. His name was Brownie. His mother had died, and the owner didn't want to deal with a young child. We grew up together. As far as he and I were concerned, his being a slave wasn't important. I know it seems strange given how things later turned out, but Georgia had an anti-slave tradition early on. It was the last of the original thirteen colonies to permit slavery. Eventually, with the development of substantial cotton and rice plantations in other parts of the state, a considerable amount of Georgia's economy became dependent on slavery. There were more slaves than whites in some counties, and in others like Harlon County, where we lived, only about twenty-five percent of the population were slaves. That may still seem like a lot until you realize how thinly settled the county is." He grinned at Bronco's expression.

"But before you think us more humanitarian than others in the south, you should know it was not because the people were more virtuous, but because the timber industry didn't require near as many hands as cotton farming." He added. "And before obtaining his Creek land, my grandfather owned several slaves in eastern Georgia. So yes, we owned a slave who became one of my best friends."

Sarge's cap hid his face as he bent down to retie his shoe. He looked up. "The truth is, I've been wondering how other parts of the South can survive without slavery. Cotton and rice are very labor-intensive." He looked from Bronco to Preacher. "Not an especially interesting story, but a long one." His face lightened into a smile. "Now, for an interesting story, talk to Preacher!"

Bronco turned toward the stocky man across the campfire. Preacher set his lantern jaw and furrowed his bushy eyebrows. He held up his hands and yawned as he seemed to consider it but turned away. "Not tonight, boys." He waved them off. "I'm ready to turn in."

4

Sarge lay under his blanket and allowed his mind to travel back in time once again to Brownie. He had not told his friends many of the details of his story. The parts he left out were the most important to him.

Sarge's given name was Madison. Before his promotion to the rank of sergeant, Sarge went by his given name. As a youth, he was wiry, long-limbed, and very energetic. His hair was light brown and faded somewhat by exposure to the sun. One morning his father told him that there would be a negro boy arriving that morning. Until then, Madison had not been in close contact with many black people. He had seen some off at a distance in the fields or lumber camps. A few had arrived bringing goods or messages from other farms, but in northwest Georgia, unless you had one or two house servants, there were fewer encounters for a child than might have been the case further east or south. He remembered watching and waiting for the boy to arrive. The boy was kind of an enigma to him. He wondered what the new boy would be like while he waited.

When the wagon arrived, he scrutinized the occupant. This boy was an inch or so taller than Madison. He was staring back at the white youth with pure terror emanating from his face. Just his expression filled Madison with curiosity, for he had no idea what fears lay behind the wide eyes. Only later did Madison piece together the whole story

The black boy also had been informed of his change of address. Two months earlier, the boy's mother, a maid at the wealthy neighboring Ingerstall farm, had died of a fever. There had been a general feeling of loss at her death, shared by the inhabitants of the main house. But as the weeks passed, the whites largely overlooked the boy as other events gained the farm family's attention. It was a slight misadventure that Brownie told Madison about later that Brownie believed turned the spotlight on him and ultimately brought the decision that led to his trip in the wagon to a new place and a new life.

Brownie's color was not a true black. His skin was smooth, clear, and flawless. His name mirrored the color of his skin. It seemed a natural enough name when applied to him. When he was a few weeks old, Mister Ingerstall observed that he was the color of dark chocolate with just an added drop of cream. After that, everyone just called him Brownie. He was younger than the Ingerstall children by many years, and as the only young black child, he had been left to his own devices under the exclusive direction of his mother until her death.

A few weeks after his mother's passing, he played with the hound near the chicken coop. The dog, too, was young and still learning its boundaries. It invented its own games, one of which was chasing chickens who escaped the coop. On one particular day, Brownie accidentally left the gate open when he collected the eggs. The dog chased a chicken back into the coop, which set up such a commotion that Mister Ingerstall felt it necessary to leave his work on the farm's accounts to look into the matter. He quickly assessed the situation and expressed his irritation succinctly. He put the hound in the shed and commanded Brownie to collect the chickens back into the coop, "or I'll skin your hide." As Madison's father explained, the story was that the thought stuck with Mister Ingerstall that Brownie needed more supervision and, minus his mother's services, served no useful purpose on his farm. As a widower, Mister Ingerstall had no one other than two elderly negro house servants to assign the boy's supervision. Thus, he said, he made the decision that brought the boy to the moment when he jumped from the wagon and with palpable fear, joined Madison at the step.

"What's your name?" Madison asked.

"Brownie. What's yours?"

"Madison," he answered, not questioning the origin of the other boy's name for a moment. He could see the nervous shaking of the boy's leg and how his eyes glanced about, trying to take everything in at once.

"My mother and father say you are going to live here now," Madison said. He observed that the words of confirmation seemed to reassure the boy, and some of the terror disappeared from Brownie's eyes. Then, the new boy looked beyond Madison to the lady who had just opened the screen.

"You boys come in; I've made cookies." Mrs. Jones stood in the doorway. She was tall and radiant in the midmorning sun. They leaped to their feet and ran inside. It seemed to Sarge that the shared cookies finally put Brownie's remaining fears to rest. As he lay so many miles and years from that home, Sarge could still smell his mother's cookies. He wondered what had become of Brownie. Then, at last, he slept.

5

At times, the three men came across stretches of road where the remains of horses and mules were lying like cordwood in the fields. They, too, were casualties of war. At times the stench was overwhelming, and the men increased their pace to find better air.

On the second evening of their trek, they camped well off the road as usual. The men used an abundance of caution as they encountered some rough-looking characters during the day. Most of the Rebels they met were pretty despondent, with their uniforms practically in rags and so emaciated they seemed to be on the verge of starvation. All of them eyed the Yankee uniforms with hostile suspicion. Blacks in groups large and small were still traveling both ways, and many seemed lost in their freedom, while others carried themselves with quiet resolve. Rebels who had horses seemed more enlivened even if the horses they rode looked to be on their last legs.

As dusk descended, Bronco and Sarge dropped their gear on the far side of a large log, and Bronco took his rifle into the nearby countryside, hoping to come across a rabbit or two for supper before nightfall. Sarge went off to forage for firewood.

The area nearby was barren of suitable fuel after the passage of earlier travelers. Preacher started to make coffee by generating a small fire with the charred ends of logs from a previous camp. He reflected that no matter how short other provisions were, the Union army did a good job supplying coffee. He was aware that it was a different story in the South. He had heard that soldiers and civilians often needed to rely on grape seeds and other substitutes to make a hot beverage. Intent on his task, Preacher didn't notice the first hoof beats until they were almost on him. Then, he was startled at the sound of a hillbilly's shrill voice.

"Well, look here. We got us a blue-belly making coffee." The man was tall, with a thick, dark beard extending almost to his shirt pocket. He was lean but seemed better fed than some of the other Rebels they had seen on the road. He wore no official uniform. He talked with a whiny, high-pitched voice. The accent told Preacher he was a southerner. He was traveling with two other weather-beaten, fully bearded men slumped in their saddles from fatigue. Preacher waved them toward the fire.

"Get off those nags and bring your cups." A flicker of dread stirred in Preacher's bones, but he motioned the men toward the fire, just starting to flame. "Plenty of coffee as soon as the water is hot."

"Reckon we will, stranger. Coates is my name. John Coates. These two are my cousins, Willard and Sam. But tell me, you're wearing a yank hat, but you sound like you might be from South of the Mason Dixon." He dismounted and moved to the side to tie the horse's reins to a nearby tree.

"Originally from the town of Pumpkin, Missouri," Preacher said. "I was late joining up until well after the shooting started."

He filled the large pot from his canteen to about two inches from the brim and set it in the glowing coals. He stepped closer to the man and stuck out his free hand but dropped it in surprise.

John Coates' gloved fist held a Colt forty-four. *Damn!*

"No call for that." Preacher nodded toward the fire. "I already offered you coffee. Glad to share what little grub I have with you."

"Hospitable of you." Coates allowed. "But I think you Union boys got paid pretty regular, and we didn't. Not that a Confederate dollar has ever bought much. We stole a couple of these nags and some chickens a few days back. Takin', instead of asking, has gotten to be a habit for better than a year. We shouldn't confuse things by getting all friendly-like."

"Horses are scarce, all right. Carcasses line the road between here and Dominion Creek." Preacher said. "Some claim there are more dead horses and mules than dead soldiers." Preacher motioned toward his pack. "It's time to get the coffee out."

Preacher had thrown his belongings down about ten feet from the charred remains of the previous fire. The pack was now almost invisible in the early Spring dusk.

"You might as well put the shooter away," Preacher shouted as he stepped toward his belongings. He waited a moment before continuing. "I'm not stupid enough to take on three men."

"Just drag your gear closer to the fire so I can see you take out the coffee. Boys, find your cups." Coates motioned to Preacher, and then the cousins, who dismounted, secured their horses with his and turned their attention to that task.

Preacher did as ordered. Coates' comments and ready resort to his forty-four sent his nerves to high alert. He quickly extracted his burlap sack of green coffee beans and rough-dumped a little into each man's cup. The men mumbled what he took for thanks and set their cups at the fire's edge to roast the beans. "So, do you intend to rob me, then move on, or shoot me cold?"

"I don't know yet." Coates dropped his weapon into his holster and knelt close to the still young fire. "Captain Owens will be along in a little bit. He tends to be more than a little blood-thirsty. Hard to say how this will go. On the one hand, you've been right hospitable. But, on the other hand, you are a southerner who went with the Yanks."

But even with the shrill danger warning going off in his head, Preacher felt compelled to speak plainly. "I hear Lincoln ordered Grant to welcome you boys back into the Union with no more than another loyalty pledge. Seems pretty generous to me."

"Lincoln's dead," Coates said the words with some satisfaction. He grinned smugly at the shocked expression on Preacher's face. "A rider told us about it this afternoon. But, hear-tell, they are beating the woods for the hero who shot him right now."

6

Preacher dropped down to his sore knees to shuffle the pot of heating water deeper into the flames. His feeling of dread heightened as he tried to absorb the news. He didn't filter his reaction. "Damn! That is sad news. He was a good man. A lot of good men have died in this war. We lost our lieutenant a few days back. It turned out he died after Lee had already surrendered, and the war was over."

"Never met a good Yankee," Coates volunteered. He touched his weapon. Without a word, the other two men settled down near the warmth of the fire. From time to time, they flicked a fingernail against the side of their cups to readjust the position of the browning beans. The light from the flames flickered across their haggard faces.

Preacher, thinking to avoid any unnecessary antagonism from the awaited captain, swiped his Union cap from his head and lay it on the ground. But, unfortunately, he concealed it a few seconds too late. There were hoofbeats and a snort. A fourth man wearing a dirty, ill-fitting Confederate uniform coat with captain's bars rode in and halted behind Coates. Preacher guessed him to be about fifty years old. He was riding a big bay.

If he hadn't been lurching sidewise so severely in the saddle and attended better to his beard, he could have favored Robert E. Lee himself. Peacher observed that the men by the fire pushed themselves to their feet, presumably in a show of respect.

"Why is this Yankee still alive, Coates?" The voice was husky and belligerent. The man looked to be two steps above a derelict. He dismounted awkwardly and stumbled forward to confront the younger Coates.

Even from fifteen feet away, Preacher caught the stink of bark juice and soured sweat. His eyes flitted between Coates, the captain, and the two cousins, who were now nervously fingering the grips of their six guns. Preacher's gun belt was lying near his bedroll, well out of his reach.

"Well, Captain, sir, given that the war is over, I knew you'd want to make that decision." The words were solicitous, but Coates' tone smacked of mock subservience to Preacher.

"War's over when I say it's over." The man attempted to square his shoulders as he put his hand on his weapon.

Coates smiled and was about to follow suit when he felt a tap on his shoulder and heard a click next to his right ear.

"Don't move," Sarge said out of the darkness. He slapped Coates' holster, took out the colt, and shoved it into his belt. The other men moved to reach for their guns but hesitated when they heard another click a few yards to Sarge's right and noticed the glint of a rifle barrel in the firelight.

Preacher intended his warning to sound ominous. He nodded toward the shadowy figure. "My friend with the rifle is a dead shot. That is a fact."

Sarge growled as he nudged Coates' ear with the barrel of his six-gun. "Tell your friends to drop their weapons. "

"The hell!" Belatedly, the captain's consciousness caught up with events. With eyes bloodshot and bulging, he pulled his sidearm awkwardly and whirled toward Sarge and Coates. In an instant, Sarge brought the barrel of his forty-four down hard on Coates' head. The sound reminded Preacher of plunking a watermelon. Then, as Coates slumped, Sarge pivoted right into the business end of the Captain's weapon. The six-gun wavered some as it sharply prodded his forehead. The man was so close that a full breadth of whisky fumes made Sarge light-headed. In his drunken state, the Captain fumbled as he tried to get his thick, gloved finger through the trigger guard. To Preacher, who watched with breath held, the passing seconds felt like death was standing at Sarge's elbow. Preacher readied himself to leap for his gun.

The captain's finger reached the trigger as Sarge's six-gun lingered almost too long under the man's jaw. The captain thumbed the hammer back just as Sarge fired. The flame singed the man's whiskers and sent a slug under the captain's chin. It exited with a bit of hair and bone out the back of his head. The cousins by the fire froze for a second, then reached for their guns. Suddenly, three guns were blazing while Preacher threw himself toward his bedroll.

Bronco's Henry rifle barked once. Cousin Sam lurched and fell, landing face down on his discharging weapon. Cousin Willard had time to pull the trigger once but did not take the time to aim. His round went wild. The rifle barked again, and he dropped, dying across his brother's body.

Preacher rolled clumsily across his bedroll. When he regained his feet, he had his forty-four in hand, but it was over.

"Whew, that was close!" He quickly verified that the two cousins were dead and dropped his firearm back onto his bedroll. With a grunt, he dragged one, then the other man into the brush, out of sight.

Sarge holstered his weapon and looked at his companions and the man on the ground. "Somebody, tie up this one." I'll fix us something to eat," he said matter of factly.

Preacher grabbed the captain by his boots to avoid his bloody clothes and dragged him off out of the firelight.

Bronco patted the bay's head, took hold of the reins, and led it to the small tree where Coates and the cousins had tied their mounts. Then he unsaddled all four horses.

When Bronco returned from his chore, he looked into his kit at his reduced rations. "Sorry, I didn't see any rabbits, fellas."

"Good thing you didn't," Sarge said. "These gentlemen are cold-blooded killers. The report of your rifle would have alerted them that you were out there. They could have ambushed both of us when we came back,"

"I hadn't thought of that." Bronco scowled. "This gold hunting is more dangerous than I thought."

"Seems so." Sarge touched his finger to his lips as a sign for silence and nodded toward Coates, sprawled against a nearby tree. Preacher had propped him up against the trunk with his hands and ankles bound with rawhide cords. He appeared unconscious, but Sarge knew you could never assume anything with vicious animals, including human possums.

7

"Shooting those two that close up was like shooting rabbits while it was happening, but it feels a lot different afterward," Bronco said, pulling his blanket over his shoulders.

"It should feel different afterward." Preacher said. He gave Bronco an understanding nod. "Sometimes, we find ourselves amid storms we did not invite."

Bronco pondered the words a bit as he did much of what Preacher said as he drifted off to sleep. He looked forward to the treasure hunting part of the journey. He hoped that they wouldn't run into any more uninvited storms.

The three men had a restless night. Each checked on Coates whenever their sleep was interrupted. Although the older men had been in numerous close-quarter situations, they were not immune to the crisis of the soul that combat to the death entails.

The following day, they awoke from an uneasy sleep and ate their biscuits with a cup of coffee. Coates, still hogtied, lay against the tree where he had spent the night. He did play possum for a bit, but finally, he let them know he was awake. Bronco gave him a biscuit and poured his leftover coffee into Coates' cup. Coates ate the food eagerly. He had spent a good part of his time during the long night wondering about his ultimate fate at the hands of the Yankees and turncoat southerner. It appeared they were planning to leave him alive, and together with his sense of relief, Coates' anger simmered over his bloodied head.

Bronco and Preacher brushed down the unkempt horses. The men assessed their condition. One had a loose shoe, and Preacher found nails and a hammer in a saddlebag to correct the situation before they saddled up. All of the horses were gaunt from long rides and little grazing time.

As they prepared to leave camp, Sarge walked over to their captive. "We appreciate the horses, Coates. They aren't much other than the bay. I reckon we'll take all four. One could go lame at any time, and besides, we don't need you lurking around our next camp in the middle of the night."

Coates had spent the night considering the deep gash on the top of his head and the smeared blood that spilled down to his chin and neck. By now, it was turning black and crusted. He still seemed pretty groggy.

"You're not going to leave me tied up!"

"Yep, we figure even if you can't get loose right away, one of your kind will come along eventually and get you out of your bindings. You've got your work cut out for you, what with three men to bury if that is what you decide to do. We're taking the horses and the guns, and with a little luck, we'll be permanently free of you."

"I won't be tracking you, Sergeant." Coates' eyes widened in fake sincerity. "I'm headed home as fast as I can get there."

"Good." Sarge stepped away and mounted the rawboned Pinto. "The war is over, Coates. The sooner everyone accepts that fact, the better."

Their ride took them through a portion of the Appalachian Plateau and into the valleys and ridges of the Blue Ridge Mountains. Bronco noticed that the only birds in sight were hawks, vultures, and crows that flew across their path from time to time with chunks of rotting meat in their beaks. He did not want to consider the possibility that some of that flesh could be from the lost carcass of a human. He wondered if the two men he shot would be buried appropriately or left out for nature's scavengers. Did they have a family who would mourn for them? Bronco looked at his two older companions and thought he detected some gloom hanging over them too. He had not known them long, but they both seemed like honorable men. He was appreciative of their willingness to allow him to come along.

After the initial repair work, all four horses seemed fit for the ride ahead. They stopped frequently to give them plenty of rest. Finally, they reached the top of a small overlook, ten miles from their last campsite.

"How far yet, Sarge?" Preacher dismounted and walked off the road to relieve himself and give the bay a breather. They had decided it was logical to put Preacher on the big bay since he was the heaviest man. He let the reins trail. He knew the animal was unlikely to wander. It eagerly attacked a patch of fresh spring grass, well off the road.

"Well, with horses and twenty miles a day, we should be in Georgia in a few days and my homeplace in a couple more,"

Sarge said. "According to the map, Sweetwater Creek is about ten miles away. I don't remember ever being there before. It looks to be a small town. I could sure use a bed for a change."

"So, could I," Preacher said. "And I think Bronco needs to spend some money before he wears it out, counting it." Sarge smiled good-naturedly and nudged Bronco. They rode on and by sunset were on the outskirts of the town, which by the looks of a small clear stream seemed well named.

Considering the threatening looks they encountered all day, they camped in a grove of trees well off the road, and Sarge hiked into town to look the place over. Preacher made a fire. Bronco went hunting. The horses were already livelier from good treatment and fewer miles. They were hobbled close by so they could graze.

After Preacher had worked with the fire for a bit, he heard a gunshot. A bit later, there was another. He smiled and drove two stakes into the ground to hold a spit. The rabbit meat would be a welcome substitute for rations. He looked around the camp area. The previous night's events weighed on him. He felt an undercurrent of uneasiness. This place, like the last, was undoubtedly open to intruders. Perhaps a night under a roof would lessen the tension for all of them.

Bronco came into camp with two rabbits he had already dressed. Preacher pointed at the spit and grinned. "Two shots, two rabbits. You don't waste any ammunition, do you?" The sight of the game already improved his attitude.

"Sorry, I looked to get another one, but these are all I found," Bronco said.

An hour later, Sarge returned with his report. "Population is about fifteen hundred people. General store, livery stable, rooming house, tavern, two churches, typical small town."

"Think it's wise for us to go tripping into town with four horses?" Preacher asked.

"You have a point," Sarge said. "I talked with the gent who runs the livery stable. He said that though he can't guarantee anything, he does sleep in an adjacent room. But it is a risk."

"I could sleep with the horses," Bronco said. "I did that a lot when I was a bronc buster. The bed old man Jacobs had for me was pretty bad." He nodded toward the sky, growing darker overhead. "Looking at those clouds, just having a roof over my head would be good enough for me tonight."

Preacher accepted one of the rabbits and threaded it on the spit.

"Okay," Sarge said. "But let's wait until full dark. The fewer people who know about the horses, the better."

8

As he watched the three men and four horses head off on the short trail back to the main road, John Coates lay quietly in place. Inside, his anger festered. His head was throbbing, and his wrists were skinned bloody from his unsuccessful struggle to release himself during the night. During his short conversation with Sarge, he had managed to contain his anger, but he was furious and humiliated at being taken and hogtied. As a child, he had suffered many similar indignities at the hands of his drunken father and uncles. Once he struggled into adulthood, he determined he wouldn't let that happen again. Even the drunken Captain Owens had accorded him the respect his cunning deserved. He also knew that his Uncle Rufus' response to the news of his cousins' demise would be swift and harsh. John had induced the two men to come on Owen's raiding party, and he would be held responsible for their deaths. As he watched the Yankees depart, his vow of revenge became a mantra repeated apace with his throbbing head. He determined the time would come when he would take sweet retribution on the Yankees and turncoat southerner.

John Coates, geared toward satisfying his most basic physical needs, had little patience for philosophical introspection. In the morning light, he could make out one of Owen's boots in the high weeds to his left. The captain had been a rough customer. Maybe that base meanness was what had drawn him to the glorified outlaw. The older man's instant and cruel mistreatment of almost everyone he encountered inspired Coates. Being an ally of evil rather than a victim seemed highly satisfying. Coates' lesson from his life, including his association with Captain Owens, was always to be the meanest man in the room.

Then, from the corner of his eye, John noticed a single wisp of smoke curling lazily from the campfire. In the morning light, he had better success untying the length of rope that bound him to the tree. He rolled closer to the smoke. Sure enough, a couple of hot coals had escaped the dousing that Preacher gave the campfire. John managed to get close enough to blow on an ember. Then it was a simple matter, though painful, to position it to burn through his wrist bonds.

Later, standing over the captain and the bodies of his slow-thinking cousins, John pulled a plug of tobacco from his pocket and tore off a chaw. If he had that fourth horse, he could get the two cousins home. But he had neither transportation nor tools to dig graves. So John gave it up and cursed the Yankees again. He wasn't feeling very charitable toward anyone, including his kinfolk. He searched the bodies for valuables and dragged the two cousins' bodies further from the road to rest behind a large tree. He covered them with some brush to help hide them from the scavenging birds. He smiled when he found a dollar's worth of change on Owens, proving the man as poor as his riders for all his airs, fancy horse, and rig. Coates pulled off the man's expensive snakeskin boots and tried them on. He had admired them since joining the captain's outfit, but they were oversized for him. John pulled the man's socks over his own to partially fill the void and decided he could live with the result. Then John looked around for landmarks and stacked some rocks knee-high beside the road for a marker on the chance that his Uncle Rufus sent someone for the bodies. Eventually, he started down the same route that the Yankees had used.

John's arrangements contrasted with his preferences, for he foresaw the reception he would get from his Uncle Rufus. He felt tempted at each step of his preparations to forget the cousins and head for New Orleans. But there was revenge to be exacted against the Yankees, and the youngest they called Bronco had mentioned gold. John had been too groggy to catch any details, but the only gold he knew about within a few days' riding distance was or at least had been in Harlon County, Georgia, which was, by coincidence, his own destination. Such as it was, his uncle's farm near Titustown was home. He looked around the area where he had stashed the two bodies to assure himself that they were well camouflaged, angrily reaffirmed the promised revenge, and then started walking.

9

After walking the horses through a short alleyway, Sarge, Preacher, and Bronco reached the livery stable. They gave the liveryman a dollar promising another if the horses were still present in the morning. Then, the three men went to the rooming house. Fortunately, the man at the front desk had a vacancy. In their room, Preacher and Sarge held a good-natured coin toss to determine who would sleep next to the wall. A restless bedmate could put the outside man on the floor. After the men arranged accommodations, they considered how to kill the evening. The tavern next door provided each with a beer. A bar of dark oak, a mirrored back bar, complete with a crack across one corner, holding a dozen bottles of red-eye, reminded Sarge of all the other drinking places he had spent time. Rickety chairs and scarred tables with unpainted floors completed the scene. Visible through the open door, the night passed gently with the soft patter of raindrops. He looked forward to a quiet evening with a beer after the long day on the road.

"I see there is a card game underway," Preacher said. "Sarge, Bronco, what do you say we jump in? "

"You go ahead, Preacher. I'll just nurse this." Sarge said. He lifted his glass.

"I'll stick with Sarge." Bronco touched his pocket holding his army wages. He could foresee a lot of evenings ahead, and until they found the gold Sarge had promised, he needed his meager funds to last as long as possible. His lower rank meant he had received a smaller amount when he mustered out than had his friends. He wasn't nearly as eager to spend it as the other men assumed.

Preacher ordered another beer and headed for the poker table by the front window.

Sarge and Bronco followed and pulled up seats at another table to his rear. The three men savored the warm beer and the comfort of real chairs.

Preacher was a cautious card player. He was also a sober one, which helped his playing immensely. He rarely looked at his cards but studied the other players' faces. He had learned two important things in playing poker; knowing the odds of improving his hand by drawing and discarding cards and determining the strength of the other players' hands. He accomplished that by catching every expression that passed across their faces when cards were dealt, discarded, and added. It had often amused him when he was preaching in his younger days to watch the congregation's faces and then ask inattentive parishioners a good-natured question as they made their way past him at the door.

"Brother Thomas, what did you think about the concept of the father, son, and holy ghost that I spoke about?" he would ask. The sputtering responses always gave him a spark of righteous amusement.

There were already four men at the table. Two were older, local farmers wearing bib overalls who kept their cards close and bantered with each other about local affairs between bids. They seemed unconcerned with the growing downpour. Preacher surmised they either had accommodations in town or farmed very close by. The third was the town banker, complete with a vest and gold watch chain, who seemed to fancy himself a bit superior, and took every opportunity to glance at the cards of the men on either side of him. He was to Preacher's left, and since Preacher seldom looked at his cards, the banker met with little success there.

The fourth player was a huge black-bearded man. He was well over six feet tall, with an impressive girth, and his thick arms strained his shirt's sleeves. His rolled-up cuffs revealed scars of various colors and dimensions. His demeanor and odor suggested he had been a buffalo hunter at some point in the recent past. He had dropped his huge hat on the floor beside his chair. He did little to protect the privacy of his cards and was well corned. As the evening wore on, winning eluded him, and he began to get irritable. His name was Curly; a tag everyone thought amusing since he had a bald spot as big as a saucer on the crown of his head.

His new-found farmer "friends" made frequent remarks about it that Curly took without quibble initially, but the joke began to wear thin with additional drinks and many poor hands. Finally, after three straight folds, his temper inched up a tad.

"Curly," the smaller farmer smirked, "They could just as well have called you Lucky.'" The big man's face reddened.

"Yeah? Well, the night ain't over as yet." He glared at Preacher, still shuffling the deck.

Preacher smiled. "You boys quit joshing, my friend." Unfortunately, his comment did not mollify the man.

"Lucky is what they should call you. You've won three hands straight. Is that what they call you? Lucky?" The big man said, glaring at Preacher meaningfully.

Bronco and Sarge exchanged a look. Bronco was starting to fidget.

"No, they call me Preacher if they're friendly." Preacher replied amicably.

"Well, you are either very lucky or finding a way to pull cards out of your hat." Curly threw back another shot of whisky.

Preacher smiled. "You will no doubt notice, my friend, that like you, I am not wearing a hat." He glanced down at the floor where both men's hats resided and let the farmer to his right cut the cards before starting to deal. "Maybe this hand will change your luck."

Sarge rose slowly to his feet and pointed at his empty glass. Bronco shook his head. He was only halfway through his.

Curly frowned but kept his peace until he looked at his new hand, then stood up cursing. "You sonofabitch!" The veins in his neck stood out, and his ample forehead throbbed.

He staggered a bit as he came around the corner of the table. "You trying to make a fool of me?"

Sarge returned with his beer in time to put his hand on Bronco's shoulder. The young man had his hand on his holster. He looked up with questioning eyes. Sarge shook his head and leaned down. "Watch and learn," he smiled.

Preacher kept his seat. "I am, by nature, a peaceable man. This is just a friendly game. As a friend, I hope that you don't make a fool of yourself."

Curly took another step. His clenched fists were huge and calloused. Preacher rose regretfully to his feet and stepped to the side of his chair. He noticed a scar on the back of the man's left hand as he ducked to the right, and it fanned harmlessly past his left cheek.

He wasn't as lucky with the right. It caught him in the ribs. Ducking inside, he put his shoulder into the big man's chest. His left hand reached down and tugged at the flapping loose end of Curly's gun belt. The heavy forty-four revolver and hoister slid down to Curly's knees.

Curly looked down, drunkenly embarrassed. He grabbed the loose ends of the belt and, in his rush, overcompensated and pulled it upward almost to his armpits. Preacher used that moment to simultaneously clap his hands hard against the sides of Curly's head with an explosive effect on his ears. Tears sprang to the man's bloodshot eyes as he reflexively dropped the gun belt and grabbed his ears in defense. Sarge's right hand tapped him firmly on the end of his nose, and the crunch of cartilage sounded like a small tree branch had snapped. Then the scarlet spurted, and Curly tasted the iron and salt of his own blood in the back of his mouth. In alarm, he tripped over his gun belt and stumbled two paces back. Sarge rubbed his sore ribs and smiled.

"Are you sure you don't want to be friends?"

Curly reflexively slapped leather, reaching for the holster now draped around his boots.

"Ah." Preacher sighed and stepped forward with an uppercut to the big man's jaw. He bent and pulled the gun from its holster before the toppling man reached the floor.

Preacher hefted the gun with authority and eyed Curly sadly. "It is so much easier to be friends." Preacher repeated. He lay the pistol on the table, unknotted his bandana, and dropped it into Curly's lap. Curly grabbed for it and sopped at his mouth and chin. Preacher questioned him with raised eyebrows and stuck out his hand. Curly considered for a moment and finally concurred.

Preacher grabbed the thick wrist and pulled Curly to his feet. "How about sarsaparilla?"

"I don't drink sarsaparilla," Curly grumbled.

"Neither do I." Preacher laughed. "Bar-keep, rum!"

10

Sarge woke at dawn as was his habit and sat at the window for a while watching Sweetwater come alive. He remembered living his whole life only fifty miles away, near a similar village. He liked this town's name better. Somehow the sound of it comforted him. He was not looking forward to his reunion with his brother, Tom. They had parted on bad terms, and the older man seemed unlikely to welcome him with open arms. Moreover, Sarge had deprived him of a valuable piece of property. Again, he remembered their argument over Brownie.

"You can't sell Brownie!" Madison had glared at his older brother. His jaw set, and his fists clenched.

"Of course, I can. Brownie is my property. Be reasonable. I can trade for three field hands. Relax, will you? It's the best thing that could happen to him. He's a good-looking boy. He'll end up in some plantation owner's house serving mint juleps to the ladies."

"He is my friend. If Mother was still alive, she'd never agree to sell him." Madison knew this was the wrong tack, but it slipped out.

"Well, maybe he shouldn't be your 'friend,' should he?" Tom shook his head. "Look, this isn't personal. I like Brownie well enough, but this is business. If it made sense to keep him, I would. The fact is we are not getting enough out of him here. When was the last time we needed to serve mint juleps? With the additional acreage in cotton, we will need more hands to hoe and pick it."

"What about the sawmill?" Madison knew they had talked the subject to death, but he wasn't willing to let it go. "If we expanded those operations, we could keep the cotton crop manageable for the three of us to handle."

Tom sighed. "We've been over this fifteen times. English textile mills are crying for more cotton. Right now, the real money is in a bigger crop. With two additional men to chop and pick, we can double our acreage easily. That means doubling our income."

"It's not all income, Tom. Expenses go up too. Food, clothes, housing, and if one runs off, your precious profit goes with him."

"Well, that's where we get to your part. Your job is to see that none of the men run off!" Tom stood up. "I'm done. It's business. It's the business of the South, and on this farm, like everywhere else, the cotton business requires labor."

Sarge contrasted the hostility of their parting with his early years. He and Brownie spent their younger years following Tom around, striving to walk like him, talk like him, and in all ways possible, be him. Sarge pursed his mouth. Maybe the best course would be to ride to the farm, find the fenceposts his father had pointed out to him years ago, and ride away with the gold without encountering his brother. He wondered if he could manage that. And Sarge had to admit, despite logic, he directed a little of his bitterness at his father for not leaving him a share of the farm. But Sarge forced himself to think logically. John Jones left him a significant inheritance in gold that, judging from the countryside they had just traversed, might be more valuable than any farm at present. And it was portable.

The lump in the bed stirred, bringing Sarge back to the present. Preacher raised his head abruptly, coming out of a dream. He slapped his forehead gently and opened his eyes, looking around the room like a wounded animal.

"Morning," Sarge said.

"Morning." Preacher mumbled and rubbed the place he had slapped. "That buffalo hunter sure could drink, couldn't he?"

"You kept up pretty well," Sarge observed.

"Well, after the first round, he was buying, so I went along. I didn't want to get him riled up all over again." Preacher laughed, grimaced, and then rubbed his head some more.

"I think I'll see to Bronco and the horses," Sarge said. "You want to meet for breakfast downstairs?"

"I won't be long." Preacher painfully swung his feet to the floor, walked to a basin, and poured water from the pitcher. He started splashing water on his face as Sarge headed toward the door.

"See you later," Sarge said.

Preacher considered a shave but dried his face. His bloodshot eyes discouraged trying to do anything requiring a steady hand and good vision.

Sarge descended the stairs and out the back to the outhouse. A few minutes later, he crossed the street to the livery stable. It had rained most of the night. He found Bronco already brushing down the horses.

"How'd you sleep?" Sarge picked up a brush to help out.

"Like a baby. I love the smell of horses and hay." Bronco moved to the pinto and stroked his nose. "How did you and Preacher sleep?"

"I was fine. Preacher slept like a baby with a hangover." Sarge said.

Bronco grinned. After tending to the horses, the two men found Preacher sipping coffee in the tavern. His eyes were closed, but his pounding head kept him awake.

11

They were in the saddle by eight. The further east they got, the more fellow travelers they encountered. Few Rebel soldiers were heading north this morning. Most of the soldiers they saw were hiking on a southern heading. Most of the men with horses had passed through this area days before.

All of the freed blacks they met were walking. The sheer number encouraged the Confederate soldiers to steer to the right side of the road. A raw enmity pervaded their frequent encounters.

"I wonder where they're going." Bronco nodded at a large group of blacks coming toward them.

"We haven't seen a lot given the number who are free to go anywhere they want. There are better routes north, east of here, and better routes west, to the south. I imagine that if I had a group of ex-slaves right now and a cotton crop to plant, I'd be trying to make some kind of payment arrangements with them rather than let them walk off." Sarge said.

"I'm betting that a lot will be headed north to the cities and factory work." Preacher said.

"Maybe they'll go west like we plan to," Bronco said. "Won't they be starting with nothing? I bet someone gave that man the handcart."

There were fewer signs of conflict in this area. Spring brought up the wildflowers, and birds were chirping happily. There were fewer animal remains along the road. Yet, even without frequent reminders, you could not pass through this way without knowing that terrible war had been raging around them only a few weeks or months before. Preacher took a drink from his canteen and wondered if forgiveness was possible after such a conflict. Love of freedom and autonomy from foreigners, especially King George, had fused the nation during and after the revolution. Could a starving, humbled South ever accept its defeat? Could a triumphant North forgive the loss of brothers, fathers, and sons? What would be the effect of Lincoln's loss? His determination had kept the Union together. His goal had been to bind the factions with a combination of strict adherence to the new order and forgiveness of the southern opponents.

Bronco was not privy to the inner thoughts of his two companions. Before working for Sam Jacobs after his grandfather's death, Bronco's intimate contact with adults had been almost exclusively with merchants, teachers, and his elderly grandparents. His first job on an Ohio horse-breaking operation taught him a lot about men and horses. After entering the military and losing a fellow Ohioan in his first test at arms, Bronco found himself shying off close relationships. Your friend today could be a casualty tomorrow. Lieutenant Adams was an example of that.

The men rarely spoke as they slowly progressed toward Sarge's birthplace, lost in their thoughts about their past and possibly shared or separate futures. After contemplating his displeasure with Tom, Sarge recollected that his parting from Brownie had been almost as conflicted. He was saddened to recall how he and his black friend followed parallel paths growing up and before separating so abruptly. Sarge corrected himself. He had separated them. At the time, it seemed like the only solution. He remembered as children how they read from the farm's well-stocked library together. They both become voracious readers. Two books, in particular, caught their imaginations.

The first, *Moby Dick*, had attracted Brownie's attention because of the whale illustration on the cover. But Brownie's education was not limited to the library. Madison attended school each morning, and at his mother's insistence, he and Brownie went over his lessons when he returned to the farm. The black boy often asked questions, forcing Madison to give more thought to his studies than he would have otherwise. Often, they took turns reading out loud to each other. In the summer, the two boys lay on the side porch and talked about going places and seeing some of the things they learned about in their reading. *The Three Musketeers* resulted in dreams of seeing France.

Many years later, as young men sitting on a step of a feed store in Bingham, Massachusetts, Brownie could scarcely believe his friend when he said he was joining the Union army.

"What about me?" He was at first confused and then hurt at the desertion. Madison did not see that flash of fear in his friend's eyes because he turned away. If he had seen it, he would have recognized the same full-blown anxiety that passed across his friend's face the first day he arrived at the farm.

"The army won't take you, Brownie. We know that. We are out of money. But, if I join the army, I'll get a bonus. I can give you part of that. If you want, you can head to New York and buy a ticket for Paris. You've always wanted to visit Paris, haven't you?"

"Well, yeah, but I figured we'd go together since we talked about it together." Brownie thought this wholly logical, and Madison could not argue the point.

"But if I don't get the bonus, we have no money to eat on, let alone for tickets." Madison could see now the anguish on Brownie's face. He felt the same himself. Madison just couldn't come up with an immediate alternative. Now, riding with Bronco and Preacher through a section of the road heavily crowded with black families heading north, he wondered if Brownie had made it to France. Sarge smiled a little, thinking about the young black man serving mint juleps to French ladies for pay. That was the destiny he wanted to believe had awaited his friend. His thoughts returned to the present as they set up camp and cared for the weary horses again.

12

The men slept in, and as their morning meal was rather late, it was well into the afternoon when they stopped for dinner. To aid in making good time, the three men pulled out the biscuits and had coffee going in short order.

As they sat drinking, Sarge watched Bronco sip from his cup. He was a good-sized fellow. The young man was energetic and eager to do his share. Bronco was a good man to join their quest to Titustown, and his skill with the rifle had already come in handy.

"Bronco, you told us how you got your nickname. How'd you get this far south?"

"I went where the army sent me, that's all."

"Do you have kin back in Ohio?"

"Not anymore. I lived with my grandparents before and after my mother died. I never really knew my pa, though I probably have met him once."

"Probably? How's that?" Preacher leaned back on his bedroll.

"I grew up with my ma and my grandparents. After my ma died, she had some kind of fever; it was just my grandparents and me. They were pretty old, around fifty, I guess. Then my grandmother died just like my ma, and my grandpa and I were left. Anyway, one day I was out in the yard playing with a group of friends. We were shooting marbles, and this stranger rode up and went in to see my grandpa. We didn't pay any attention. I was winning, so I had my mind on the game more than anything else."

Bronco stretched his legs out to relieve a cramp in his calf. "Then there was a lot of hollering coming from the house. My grandpa was a feisty old wart. I could hear he was letting the guy have it with both barrels. Then the door opened, and the man came out in a hurry. He walked over to us kids and stood there for a minute, watching us shoot. Then for no reason at all, as far as I could see, he reached in his pocket and pulled out some change. He gave each of the other boys a nickel. He handed me a dime. Finally, he patted my head, jumped on his horse, and rode away." Bronco looked from one man to the other. "Turned out he was my pa."

"How do you know that?" Sarge said.

"Well, I had never owned a dime before in my life. The other boys had never had a nickel. The game was over because they hightailed it home to tell their ma's. I went running inside to tell my grandpa. When I found him in the back room, he had a strange look on his face while he sat looking at a tintype of my ma. I told him about the nickels and the dime, and he told me right off that the stranger was named Randolph Brumley and that he was my pa." A shadow passed over Bronco's face. "I asked how come he gave me a dime. Was it because I was his son? Grandpa just said, 'He probably ran out of nickels.' After that, I never saw him again. My grandpa didn't like him much,

I guess. He said he was a riverboat gambler. I don't think my grandpa ever had much truck with gamblers."

The number of Rebel soldiers headed their way was diminishing, it seemed. Most of them had walked a long way, and some eyed the horses and blue caps with intense interest. Sarge suggested they keep their hands close to their firearms. It was an hour later when, far ahead, they spied a lone Rebel hobbling along on a crutch. He had copper red hair and stumbled along, clearly worn out. They could see that he had lost his foot.

Preacher remembered his thoughts while examining Lieutenant Adams' leg after their narrow escape from the thicket. This young man could have been a southern version of lieutenant Adams if the lieutenant had lived. He pulled up and motioned to the others to do the same.

"Boys, I was watching that young goober grabber up ahead. He has a tough road ahead of him, what with that missing foot. We, on the other hand, actually have an extra horse." He stopped to read the expressions on his companions' faces.

"Yeah, and our extra horse is what gets most of the attention from the Rebels," Bronco said.

"It does seem like an unnecessary luxury at this point, doesn't it?" said Sarge.

"So, you boys wouldn't object to unloading our extra oat-eater on that young fella up there?" Preacher said.

Bronco and Sarge exchanged glances. "Great idea," Bronco said.

"Suits me." Sarge agreed.

"Okay." They spurred their mounts and overtook the red-head again.

The young man looked at them warily when they came alongside. He tilted his chin defiantly.

"If you Yankees are thinking of robbing me, you're too late. A gent took what little money I had two days ago."

"Sorry to hear that, Reb," Preacher said. "Do you have a fair piece to go yet?"

The young man's face cleared, reacting to Preacher's tone of voice.

"I turn due south in about five miles and then have another twenty miles or so."

"Well, you might notice we have an extra horse," Preacher said. "We were wondering if you'd take it off our hands?"

The redhead looked incredulous, then turned his face away for a minute. When he turned back, he said, "That would be right generous of you."

"I'm Preacher." The stocky man motioned toward his companions. "This here is Sarge, and that's Bronco. We thought we might need a spare, but our horses are holding up well, and we're only a day or so away from our destination."

Preacher dismounted, untied the fourth horse's reins, and helped the young confederate into the saddle.

"I'm David Boyd," he said, taking the reins and rocking back and forth in the saddle. "I forgot that sitting up here is like being on top of the world! Think we can ride together for the next five miles before I turn off?" The three men grinned and nodded, and after a few minutes of chatter, they all lapsed into silence. It occurred to Sarge that they made an incongruous sight, three

Union soldiers and a single Rebel riding down the road together with no one holding a gun on the other. He wondered if that would ever seem normal again.

Finally, Bronco spoke up. "What did you do before the war?" He could tell the boy was a few years younger than himself.

"My grandfather operates a General store in Thomasville, Alabama. So I expect I'll go back to that."

"I lived with my grandparents when I was younger," Bronco said.

"My parents died of the fever when I was five," David said.

"You seem a bit young by Union standards," Sarge said.

"I'm not even close to the youngest," David answered. He patted his new mount's neck. The reduced daily mileage and plentiful grass had improved the horse's appearance in just a few days. After a while, David pulled up and pointed to the fork going south. "This is my turn-off. I appreciate the horse. I promise I'll take good care of her." He shook the hand of each man in turn.

They watched as he took the right fork and waved back at them. "Nice fella," Bronco said. "I'm happy we gave him the horse."

"Yep," said Sarge. And just think of the boarding fees we'll save."

"And the brushing and feeding and watering," teased Preacher. Then they grinned at Bronco.

The town of Titustown, Georgia, lay twenty-two miles east of the Georgia-Alabama border and was located in a valley used as a campground by the Creeks. According to town lore, the name used by the Creeks meant 'good valley.' The town got its name from an early settler. They were approaching from the northwest and were dried out and thirsty when they came to a stream. Bronco was the first off of his horse. He let the reins drop, knowing his mount was as interested in a drink as he was. He walked a few paces upstream from the animal and was soon down on his knees. With much splashing, he brought up double handfuls to his face, neck, and mouth.

The older men dismounted and watched for a second, then Preacher motioned to Sarge, and they leaped on the kneeling Bronco. Moving quickly, they picked him up by his belt and collar, rocked back once, and tumbled him into the midst of the stream.

Bronco came up, sputtering. "Hey, what was that about?" He was not happy to have his boots wet, although the coolness of the stream felt refreshing.

"Aren't you forgetting your military training?" Sarge said with mock seriousness.

"What military training?"

"The training about keeping a lookout when you drink? What if we had been Rebels or, worse, Indians? What if we were road agents ready to relieve you of your valuables? Giving you a dunking as we did is a time-honored army tradition."

"What if a pretty girl walked by, and you missed her because you were embarrassing yourself drinking like a horse?" Preacher added.

"Looking out is what you two were supposed to be doing," Bronco grumbled. He waded back to shore and glanced around at the thought of a witness to his embarrassment. "As far as tradition, maybe so, maybe not. Either way, we aren't in the army anymore." Bronco took off his cap and shook some water out of it.

"It's getting late," Sarge said. Let's make camp here. My home place is three miles on the other side of town. I'd like to get the lay of the land before doing anything else." Then he grinned. "Bronco, since you are the cleanest of us, do you think you could go in and look around without being too conspicuous?"

"Good idea." Preacher grinned at the 'cleanest' part and knelt to splash water on his face and neck. He wiped his face with his sleeve.

"All right." Bronco agreed. "But I'd rather have ridden in without wet clothes."

13

John Coates relished his last biscuit. He sometimes had southern-bound companions while walking for the first day and a half, but he came across no one he knew from Harlon County. Most planned to turn south a few miles ahead, whereas he would go east. His fancy oversized boots had rubbed blisters on his feet despite the extra layer of socks, which hindered his progress. His head still throbbed intermittently. He took the opportunity to wash the blood from his face and clothes when he came across the first stream of fresh water. His clothes dried on his back as he continued to walk. Then, just at sunset, he decided to give it up. A narrow path angled from the main road. He turned in and walked deep into a large grove of pine trees. He resigned himself to another long night curled up on the hard ground until he heard a horse's faint neigh.

John's steps slowed. The possibility of obtaining a horse quickened his pulse. In his present circumstances, he would not hesitate to acquire a horse by any means necessary. The trees were old-growth pine. The trunks were as wide as his shoulders and offered good cover. Dust motes and gnats drifted in the fading rays of sunlight. Coates prided himself on his stealth. He peered around the tree and, seeing nothing, moved swiftly and quietly to another. Then another. Still nothing. He sniffed the air. He caught a whiff of horseflesh and a more disagreeable something else. Another whinny and hoofs pounded impatiently.

Then he saw a bay very much like Captain Owens' mount. It stood a hand taller and had grazed out an area ten yards from the remains of a campfire. John could see that it had been there a while. He moved closer and saw a figure lying close to the dead fire. It looked like a man in a blanket. Given the time of day, he surmised that the man could be sick or dead.

Coates wished he had his revolver. He cast around for a weapon, and his eyes fell on a large piece of sandstone. He picked it up and hefted it. It should do the trick. Slowly he moved forward, casting his eyes around for any companions of the man in the bedroll. He was almost on him, and there was still no movement.

The anxious horse stamped its hoof again, then calmed when he caught sight of a human. There was still no movement from the bedroll. He raised his chunk of rock to shoulder height and moved within view of the man's head. The reclining man was still. He was already dead.

Coates threw the rock to the side and walked over to the horse. He ran his hand over its sleek neck. He had never owned such a fine mount. Searching the dead man's belongings netted him a small amount of money and some food. He could scarcely contain his delight at such good luck. At the same time, his head still throbbed, and his thoughts returned to obtaining vengeance. With the horse, he had the means to bring that day much closer. He walked the animal to the stream, found another blanket, and restarted the fire. He folded the soiled bedding to enclose the remains and dragged the body out close to the road. He ate, and as he started to doze, his last thoughts were how lucky he was that his trail home included coming upon such a fine horse. Finally, as a bonus, the man's old six-gun could afford him a means to obtain his revenge. It was good!

Titustown was a bustling village of close to two thousand people. The nearby garrison of Union soldiers further increased the area's population. Bronco kept his eyes open as he rode from one end of Main Street to the other and back again. He held up at the small Lucky Star tavern attached to a boarding house at the end of the block. He dismounted at a water trough, double-tied the pinto, and loosened the cinch strap.

There were only a few customers inside at scattered tables. Bronco spotted a place next to the window and took a seat that gave him a good vantage point to keep an eye on the pinto. He felt pretty confident of its safety with the Union soldiers around. He took off his cap and placed it on the table. A moment later, an elderly lady took his order without pleasantries.

Bronco's shoes were still wet, and his damp pants made the back of his legs and butt itch. He groused to himself about his dunking in the stream and was unprepared for the young lady who brought him his food. He stared out the window at his horse until she approached with his plate. Then, looking up, he was startled to realize that she was the prettiest girl he had ever seen. Everything about her testified to the truthfulness of all the tales of southern beauty he had heard. As he looked up into her high-cheek-boned face, she captured him with the calm green eyes, flared nose, and a mouth that made his heart lurch. She wore her cloud of dark hair an inch longer than shoulder length. She saw his expression of admiration, and her semi-smile faded to neutral; but not before he had time to admire the small perfect white teeth. Her change in demeanor surprised him until he remembered that he and all the other Union soldiers in the room were still considered the enemy of every southerner they encountered. His face sobered.

"Your order, sir." She said flatly. She placed his food in front of him. He noticed she directed her gaze at his hairline to avoid meeting his eyes.

He barely remembered to stutter his thank you. Bronco suddenly had no interest in food. He wanted the girl to stand there permanently so he could drink her in. The intensity of his expression must have given her the idea that he was about to say something.

"Can I get you anything else, sir?" Her voice was low for one so young and had a bit of a warble reminding him of the loons that had drifted on the pond down the road from his grand-father's house back in Ohio.

"No, thanks." He gave his head a quick shake and then cor-rected himself. "Yes, yes! Could I have a glass of milk, please?"

"Yes, sir."

He watched her move effortlessly across the floor, oblivious that every other man in the room was doing the same. Time stopped until she returned and sat the large glass before him.

"Let me know if you need anything else." Her tone was still perfunctory, he thought. He nodded dumbly and watched her move to another table where three Union soldiers were seated. She stopped for a moment. Then, unexpectedly, one of the men's large paws reached out to encircle her slim wrist. The big man with corporal stripes said something to her. Bronco could tell that his comment was not appreciated. Her eyes glanced around the room, then fastened on Bronco for a second mid-circuit. Finally, she attempted to pull her arm away—the big hand-held fast.

Bronco was on his feet in an instant. Another corporal sitting with the big man spoke into his ear as he leered at the girl. The man grunted before releasing her. He did not take her rebuff lightly. He glowered at her for a moment, then returned to his food. The girl grasped her wrist where he had restrained her. She glanced again at Bronco as he regained his seat. She had correctly read his intentions. She turned and pushed through the swinging door to the kitchen. Bronco watched her disappear, and his hardened eyes returned to the three soldiers.

"The queen of Harlon County, Georgia," a wheezy voice murmured close behind him.

"Huh!" Much surprised, Bronco pulled his attention away from the three men and turned abruptly to face a grizzled older man sitting at a table to his rear. "Sir," Bronco responded honestly. "She is the prettiest gal I have ever seen."

"She is a vision from heaven, all right." The older man took a sip of his coffee and grinned. "I'm Matthew Jordon. People call me Pappy." He stuck out his hand. Bronco grasped it, and it flitted through his mind that most southerners he encountered would not have made the gesture. Bronco shifted his chair so they could sit face to face.

"What is her name?"

"Sarah Tyson Jordon, last name the same as mine." The man replied. He laughed at Bronco's expression. "No, no, we're not closely related. She is married to my great-nephew."

"Married!?" Bronco looked incredulous.

"Yep. You would have noticed the wedding ring if you hadn't been gazing into those pretty eyes. She and Jimmy was married just before he went to Atlanta and signed up with the Army of the Confederacy."

Bronco's expression of dismay made the older man cackle. "Right now, what you're thinking is exactly what every other young scallywag in this room is thinking. I thought for a minute there; I'd have to pull my iron on that northern clodhopper over yonder." He motioned toward the three soldiers who were getting up to leave. Bronco and Pappy watched the men exit before the older man continued. "Well, except me, of course," He brushed his fingers across his mustache and pursed his lips.

"She turned down every eligible man in town before marrying my grand-nephew." He lowered his voice. "But I'm afraid she might be a widow already. Word came back that Jimmy was killed over three months ago, but no remains have come in and no official confirmation either. So every day without a word worries us that he's not going to make it." The man's expression turned fierce. "He is a good boy too!"

Bronco nodded and dug into his food. He learned that Pappy Jordon rented a room in the back of the house next door to Miss Emmy, the elderly lady who owned the Lucky Star. The ride from his farm to town was fatiguing for the old man with his bad back. Bronco learned that, Howie, who ran their farm, injured his leg in a logging incident, which kept him out of the Confederate army.

Though Pappy didn't confide the information to Bronco, both father and son were highly skeptical of the unrest and 'state's rights' arguments that had accompanied the run-up to secession and the war. They were confident that the state's rights claim was politicians' talk for the right to enslave black people. Not that the states made any attempt to deny that. Since they did not support the 'peculiar institution,' they maintained support for the warriors if not for the war.

Now they were particularly impatient with those who sought to continue with the skirmishes when the conflict was officially over. Pappy didn't know why he had spoken to the young Yankee. He usually tried to avoid any interaction with the foe, but the boy's admiration for the girl he felt such a strong attachment to lead to the impulsive decision to speak up. He, too, had seen Bronco rise in preparation for her defense.

Bronco nodded, and though he was cheered by the news of the absent husband, he could read the older man's pain in his face. He kept his eyes on the back of two middle-aged red-headed men sitting across the room and tried to emulate their apparent disinterest in the pretty girl. He visited with Pappy while they ate and reluctantly followed the older man to the door after they finished. He feared that if he hung around, he'd embarrass himself with the girl.

14

Sarge and Preacher noticed a change in Bronco's disposition as soon as he returned to camp. His description of the town and his activities while there were fragmented. It seemed clear that his mind was somewhere else. The two men eyed each other and speculated about what could have caused the change.

The following day, they rehashed Bronco's story with him but didn't get much new information.

"So, to sum up, the town is occupied by Union soldiers; the food at the tavern is okay; the pinto didn't get stolen, and you didn't notice if there is a boarding house," Sarge said.

"That's about it. Well, I'm pretty sure there is a boarding house." Bronco looked off into the distance.

"Preacher, let's pack up and go see for ourselves."

"Yep." Preacher poured water on the coals and started kicking dirt to smother the fire.

They saddled the horses and were soon riding down Main Street. The town experienced some growth with the Confederate and then the Union forces stationed in the area. Thanks to its north-western Georgia location, it had not suffered the scorched earth march by Sherman. There were a couple of new storefronts, and on a vacant lot, tents erected with signs promising unknown pleasures within.

"I got it." Sarge laughed. He pointed at one of the signs and motioned toward Bronco. "Our buckaroo got more than supper last night. I thought that look was familiar."

"That could be it, alright," Preacher said. Sarge and Preacher laughed while Bronco turned his head away, red-faced. He didn't honor the suggestion with a response.

As they rode up to the boarding house, Preacher noticed that Bronco was craning his neck to see through the windows of the attached tavern, the Lucky Star.

"Sarge, let's stop in the tavern for some breakfast." Preacher said.

"Good idea."

"How about you, Bronco?" Sarge watched his friend's face.

"Yeah, okay," Bronco said casually. "If you men are hungry, I could eat some pancakes."

Once they were seated, the older lady Bronco had learned was called Miss Emmy the previous evening came around, poured coffee, and took their orders. Preacher looked around the nearly vacant room and exchanged looks with Sarge, who shrugged. Both men had been suspicious of Bronco's expressed disinterest in the establishment.

"I guess I'm stumped," Sarge said.

"Me, too." Preacher said.

"About what?" Bronco looked from one to the other. He had seated himself, so he had a view of the entire dining area. Now he picked up his cup and started to bring it to his mouth but only got halfway.

The other men saw his change of expression and looked around. "I'm not stumped anymore," Sarge said.

"Nope."

Unlike the previous evening, Mrs. Sarah Jorden greeted Bronco with a hint of a smile. His apparent readiness to act in her defense and his lengthy conversation with Pappy seemed to have softened her opinion of him a bit.

"Be careful, sir; these pancakes are right off the stove."

"Thanks!" Bronco, again entranced, made no motion to pick up his fork.

"Ma'am, this is mighty good coffee," Preacher said. "You suppose I could have some more?"

"Yes, sir." All three men watched her go for the coffee pot."

"Notice how she seems to float across the floor," Sarge said.

"I'll be damned if she doesn't," Preacher agreed.

Bronco finally put his cup down without drinking. While she topped off Preacher's cup, Sarge spoke up.

"If you don't mind my asking, what's your name, ma'am?" Sarge asked. "I grew up around here, but I've been away for a long while. So I'm thinking I might know your family."

The girl's eyes lifted quickly from the flowing stream of coffee in surprise at the sound of his southern accent. "My pa was George Tyson. He and my mother passed away from malaria when I was eight years old. My married name is Jordon, Sarah Elizabeth Jordon."

"Well, I'll be! I used to know your pa. My name is Madison Jones. Your father, my father, and I went squirrel hunting a few times long ago. Maybe you know my older brother, Tom?"

Her face darkened. She paused. "You're Major Tom Jones' brother?"

Sarge smiled, but then he saw her expression. He leaned forward. "Is there a problem with that?"

"Well, sir, your brother is in a peck of trouble. Our Confederate garrison used his place as headquarters for this area when they operated out of here. Now, the Yankees have run our boys out and taken over his house."

"I see." Sarge looked from the girl to Preacher and Bronco. His face registered mild concern. "So, how is he in trouble?"

"The Yankees claim that he stole a payroll. They say he had access to the strongbox through a secret passage." She looked around and, satisfied that her services weren't immediately needed elsewhere, pulled a chair over from another table. "The word is he won't admit to anything. And being a prominent local Rebel, the commander threw him in our local jail yesterday."

Sarah could now see the family resemblance between Tom's and Sarge's features. However, the Union uniform on the brother of a local Confederate Officer seemed passing strange.

"Impossible!" Sarge said, his face incredulous.

Sarah shrugged. "Everyone in town agrees with you. I have to get back to work." She gave Bronco and Preacher a glance but spoke to Sarge. "Are yah-all going to be back tomorrow?"

They assured her that they would. After she left, Sarge motioned the other two men closer. "This sounds serious. I think I need to talk with the sheriff. Why don't you boys see if we can get a room in the boarding house? I'll join you after I've talked with him."

Sarge walked the two blocks to the Titustown jail, his head buzzing with questions. He opened the door and found the sheriff at his desk. He was older than Sarge. At first assessment, Sarge guessed that the man was a couple of years older than his brother, Tom. His mustache was graying, and he read the newspaper on his desk through spectacles. But when he faced the door, Sarge realized that he looked familiar.

"Morning, Sheriff," Sarge said as he shut the door. "I hear you have my brother locked up here."

The older man looked up and squinted for a long moment. "I'd ask which man, but I recognize you, and I only have one man in custody. Madison Jones, isn't it? I see you're wearing a Yankee cap. I wondered what would happen to you when you hightailed it out of here, what, ten years ago?"

"About that. It's good to see you, Sheriff." Sarge took his hat off and stuck out his hand. The lawman stood up and made a point of hooking his thumbs in his belt instead. His eyes flashed irritation for a second. "I hope you aren't expecting a parade wearing that uniform around here. Tom took some unfriendly ragging from his neighbors when word got out that you helped his slave run off. Once word gets out one has escaped, they all start scheming," He hesitated, " But I guess that don't matter none now."

"I was in the Union army before the war and saw no reason to make a change," Sarge said. "The rest of it is between Tom and me. Are you and Tom still friends?"

"Of course, we are." Sheriff Beckett paused for a moment.

Sarge pursed his lips and stuck his hand out again. The hooked thumbs didn't move for a few heartbeats. Finally, the sheriff extended his right hand, and they shook.

"Well, I want to see about getting him out."

"That is easier said than done." Beckett motioned to a chair and sat down. Sarge did the same.

"I hear the army has accused him of stealing? You have to know Tom never stole anything in his life. He's as hardheaded as a billiard ball, but he's no thief."

"Oh, I know that." The sheriff leaned back. Sarge's comment seemed to tickle him a bit, but he didn't acknowledge it."It looks like a trumped-up charge, alright. But the Yankee commander is pressing charges, and he has the guns to make it stick."

"He can't have proof. He still needs proof."

"Well, he thinks he does. He says they stored the payroll in the library. There was a guard at the door. Last Wednesday evening, the strongbox was there. Thursday morning, when the guard changed, the box was gone. In the process of turning the place upside down, the Yankees found the secret entrance." The Sheriff smiled. "I remember when you was kids, You and Brownie figured out that moving bookcase."

"I remember." Sarge smiled. "Brownie and I used to play using that secret entrance with a couple of my friends."

"Well, as far as the major is concerned, that secret entrance nails Tom."

"I see. I'd like to see Tom."

"Sorry, Madison. The major has ordered no visitors other than a lawyer. So if you want to get in, you'll have to get permission."

"But, you're the sheriff!"

"I'm the sheriff, but this is an army matter, and we're under martial law here because of the idiot yahoos still carousing around the county stirring up trouble."

Sarge's face reddened. "I'm not going see my brother railroaded, Sheriff." He stood abruptly. "I'll be back!"

The sheriff stood. He came around the desk. "Good luck with the major. Be sure to wear that Yankee cap when you go in. It may be the only thing you have going for you."

Preacher and Bronco spent the next couple of hours checking into the boardinghouse and taking a ride around the town and nearby countryside, getting the lay of the land. Titustown included Baptist and Methodist churches. In addition, there were two general stores, a feed store, two hardware stores, an assortment of other stores, and a probable brothel. The boarding house was attached to the Lucky Star, where they had eaten breakfast and a few other miscellaneous establishments. After perusing the contents of a dry goods store, they returned to the street.

"Dang!" Bronco said. He nodded toward the other side of the street.

"What?" Preacher's eyes followed his motion. "My Lord, bad pennies keep turning up, don't they? Of all the places for Coates to land, why here?" Preacher murmured.

John Coates sat on a bench in front of the livery stable. Coates pretended to carve on a length of wood. He had already spotted them and, noticing the two men looking back, tipped his hat and gave them a malicious grin. Then John lay the piece down, stabbed it with the knife, and held it up for display. Next, he pointed to the blade and then at them.

"Let's go back by the Lucky Star. I'm hungry again," Bronco said. Coates seemed pretty harmless at the moment despite his gestures.

"Well, this place is closer. Let's try it out." The Preacher pointed to the café sign over their heads and suppressed a grin.

"I bet this one doesn't have a girl as pretty as Miss Sarah," Bronco said and mulishly headed down the street toward the tavern.

Preacher sighed and started after him. Soon they were installed at a table with Bronco's new friend, Mister Matthew 'Pappy' Jordon. Briefly, they shared with him their concern for Tom Jones. The conversation trailed off when Mrs. Jordon brought out the food.

John Coates watched the pair move away from his perch in front of the livery stable. His beard itched, and his feet still ached from walking. He had tuckered out the bay, pushing it to get to Harlon County as quickly as possible. He had just used two bits of his found money to get his newly acquired mount into the livery stable. It was too good of a horse to risk for very long on the street. Fortunately, the man whose horse he had rescued had a small amount of money on him, but not enough to make Coates careless. He was hungry but knew that once his remaining money was gone, he'd have to depend on the generosity of his Uncle Rufus. John's holster was no longer empty. He had obtained a replacement from the same gent who provided the horse. His head rotated while he tracked the men as they passed the bank and into the tavern. His eyes blazed. His head still ached due to the never-to-be-forgotten or forgiven wound on his scalp.

15

Sarge rode out to his old home place and felt his initial anger transform into anxiety. It was only a short ride past the last stores to the first farms. Here the indirect toll of the war was evident. He could see long sections of dismantled split rail fence. Fenceposts leaned as if ready to topple, and hayfields lay barren of crops and full of weeds. Cotton fields lay dormant with no sign of preparation for planting. Only patches of subsistence vegetable gardening grew close to some of the houses. Although spared the onslaught of intentional damage, it suffered much from neglect. It was mid-spring, and the unworked land waited, but the disarray suggested neglect going back for years—a noticeable difference, the acres of pastureland, now devoid of animals.

Soon, Sarge reached the road that led up a slightly inclined curve to his family's big house. Through a grove of massive oaks, he could see the interrupted outline of the house and out-buildings. It was not a plantation house with massive columns but a large farmhouse that could have easily stood in Ohio or Kansas. He pulled his horse up for a minute and let himself absorb the vista. *Home!* Here too, upkeep was minimal. He felt a surge of anger. Why didn't Tom take better care of the place? Farms had seldom relied on slaves in this part of Georgia in his father's time. It was primarily forested land with some cotton fields with hay meadows set aside for winter fodder at lower elevations. He wondered if Tom had followed through with his plan to buy additional slaves. He dismissed the question once he saw a couple of dilapidated newer buildings built since he had left the county. But, of course, he did, and from appearances, the men were now long gone.

A small group of blue-uniformed Union soldiers marched along the east side of the house where he had played as a child. He was sure that the outbuildings had been left unpainted since the beginning of the war. No one confronted him as he approached the house, now the headquarters of the local Union commander. The Stars and Stripes were flying on the flagpole out front. Sarge dismounted and walked up to the two guards slouching in the doorway. He wished he had been able to salvage his full uniform. They eyed him closely but let him pass, noting his Union cap and partial uniform.

He entered the building. A formidable, thick-necked corporal sat at a desk against the back wall. Sarge was standing at the edge of a large area that, in his youth, had been the parlor. He recognized most of the furnishings. Everything seemed shabby. He had to remind himself that it had been over nine years since he had last seen the room. A framed poster bearing Abraham Lincoln's likeness, framed in black, replaced his mother's painting over the fireplace. He imagined her portrait sitting against a wall in some back room. Both the loss of the President and the absence of his mother's image filled him with a sense of injury.

"I'd like to see the company commander." He addressed the huge corporal at the front desk. The clerk's hand-carved desk plaque read, "Corporal Yates." He was massive, easily as big as two men. His beetle brow furrowed. His cigar-sized fingers gripped a pen that hovered over what looked to be a logbook.

"What's your business?" He hesitated, taking in Sarge's attire. Sarge's civilian coat gave no hint of his rank, but his age and manner suggested seniority to his own. The huge man had dark eyes looking out over fleshy cheeks. His hair was black and hung down over his ears. His one nod to fashion was a shapely handle-bar mustache. He had an air of authority that exceeded his rank and suggested that he took personal pleasure in his position as gatekeeper to the officer in the office behind him.

"I'm Sergeant Madison Jones. I want to discuss my brother's release."

"Brother?" The corporal seemed at a loss for a moment, and then his eyes cleared. "Brother! I'll see what I can do, Sergeant." He rose abruptly like a behemoth from the deep, disappeared behind the door, and reappeared a moment later. "Major Rogers can see you. Go on in."

Sarge entered a modest bedroom converted into an office. The major sat with a captain at a small campaign desk in the middle of the room. He appeared of medium height and cleanly shaven, except for the mustache. His eyes were intelligent but, to Sarge, lacked the spark of ingenuity. Sarge could sense the officer making a quick assessment of him as well. The captain gave him a sidelong glance. He seemed to be watching the major for a clue on how to react. A bed had been pushed to one side and made up in army fashion.

Sarge approached the desk, stood at attention with his hat in his hand, and announced himself without saluting. "Former Sergeant Madison Jones, sir."

"At ease, Sergeant. You are out of uniform."

Sarge stood at ease and responded in a level voice. "I am a civilian, Sir. I mustered out of the third army in Alabama."

"I see." The major leaned back in his chair, gave Sarge a second once over, and glanced at the captain. "Corporal Yates said you were here about your brother?"

"Yes, Sir. I believe him unjustly arrested." His eyes did not waver.

"Well, that's interesting. How did you come to that conclusion without the facts? You must have just arrived?" The major leaned forward as if to give the matter his full attention.

"Yes, Sir. I got into town today. I've talked with the sheriff." He pressed the back of his hands into the small of his back and stood even straighter. "My brother is not a thief. He would never steal. Taking money is not in his nature. The sheriff has known him all his life and can corroborate that."

The major spoke with his head tilted back and his jaw jutted. "Well, the evidence suggests otherwise. I believe he used a secret entry into the library to gain access to the payroll. I suspect he didn't think we'd discover his methods, but our men were either more thorough than usual," He glanced at the captain, "or just lucky when they searched the room. The money was gone, and obviously, he had the means to obtain it, and looking over the condition of his farm, I'd say he had a motive, wouldn't you?"

"Sir! The evidence you mention is circumstantial. At least a dozen men in the community are familiar with the bookcase entrance. The sheriff and I talked about that half an hour ago in his office. Tom and I often brought friends into the library via the "secret" entrance, so it doesn't prove anything."

"Really? The passage does open to his bedroom." The major rubbed his jaw. "But whatever my conclusions, it is not my place to make the final judgment. Guilt is for a legal tribunal to decide. In the meantime, he should retain a local lawyer if he hasn't already."

"I'd like to see him as soon as possible, sir." Sarge struggled to keep his tone in check.

"As for your seeing him, that is impossible. No visitors other than his lawyer are allowed."

"But why?" Sarge was incredulous.

"I, too, have my orders, Sergeant. The strongbox that he stole contained the pay for every man in my command. Its theft under my watch does not enhance my military aspirations." He nodded at the younger captain to his left, who was nervously drumming his fingers on the desk, "or those of Captain Rumpole, who is the company paymaster and whose detail guarded the room." He gave the captain a hard look before returning to Sarge. "Your brother will be tried for theft and murder in five days. If convicted, he will face a firing squad." The major stood to signal that the interview was over.

"Murder?" Sarge took a step back. "Murder!" He was stunned at the additional charge.

The major nodded as if unaware of the surprise his statement would elicit. "Yes, there were two guards in the house. One in the room with the strongbox and one outside at the door. The guard inside was knifed during the robbery."

Sarge staggered in disbelief. "Tom would never kill anyone."

"He was involved in the killing of men very recently. He certainly had lots of opportunities. Your brother is a decorated Confederate soldier."

"It's not the same. You know it's not the same." Sarge could not grasp the news. The implications were stunning.

"For most men, it isn't the same. But most men don't have the motive and opportunity that are obvious in your brother's case." The major stepped toward the corner of his desk. "Get your brother a good lawyer, Sergeant. I'd suggest he turn the money back in. It might help with the robbery charge and establish a slim chance for him to avoid the firing squad." He motioned toward the door. "Good day!"

Sarge clenched his fists. He fought the impulse to climb over the desk after the self-satisfied officer. A small voice of reason managed to prevail. Instead, he turned and staggered from the room past the big corporal still staffing the desk. The big man's eyebrows arched. There was a flicker of a smile as he watched Sarge pass without a glance and go out the front door. Then he returned to his work. Back in his office, Major Rogers looked at the captain and cocked an eyebrow.

"There is something in what he said about the evidence being circumstantial, but he's the only suspect we've got."

"That fact does not rule out a conviction, sir."

16

Preacher stood in the open window of their second-floor room. He enjoyed watching the street. He had noted that Coates' eyes followed them to the tavern. He had reentered the hotel via the throughway between the two businesses to avoid the man. What had been the primary motivation for Coates' presence? Was he intent on retrieving the horses or his gun? Was he going to seek revenge? For some men, losing a relative or friend justified revenge, even in a case of justified self-defense. In Coates' case, he suspected a very low threshold for retaliation. Then, he heard heavy steps in the hallway, and the door burst open.

"Good, you're here!" Sarge threw himself onto the corner of the bed. "They've got Tom up on murder charges!" His face stricken, Sarge panted as much from exasperation as the climb up the stairs.

"What!" Preacher grabbed the chair and sat down. "Murder?" His friend's contorted face revealed his distress.

"Where's Bronco?" Sarge looked around.

"Over in the tavern trying to spark the young widow." Preacher said.

"I hope he is having more luck than I did," Sarge said. Then, he laid out the situation for Preacher, including his discussion with the sheriff. From time to time, he kneaded his forehead as he talked.

"I'll be." Preacher ran his open hand over his head and the back of his neck. "This looks bad. You're right about the circumstantial part, but that doesn't mean he will get off." He looked pensive. "By the way, we aren't shed of John Coates. Bronco and I ran across him down by the livery, and then he kept track of us to the tavern. No telling what his scheme is."

Sarge's eyes widened for a moment before his mind returned to the more immediate problem. "Well, we'll have to keep an eye out," Sarge said. "I need to get word to Tom that I'm working on this. I honestly don't know if I can count on the Sheriff as a go-between. Tom needs a lawyer in a hurry. I used to know a good man who knew my brother. I'll see if he is still around after all these years."

"I agree. I wouldn't bet you can depend on the Sheriff to be on the square with you." Preacher said. "Why don't you find your lawyer, and I'll see if I can round up Bronco."

"I appreciate your letting me walk you home, Miss Sarah," Bronco said as he and Mrs. Sarah Jordon reached Miss Emmy's porch. He took off his Union cap as she turned to face him. It had been comforting for her to let him ramble on about his growing-up years in Ohio. It seemed like a long way off, but he made it sound normal and peaceful. His friendship with Madison Jones, a southerner, though a scallywag and his friendly conversation with Pappy Jordon had made him seem a lot less villainous than other Yankees she had to deal with at the Lucky Star. Although she ignored some stares from people she knew, he made her feel normal. She was darkly aware that it could be a long while before walking down the street in Titustown, Georgia, with a Yankee soldier would be a common sight.

"I appreciate your company, Mister Brumley. You wouldn't believe how rude some of these Yankee men are." Her eyes shifted to the street and back to his face.

"If they trouble you, just let me know!" Bronco stuck out his chest and glanced around to verify that she was not in imminent danger.

"We could sit in the swing?" She knew she was pushing convention with the offer, but she wanted the feeling of normalness to last a little longer.

"As long as I can look at your pretty face, I'd sit on hot embers," Bronco said solemnly.

That made her laugh a bit. They sat, and Bronco pushed off the porch floor to start the slow swinging. She removed her wide-brimmed straw hat. "I bet you have made many ladies laugh, haven't you?"

He grinned teasingly, "Maybe not always on purpose." His face became serious. "I think you are the most beautiful girl I've ever seen," he said emphatically.

"Thank you, Mister Brumley, but don't forget, I am a married woman. I pray continuously that Mister Jordon makes it home safe." Her lip trembled a little.

"Well, to be honest, I'm sorry he hasn't come home for your sake and yet hoping a little that he won't for mine." Her words subdued him but couldn't extinguish his feelings.

Sarah looked at him closely. "I bet if this horrible war had not started up, Mister Brumley, that you and my husband could be friends. He is a good man. He's a good worker and honest as the day is long, but he doesn't speak out much, not even back during the short time we were courting. I guess the most I've ever heard him say at one time is when he asked me to marry him before he left for the army." Her eyes drifted away with her thoughts.

"If you weren't already married, maybe you would marry me?" Bronco exclaimed. She looked sidewise at him.

"I don't know, Mister Brumley. After all, we've only known each other for two days." He liked her laugh.

17

Preacher stuck his head in the tavern and looked around. The elderly Miss Emmy saw him and pointed south with a backward wave of disapproval. "Brown house four corners down and turn left. I expect you'll find what you're looking for."

Preacher tipped his cap and glanced up and down the street. He celebrated a little that there was no sign of Coates since early in the day. Maybe he had moved on? He headed south down the street. Now, he had heard enough about the robbery to wonder if Sarge was too confident of his brother's innocence. Slavery was a nasty business, and Tom's use of slaves was a decidedly adverse factor in Preacher's opinion of his character. He stopped to look in a shop window.

Mister John Coates stood next to a hitching post a block down the street, watching the young couple rock gently in the swing. He frowned at the picture. Another randy Yankee was looking to despoil southern womanhood. And a married woman at that! His blood boiled at the thought. He never had much use for her husband, Jimmy Jordon, but still! He was to their rear. He knew he could easily approach them and put a bullet in the man's head without resistance. It was tempting. It was very tempting.

Yet, as he moved forward, he hesitated. If this was to pass as a mission to restore honor, it must have all the trappings of fair play. Doing it according to the code of the times would serve to leave him cleansed. Then, of course, there was the additional fact that at least half a dozen citizens in the immediate area knew him and his family, in person or by reputation. Since that reputation was not very virtuous, he needed to make this a clean, self-defense situation for the local law's benefit. His worthless cousins deserved no less. A sneer broke the solemn planes of his face as he put together a prospective explanation for the sheriff.

Coates moved closer until only a few yards away. His right hand dangled tensely in front of his frock coat, which he had tucked away from his holster. The revolver John had rescued from the dead man on his trip east seemed adequate for the job ahead, though not in the best condition. He was practically at the porch railing when he spoke.

"Step off the porch, Yankee," Coates commanded. Venom governed his tone. He stepped back and around so that only fifteen feet separated him and his prey.

Bronco and Sarah stiffened. The familiar drawl was an octave lower now, and the sound raised the hackles on the back of Bronco's neck. He turned his head, and his eyes met those of John Coates. He immediately recognized that the man tapping his holster wanted revenge. Bronco lay his hand protectively on Sarah's arm. Despite the immediate danger, that contact sent a thrill through him. First, touch! He gently squeezed her arm and slowly rose from the swing. Bronco was mindful of the girl's scent, her stiffened body, and her terrified face so close and beautiful. The gunman standing in the street obscured his thoughts of the absent husband.

Bronco could not know Coates' plans, but he grasped that outright murder was not the aim of this day's play, or he would already be dead. So, with that confidence, he calmly opened the screen door and gently pulled Sarah up from her seat and into the protective shelter of the house. He closed the door firmly and turned. The situation seemed so surreal that he half-expected the strange dark figure to be gone when he turned again toward the street.

But Coates was still there, as tense as a coiled rattlesnake. Bronco stepped stealthily down from the porch. He moved away from the house toward the center of the street, knowing that each step made Sarah safer from a stray bullet.

"I'm challenging you to a duel." Coates fairly shouted the words. After a moment of confusion, people in the area started heading toward any available shelter. John liked the sound of the word duel. He noted that though he had killed before, he had never used the word duel before.

Bronco took a breath. His forty-four was holstered high on his hip, army fashion. Then, with Sarah still in mind, he stepped further from the porch.

"I won't draw." Bronco's gaze swept the street. There were several groups of citizens in the shadows. They were faceless from his vantage point.

"I don't care." Coates tapped his holster with his middle finger. He enjoyed the drama. He glanced around. And he liked the attention.

"It will be murder." Bronco hoped that the longer they talked, the better the chance of the gunfight getting broken up.

"Not in this town. You are a blue belly, and you have a gun. "

"What if I drop it?" Bronco smiled tightly at the mental picture the statement conjured up.

"When you touch it, you're dead."

"What if I turn around and walk away?" Bronco moved slowly closer to the middle of the street.

"You're dead. "

"What if my friend, Preacher, standing behind you, pulls the trigger?"

Coates' finger stopped tapping. He looked hard at Bronco. His senses waited for a repeat of the well-remembered clicking sound next to his ear. His head was not yet healed from the hard blow to his skull just a few days before. He heard nothing. He smelled a whiff of fresh bread from Mrs. Dawson's bakery down the street. He swore at the bakery, for the scent could be distracting him from the presence of a man behind him. The sky was robin's egg blue. A horse was trotting away in the distance, its rider oblivious to the two men in the street behind him. Coates' forehead creased. A drop of sweat gathered on his eyebrow. He looked into Bronco's eyes for some sense of the depth of his confidence. The solemn face told him nothing. He wondered if the young man played poker. John Coates remembered how loud the revolver sounded when Sarge discharged it an inch from his ear. Captain Owen's head had not been pretty the next morning. Was it possible? He was sure he would have heard something, but still, John had been unaware of Sarge's approach as he came up behind him. This young Yankee seemed strangely confident.

Coates' head swiveled ever so little to the left. Nothing was visible in his peripheral vision. He turned a couple of inches further. He still saw nothing. He smiled in satisfaction and swung his head back to face Bronco. His smile soured into a grimace over tobacco-stained teeth. Bronco's forty-four leveled at him with disconcerting steadiness.

"Drop the gun," Bronco ordered. Coates froze. Bronco took a pace closer. The forty-four did not waiver. He took another step. Then another. Coates knew that the closer Bronco advanced, the better his chance of a clean kill shot.

The men were now only six feet apart. Even a tenderfoot could plug him dead center. He quickly reminded himself that this youngster was not a tenderfoot. The question of whether he was as good with a six-gun as he was with a rifle was no longer relevant. Even if only wounded, no wound was painless. The longevity of the pain from Sarge's crack to the top of his head affirmed that. He slowly brought his gun hand away from the holster and up to his vest pocket. He drew out his pocket watch and looked at it meaningfully. "Looks like time for dinner."

"Yes, it is. Turn around," Bronco ordered.

Coates turned, eager to have his decision validated by the presence of Bronco's friend. He stood alone. He cursed himself. There was no sign of the man they called Preacher. He heard the crunch of Bronco's boots in the gravel and felt the swish of metal against leather as once again his gun slid from the holster. His scalp tensed in anticipation of another blow to the back of his head.

18

The sign read, *Mister Anthony Dulles: Attorney*. Sarge opened the door and encountered the back of a white-haired man looking for a book on the shelves. "Good afternoon; I'm looking for Anthony."

The man turned, and Sarge smiled. "Good grief, Anthony, what happened to your hair!"

The man looked at Sarge. For a moment, he seemed mystified. He blinked and then laughed. "I always tell people it's the war." He said. He strode forward and shook Sarge's hand. He took the measure of this younger version of Tom Jones. The likeness between the two brothers was strong, but the Yankee uniform made his mind recoil a bit.

When Madison told him his business, the attorney worked to keep a straight face. Tom had not held back his disgust for his younger brother all those years ago when he lost his slave, Brownie. Tom had called Madison a thief. As they discussed Tom's dilemma, Anthony thought how ironic that the more youthful "thief" was now trying to deliver his older accuser from the same charge compounded by the more ominous charge of murder. Anthony agreed to represent Tom, though he said he badly needed details to do so effectively.

"Thank you, Anthony. Simultaneously I seem to be an outsider both in my hometown and with the army I fought with. Will you check on Tom as soon as you can? I want him to know I'm here. I'll do whatever it takes to get him out."

"Hey, everyone! This here Yankee tried to kill me," Coates called out loudly as people started coming out of hiding. Both of his hands were over his head.

"Shut up, Coates. I'm taking you down to the sheriff's office," Bronco said evenly.

"I saw it." A man stepped up. Bronco knew that his uniform was all the man needed to see.

"Hey, Bob." Coates waved one of his hands. "This Yankee just pulled a gun while I was peaceably walking down the street." He pointed over his shoulder. "That damned Yankee uniform is a sure giveaway."

"That ain't right." Another man piped up.

"What do you expect from a Yankee!" A man shouted as he jumped from his wagon down to the street.

A woman moved closer. Another man came up behind her, and two more people edged in from the right and three from the left. Finally, a man dragging his foot came up to Bronco's right side.

Bronco gauged the group nervously as more people gathered. He could feel the beginnings of a mob. A clamor rose from the rapidly growing crowd. He was suddenly conscious that these people had recently lost loved ones to men dressed in the same uniform he wore. A few voices protested Coates' version of events, but they seemed to be a minority and drowned out by the shouts of affirmation. He caught the voice of Sarah from the porch, but he doubted anyone else did.

Bronco swung his revolver right to left to ward off the crowd, but the people edged closer. Then, someone, perhaps in jest, or maybe not, mentioned a rope, and a rumble of voices agreed.

"Hey!" A new voice shouted above the din. "I know this boy. He's alright."

A hush settled over the crowd. Bronco looked sidewise and saw that it was Mister Pappy Jordon from the Star. The older man drew himself up to his full height and spoke with surprising authority.

"This here is a friend of Madison Jones." He looked around. "Yes, Tom Jones' brother. The Tom Jones that is sitting in our jail right now falsely accused of robbing the army." He glared at the crowd with such furious intensity that those in the first row shrank back a step.

Pappy pointed at Coates. "Every one of you knows Tom Jones by hisself has more principles than the Coates clan all put together." He looked at Bronco. "What say we take this skunk to the sheriff's office?"

"Just what I was planning to do!" Bronco agreed.

"This is the sheriff's business, all right," Pappy said. "The rest of you move on before I pull out my iron."

The crowd started to disburse, and the older man looked at Bronco. He ran his finger across his mustache. "See how they skedaddled when I mentioned pulling my iron?" He cackled and jabbed Coates in the ribs with his finger. "You know where the jail is, Coates. Lord knows you've spent enough time there."

Preacher stood rooted in place a bit down the street, away from the commotion. He was late for the party and decided that old man Jordon and Bronco seemed to have things well in hand. Besides, his head was still buzzing with a hangover.

19

Sarah watched Bronco and Pappy march Coates down the street. Then, finally, she sat on the swing again. After all the excitement, she had a chance to be a bit shocked that Bronco had taken her hand without encouragement. But he was so earnest and protective that it was hard to hold his boldness against him. But she was still troubled remembering Jimmy.

Everything with Jimmy had happened so quickly. Well, she thought, not fast so much as unexpected. They had known each other since grade school. But then the war started while she was a senior. Jimmy was only one of a half dozen boys in the county interested in her. She rather enjoyed the attention. There was Bobby Roy, whose father owned a hardware store. Rob Masters' father was a barber for as long as she could remember. Clarence Todd's father owned a farm just out of town. They had all been kind to her. They competed with each other for dances, and they bid up her pies at the pie socials.

It made her feel like a princess or even a queen! She knew she was pretty. Even the other girls agreed on that. But once, when Mary Jane's boyfriend was ogling her, another boy reminded him that he had a girlfriend. That set off an argument, and they even wrestled a little. It embarrassed both Mary Jane and Sarah. Later, Sarah tried to apologize, but Mary Jane took a long while to get over it.

When the war began, and many of the local men took off, it was kind of a lark. The oldest boys sometimes went with their fathers. Everyone expected it would be a short thing. Then some of the patriots came back shot up. Judy Clark's father returned in a box, and everything suddenly became serious. Those Yankees weren't giving up. They turned out to be pretty good shots, and there seemed to be more of them than anyone realized.

Sarah gently rocked the swing and thought about all those boys. Every six months after the war started, a recruiter appeared in town and told the local boys that Robert E. Lee needed them. He said the Confederacy was in danger and needed more men right that day. So first, one boy and then another signed up, and without anyone knowing how it happened, the boys started asking the girls, even those still in school, to marry them! It was crazy!

First, George Massy had approached her, and she said absolutely not. Then Bobby Roy knelt there on that very porch and said he was going to war and didn't want to be so far away and not know she was waiting for him. It was painful to say no to Bobby Roy. He was such a sweet boy. He stuttered a little when he asked, and she looked away and said she couldn't. But saying no so many times kind of wore her down, and then there was Jimmy Jordon. She had always liked Jimmy best. He was quiet and never teased her like other boys—he just stood by and admired her. So, when Jimmy finally asked her in his halting shy way, she couldn't say no! It had seemed patriotic to say yes and send him away happy. She wasn't sure what would happen when he came back. His folks did own a large farm. She guessed she'd be a farmer's wife. Then she thought about the last four months without a letter or word. She painfully corrected herself-if he came back.

She tossed her tresses and twisted the wedding ring on her finger. She did love Jimmy, and she so wanted him to come home. He had written her almost every day for over a year, and she replied to every letter. But sometimes, his letters didn't arrive for a couple of weeks after being posted. Now, over four months had passed with no word. Then the worst of all possible moments arrived when word came of Jimmy's death east of Atlanta. But it wasn't for sure, and there was nothing official. She had cried then. Wasn't it okay to cry? It hurt so much. Jimmy, sweet Jimmy! Her brother Luke had invited her to come live in San Francisco when she graduated from high school, and she had considered it until she married Jimmy Jordon. It seemed unlikely after that.

And here was Bronco, and the war was over, and he was obviously interested in her. She had not invited that. She knew she just wanted to be comforted. She wanted to feel safe with things settled. She mostly wanted to hear Jimmy speak those cherished words of love out loud! Jimmy had always seemed so hesitant to speak up. When would everything be resolved? After acknowledging that, Sarah jumped up from the swing and opened the screen. With a last glance down the street, she moved inside and closed the door.

Preacher intended to return to the room and lie down in hopes of alleviating his aching head until he spotted a church steeple over the nearby rooftops and ambled in that direction instead. When he turned the corner, he found a Baptist church. He supposed it didn't really matter what denomination it was, as he always felt a pull from any church. It was a place that held the reminiscent scent of hymnals and the sound of familiar music that had played such an essential part in his life.

As he got closer, he realized that someone was playing the piano. He mounted the two steps and quietly opened the door. A middle-aged lady sat erect over the keyboard to the right side of the chancel with her head cocked forward a bit, reading the music. He sat down carefully in the pew second from the back. He smiled, remembering the number of times he had joked from the pulpit about people sitting in the back pew. That seemed so far away now, but the feel of a church was the same. He sat and leaned gently against the armrest and listened. He closed his eyes and just let the music roll over him. How perfect the old hymns were. Maybe the cadence would simply wash his headache away? He sang the words silently, remembering all the times he had stood beside the pulpit and enjoyed the sweet harmony of a choir. An ache in his heart now melded with the pain in his skull. His big head slumped forward, and he thanked his Lord for the life he had enjoyed, for his time in the church, and the peace the music gave him. It took him a moment to realize that the music had stopped. When he looked up, the little woman was gathering up her music. He made to rise and caught his big foot on the edge of the pew.

The little woman looked over in surprise at the sound of the impact. He straightened and side-hopped out to the center aisle.

"Hope you don't mind my listening in." Preacher said.

She recovered quickly from her surprise. "Not at all, young man." She walked toward him with a half-smile.

"Well, not as young as you seem to think." Preacher laughed.

She approached him and hesitated a moment before putting her hand out. She was small, tidy, he thought, and the veins were prominent on the back of her hand. Preacher always admired small hands on a woman. He took it in his big paw and felt her squeeze his fingers briefly.

"Well, I'll be on my way, ma'am. I'm kind of passing through with a couple of friends."

"I know who you are!" she exclaimed. "The whole town is talking about Major Tom Jones being in jail, and now Mister Madison Jones is back. We were worried, but we know Mister Jones will straighten things out." The words came out so rushed that she had to stop and catch her breath.

"Well, ma'am. I hope you're right. Things are looking kind of iffy right now," Preacher said. He looked up at the high ceiling. "It is good to be in this place."

"It is, isn't it!" she agreed. Do you go to church regularly, young man?" Her eyes took in the width of his shoulders.

"Yes, ma'am. When I can. Not as often as I'd like while I've been in the army, but I'm out now and will be going more often."

"I forgot to tell you my name." the woman pointed at herself. "I'm Miss Maggie Taylor. I've been going to this church since the day the doors opened when I was a girl."

"I'm Pre...., Robert Gracey." Preacher caught himself and gave her his given name and then felt embarrassed that he didn't tell her his nickname instead. "People call me Preacher, ma'am." He cast his eyes down for a moment with some confusion. "I served as a pastor for a good while before joining the army."

"That's interesting." She motioned him toward a pew. They sat side by side. "So, were you a chaplain in the army?"

"No, ma'am. At first, I thought I'd serve as a chaplain, but the chaplain corps is comprised of commissioned officers. It is a very small command, and unfortunately, a bit of political clout is required, which I could not summon at the time. But they did need soldiers, and I just signed up in the infantry."

"We lost our pastor here a year ago. He was the only one we've ever had. It seems like only yesterday when he preached his first sermon." Miss. Taylor gave Preacher an appraising look and rose to her feet. "Well, Mister Gracey, I should be off. I have other preparations to make. I hope you will be able to join us this Sunday!"

"Thank you, ma'am." Preacher stood and followed her out. He stood on the sunny church porch and breathed deeply in the midday air as he watched her walk away.

<h1 style="text-align:center">20</h1>

The three men sat together in the tavern for supper enjoying mashed potatoes, cabbage, and pot roast. Bronco related his run-in with Coates.

"I wonder what our friend, Coates, is having over at the jail." Bronco smiled.

"It's probably pretty good. Jail looks well run." Sarge said. "What is Sheriff Beckett holding him on?"

"Disturbing the peace. Pappy Jordon's complaint made it stick. Coates wanted us arrested for what happened over in Alabama, but the sheriff said it wasn't in his jurisdiction and no concern of his."

"I saw you and Jordon heading toward the sheriff's office." Preacher volunteered. "Looked like you had things well in hand."

"It was pretty sticky for a while." Bronco acknowledged. "First with Coates getting the drop on me, and then the crowd wanting to hang me. Doesn't this meat taste like the embalmed beef we used to get once a week in the army?" Bronco took another bite.

"I suppose someone in the local quartermaster's office could be benefiting from his unique position," Sarge said with a smile.

"Black market for just about everything, I expect." Preacher bit off a chunk of warm bread. "Now, this homemade bread is to write home about."

"We've got to come up with a plan." Sarge frowned. "Otherwise, Tom will go into court on Monday and in front of a firing squad by Tuesday." Sarge rubbed his squinted eyes.

"Well, we think he didn't do it." Preacher said.

"Not think, know! Someone else did it!" Sarge exclaimed. He gave Preacher an annoyed look.

"Who else had access?" Bronco said.

"The men stationed at headquarters," Preacher said.

"The major for one?" Bronco ventured.

"The strongbox probably weighed at least a hundred pounds. Not knowing about the secret entrance, the thief would have had to haul it out right in front of the guards and office personnel hanging about. Then, of course, he could have paid someone off."

"A local? Seems a stretch." Sarge said. "A local could have known about the secret entrance. But he would have had to get past guards just to get in the house."

"The guards themselves?" said Preacher. He answered his own question. "But then you have the same problem as the major compounded by lack of rank."

"What if the guards were in on it together?" Bronco said. "One of them is greedy and kills the other."

"Maybe, but wouldn't it make better sense to kill your accomplice somewhere else rather than in the room?" Sarge said.

"You've told us there is a secret entrance into the library. But how does it work?" Bronco asked.

"There is a bookshelf that pivots out in the library. It is hinged on one side and has rollers on the floor. When you swing it open, you are looking at the back of another bookcase in Tom's room that works the same way." Sarge said.

"Has it always been Tom's room?"

"No, it used to be my parents."

"Are there any other exits from that room?" Preacher asked.

"The door out to the hallway had a guard. I know of no other way out besides the hidden door to Tom's room. Well, I suppose the killer could have climbed out the window, but he would have to deal with the two guards stationed on the porch. Even if he knew about the secret door, the thief would have had to carry the strongbox through Tom's room while he slept. Tom was always a light sleeper. I don't see how that could happen."

"I wonder if the major's men searched Tom's room as thoroughly as they did the library. If so, they might have found the strongbox hidden in the room or perhaps another hidden passage." Preacher avoided Sarge's glare.

"I told you, Tom didn't do it!"

"I'm getting dizzy," Bronco said. He winced with some alarm at the tension between his two friends. Bronco remembered seeing people turn on each other in a pinch.

"I'm going to pay another visit to the sheriff," Sarge said. "Maybe I can sweet-talk some more cooperation out of him."

Bronco walked the few blocks toward Sarah's house. Her absence at the tavern had been disappointing. He strode down the street in happy anticipation, for the potential return of her husband hardly entered his mind. Even though she had reminded him repeatedly that she was married, in a way, it seemed like her husband Jimmy didn't exist. In Bronco's reality, there were just the two of them. He knocked at the door and was pleased to see her look through the curtain.

Sarah flung the door open and stepped out on the porch. "Oh, Mister Brumley! I'm so glad you are all right!"

"Well, you weren't at the Lucky Star, Miss Sarah, so I thought I'd check up on you." Bronco took his hat off and held it in front of him.

"It's my evening off." Sarah's mind was conflicted because of the scene she had seen earlier in the day. *My Aunt, Emmy, would have had a fit if I'd shown up to check on you, even though you survived a life and death situation,* Sarah thought to herself. She moved toward the swing. The early evening was alive with the scent of lilac; the street was almost abandoned. She sat down, and he followed.

Bronco shrugged. He tried not to show his pleasure at her concern.

"I watched through the curtain," She said. "I couldn't hear what you said, but I almost fainted when you made that evil man look away and then got your gun on him. I was so scared he would just shoot you!" Her face turned ashen. "To lose my husband and then a friend would have just been too much." She whispered.

"Well, I'm not saying it wasn't a close call, but it worked out alright." Bronco dared to lean closer and take her hand to comfort her.

Sarah startled and looked up. Then she gently disengaged his fingers from her hand. Then, after a pause, she spoke to him softly.

"You should go, Mister Brumley," she whispered.

"Yes, Ma'am." Bronco stood. He felt they had come perilously close to some meaningful moment. His breath came quickly.

She gazed up at him. Then, in the deepening dusk, he thought he saw a gleam in the corner of her eye. "Good night, Mister Brumley." She stood and took a step toward the door.

He waited as if anticipating something but not knowing what.

She took another step. She pulled the screen open, and her hand grasped the knob. She took a deep breath, and Bronco sensed she forced herself to speak lightly, "Good night, Mister Brumley. I'll see you tomorrow?"

"Yes, Ma'am," Bronco said softly. He wheeled about and put his cap on. He stepped off the porch and took a few steps. Looking back, he could see her face framed in the window for a moment. He carried that image down the street and into the livery stable as he brushed down all three horses singing softly to himself.

Sarge cracked open the door to the sheriff's office and gave it a quick knock before entering. "Hello, Sheriff," he said.

Sheriff Beckett looked up from his newspaper and removed his glasses. "Hello, Madison. Come in." An elderly deputy lounged in a chair on the other side of the desk. "This here is Deputy Boggs."

Sarge shook hands with the deputy, who appraised his Union hat with some suspicion. Sarge then took a seat and was silent for a moment. The sheriff folded the paper and set it aside.

"What can I do for you, Madison?" He leaned forward on his elbows. "How did things go with the major?"

Sarge struggled for a moment against an outburst, then quietly asked the question weighing most heavily on his mind. "Why didn't you tell me Tom is charged not only with robbery but also murder?"

The sheriff straightened upright in his chair. "What?"

"The major didn't tell you?" Sarge watched the man's eyes carefully. He glanced over at the deputy as well. Both men registered surprise.

"I don't know what you are talking about." Beckett's voice sounded strangled. His jaw worked.

Only half convinced of their surprise, Sarge told the two men about his visit with the major and reiterated the theft and murder charges.

Sheriff Beckett shook his head with amazement. "I'm sorry, Madison. They brought Tom to me for housing in my jail. They said the charge was the theft of the strongbox. They didn't mention anything about the murder."

"Doesn't that seem odd?" Sarge asked.

"Yes and no. I can see that the major might be afraid that locals would be more apt to spring him if the charge was murder, him being a local hero and all. I can see that the major wouldn't want to trust a local jury under any circumstances. But..."

Sarge interrupted. He bent forward and grabbed the corner of the desk. "What do you mean by that?"

"Why I thought you'd know, what with you being in the Union Army. We're under martial law. A military court will try Tom. The offense, or offenses, occurred on property occupied by the army against a Union soldier."

"Why, Tom doesn't stand a chance!" Sarge was on his feet. He could feel the sweat starting to slide down the back of his neck. "He's a civilian!"

"I guess that doesn't matter on army turf." Sheriff Beckett looked at Sarge in alarm. He had never seen a sober man so worked up. "I discussed this with Dulles when he was in earlier. Anthony went back and talked with Tom for a while. As far as I know, the military court part is on the up and up."

"Sheriff, I've got to see Tom! Please, just for a few minutes."

Beckett waved him off. "I have orders for no one other than Tom's lawyer to see him. I understand your wanting to, but I have no excuse."

"Sheriff, you claim to be his friend!" Sarge said tersely.

"Yes, we are friends." The sheriff looked at the deputy. "Amos, why don't you go make the rounds. I can tend to this."

The deputy rose to oblige, and Beckett held up his hand to pause the discussion for a moment. He fiddled with papers on his desk until the deputy was well on his way.

"Madison, I shouldn't do this; it could be the end of my sheriffin', but Tom and I go way back, and given the seriousness of the charges, I agree you need to visit with him regardless of the major's rules. I'll let you go back. But this is between the two of us. Agree? "

Sarge nodded, grabbed the sheriff's hand, then stepped back as Beckett retrieved the keys and opened the door to the lockup.

"I let John Coates out earlier. I didn't want to feed his ornery butt any longer than I had to."

21

Coates mounted his horse and headed back to his Uncle Rufus' farm. A shortcut earlier in the day had permitted him to stop by to report his cousins' loss before venturing into town close behind the Yankees. Presumably, another cousin or two would be assigned the task of making the two-day trek back to recover their brothers' bodies. The father's apparent grief at the news surprised John because while they were growing up, the old man's response to even trivial misdeeds was usually a thrashing.

Coates gritted his teeth. The old devil was going to get his due someday. At the moment, John's immediate concern was avenging the wound on the top of his skull and the humiliation he suffered being hogtied to a tree. During his ride, John fantasized about separating Sarge's brother from the gold Bronco mentioned. But then, learning of the presence of the company of Union soldiers at the Jones farm put a cap on that idea. John's need for personal revenge ate at him. He would have it even under the guise of righteous vengeance for the loss of the war. He was already thinking of how to mesh vengeance with the older man's supposed bereavement.

He dismounted. The older man was coming out of the out-house out in the back. He was still drawing up his suspenders when he saw John. He scowled.

"Schooley and Barney are headed toward Sweetwater right now. I think it would have been better if you had gone too. What if they can't find the bodies?"

"I'm right, sorry, uncle, but you can see the condition of my horse, not to mention myself. I'm plumb tuckered, and there's just no time for laying around here resting up. They know how I marked where I left them, and I did the best I could for the bodies, but it's already been over two days."

"So, why are you back out here now?"

"Revenge, Uncle, pure and simple revenge. I want to discuss my ideas about attacking that Union post and killing a few Union criminals. Plus, I want to 'specially get the three who killed Sam and Willard."

Rufus looked at John with suspicion. "You are stupider every day." He spat and turned to mount the steps. He seemed to have a second thought. He turned and grabbed the rail to steady himself. "You ain't doing no night ridin' till my boys get back. And you won't be telling me your ideas. You'll be getting my orders. Get your ass out of my sight before I lose my temper." He climbed painfully up the remaining steps, and the door slammed behind him.

Having been uninvited into the house, John headed for the barn where Rufus made his moonshine. His face was red.

"I'll get your carcass eventually," he vowed.

The sheriff led the way back to the cells. They were about ten by eight feet in size, arrayed along the back of the building in a set of four with a heavy door opening to the back alley to one side. There was just room enough for a bunk, a small table, a chamber pot, and a chair in each cell. Each cell had a small barred window high up on the back wall. Sarge could see that someone had swept up recently. No signs of pests that often infest jails. The bunks, though primitive, were made up and looked clean. His heart was racing when they reached Tom's cell. The man lying on the bunk looked older than Sarge expected. His slumped posture made him appear shorter than Sarge remembered and spare. The man heaved around at the sound of their approach and dropped his feet to the floor. He squinted his eyes in the pervasive gloom. The click of the key in the lock brought a look of anticipation to his face.

"Tom, I've got someone you'll want to see." Sheriff Beckett swung the door open.

Sarge stepped into the cell without a word and reached out to grab the older man's shoulders before he could stand. He could feel the bones through his flannel shirt. After the perfunctory embrace, Tom reached out his left hand and turned it sidewise as if to shake Sarge's right hand. Sarge grabbed the extended hand and pulled his brother to his feet. Tom seemed so diminished. His eyes were sunken, and his hairline had receded.

"Madison! Anthony told me you were here in town. I can't believe it." Tom said.

Sarge reached out, took his brother's scrawny shoulders in his hands again, and steadied him.

"I wasn't sure I would ever see you again," Sarge said—moisture formed on the inside corners of his eyes. Sarge looked down, pushed away, and stared at his brother, incredulous. "Your arm! What happened to your arm?"

"Damned Yankee sniper. Probably aimed for my head." Tom glanced down. His right arm stopped at his elbow.

The sheriff excused himself. He duly locked the cell, and they sat in silence for a moment until the door to the office slammed shut. The quiet hung in the air like an evil cloud.

"At least part of it is still here." Tom broke the silence and waved his right stump to demonstrate. "And I've still got my legs." He slowly got to his feet and did a couple of march steps to prove it and almost fell as a knee gave way. He dropped back against the bunk groggily.

"But how?" Sarge couldn't finish the question. He allowed Tom to pull him down to sit beside him. His mind raced. Pictures of their youth flashed through his mind. Growing up, Tom had been the hale and hearty one. He was the best runner, swimmer, and worker in Harlon County. Sure, Sarge and his friend Brownie had been good at those things, but Tom had always been a bit taller and stronger. Now, this!

"I caught the mini ball about six weeks ago." Tom's speech seemed a little off. "I came home to recuperate, which worked fine until the Yanks ran off the Home Guard boys stationed here and commandeered the house for their headquarters three weeks ago." He tucked the stump against his side like a hen tucks her wing. "Things have been crazy for the last week."

"I just got into town yesterday," Sarge said, trying not to stare at his brother's dangling limb. "As soon as I learned about the charges, I came in to see Beckett and then visited with the major out at the farm. Do you know that they have you up for murder?"

"Murder? First time I've heard of it. I tell you, Madison, things are just going by so fast I can't keep up. Mind if I lay back?" Sarge stood so Tom could swing his legs around and resume his prone position.

Sarge pulled up the chair and sat facing him. "It's a whirr, all right. Beckett didn't say a thing about the murder charges. I got the news from the major. You have a trial in three days."

Tom closed his eyes. "The charges are absurd. But the major holds all the cards, I guess."

Sarge noted that there was no fire in his brother's eyes. "We aren't giving up." Sarge wondered at his brother's fatalism. His tone didn't sound like the Tom he knew.

"What can you do?" Tom sounded resigned. "I need to rest. Just let me rest." He closed his eyes.

Sarge shook him roughly. "Not until you tell me everything that happened from beginning to end. Every detail. Leave nothing out."

22

As the two men sat together in the darkened jail cell, Sarge pressed for details. Tom sighed deeply. Then he began. Addressing the questions, he covered everything between his medical discharge from the Confederate forces and his arrest.

"The local Home Guard boys had control of the farm. When I got back, they were cooperative, of course. They were on my property, and as a major, I had rank on everyone else locally. The local commander turned my bedroom back over to me. A couple of local women changed my bandages. I am mending all right, I think, but I'm not completely healed yet," Tom said. He raised his stump as if to illustrate the point.

"Then we got word that Lee had surrendered, and the locals disbanded. A week later, the Union troops arrived and took over where our southern boys had left off. Major Rogers made allowance for my wound and left me to my own devices. I could do whatever I wished. There are still some ragtag gangs in the area stirring up trouble, so he has been vigilant. I pretty much went back to my old routine."

"Do you have any ideas about the stolen strongbox?" So far, Sarge had learned nothing useful.

"I can't seem to keep a train of thought since I've been home. I woke up Wednesday with that big corporal standing over me. He said I stole the payroll. I was so baffled at the situation that I just brushed it off."

"Have you noticed any neighbors on the premises who may have known about the secret door? Give me something to work with." The lack of helpful information aggravated Sarge. "Did you ever see the strongbox? Did you notice anything suspicious with the Union troops? Is it possible that major is behind it? Come on, Tom!"

Tom frowned. He didn't like the cross-examination. "No, no, and I doubt it!" He threw his hand up. "Just leave me in peace."

"How could a strongbox be moved into or through your room without waking you up? You have always been such a light sleeper," Sarge said.

Tom sighed. His eyes shifted from Sarge's face to the table where two items rested, a bottle and a spoon. Sarge picked up the bottle. He read the indistinct label with the skull and cross-bones. *Laudanum! Damn, the answers to my questions were right in front of me?* Sarge looked over at his brother.

"So, you were knocked out? They could have run a train through your room that night!"

"I'm afraid so," Tom dully lay in his bunk as Sarge speculated on possibilities for a while without uncovering any new ideas.

A half-hour later, the sheriff came back. He could tell that Sarge had little to celebrate from the look on his face. Beckett opened the door for him to leave the cell and then the outside door. He glanced up and down the street as he let Sarge out. "Good luck, Madison. I know you'll do everything you can."

23

Tom watched Madison leave with the sheriff. Everything was so hazy. It had taken him a month to get used to the stump. How many times had he reached for something with his right hand and literally come up short? From appearances, his arm seemed healed now, but he still felt like he needed his medication. Since he had lost half of his arm, everything that had once been easy had become a chore. Tying his shoes required a degree of dexterity never needed before, so he had switched to boots. He had always been a big, strong man who could bull his way through work and life. Now he felt weak and lifeless. He was almost glad that Jenny, his beautiful wife, had died before she had to see him in his misery. Her passing had spared her this drama, and he half-wished the same for himself.

Madison! The last person he had expected to see again was Madison. When he first disappeared all those years ago, Tom immediately realized that Brownie had left as well. It was embarrassing the next day when the trader delivered three field hands, and Tom's end of the trade was not available. He cursed Madison that day. He'd dipped into cottonseed money to pay for the men. He even considered putting a bounty on Madison and

Brownie's heads but thought better of it. It didn't seem likely they'd be caught, and if they were, it would just be more of his cotton money going out the door.

He cursed his brother daily as he put the new men to work building a bunkhouse and plowing for spring planting. Unlike Brownie and Madison, these men, not accustomed to working with construction tools, relied on brute strength and stamina. Gradually he learned that they each had a story of their own. One had been mistreated, and the other two separated from loved ones. All resented their status. They didn't parade their angst around or attempt conversation with him, but it hung over and around them. He learned their stories indirectly, from the exchanges he overheard and songs they sang as they worked. It took a while to appreciate that they were more than muscle and sinew. They could learn to take pride in their work. To his surprise, they seemed to grow a slight sense of attachment to him over time, at least until he left to fight for the southern cause.

So, in his heart, he blamed Madison for Brownie's absence while intellectually acknowledging that Brownie would be gone via the planned trade even if Madison had not helped him escape. Eventually, he permanently erased his younger brother from his mind, but doing so did not eradicate the overshadowing feeling of betrayal.

In the fall and winter, after the day's work, Tom went to the library and sat at the oversized desk or lay on the big leather sofa surrounded by books and tried to read. He had never been a big reader. His mind would stray, and Tom would worry about his farm. As the years passed, things got worse with Washington, and he worried about the wild talk of secession. In the summer evenings, he sat on the wide front porch, looked out over his land, and listened to the slaves out behind the bunkhouse enjoying an elemental social life he had lost when his brother disappeared. His loss of Jenny and the boy who had died during childbirth was an endless drain. Day by day, his list of grudges grew. Somehow, he lay every setback on his absent brother. He told himself that he never wanted to see Madison again. Eventually, he resigned himself to a life alone. Tom reached for the bottle next to his bunk and took a swig. He was too tired to fool with the spoon. The bitter liquid soothed the gnawing in his soul.

After his time with Sarah, Bronco returned to the livery stable to check on the horses. He would have uttered a "yea-haw" if the street had been less busy. After a brief stop, he strode toward the boarding house, his feet dancing in tune with the spinning in his head. Sarah was so pretty. Bronco felt he had only imagined love in his past, not experienced it. He admitted he had been in love with two girls in school. They were pretty and provocative when they batted their eyes. But he assured himself that it hadn't been 'pure love' like he felt growing for Sarah. She was the prettiest. So, his love for her must be the strongest he would ever feel.

Though conscious of Sarge's problem, it somehow seemed abstract since he did not have an active role. It was hard to believe that an innocent man could end up in front of a firing squad. Was he innocent? Sarge thought he was innocent, but could Sarge really be sure? Then Bronco hastily erased the possibility of Tom being guilty from the equation. If Sarge said he was innocent, then he was innocent. That was that. He wasn't sure what he could do. Sarge seemed to have taken the bull by the horns without assistance from either Preacher or himself. He decided to check the boarding house for an update.

24

Preacher was sitting in the parlor with his Bible when Bronco entered. Bronco stopped beside him and stood awkwardly, unsure if he was interrupting anything.

"Have a seat, Bronco. Sarge is up in the room. I thought I'd give him some time alone. He is feeling pretty discouraged."

"How did things go with his brother?"

"Not well. Tom is addicted to laudanum and has no ideas about the night of the robbery, who might be potential suspects or the aftermath."

"I guess I'll sit with you then?" Bronco dropped into a nearby chair. "I see you're reading the Bible. My grandmother used to do that a lot. She said it comforted her. She read some to me, and I've read it a little myself. I guess you've read it a lot, being a preacher and all."

Preacher closed the book. Then he opened it again. "Yes, I've read it a good deal. It's the only book I know that can speak to you from every page."

"I've wondered about your preaching days. Why did you quit?"

Preacher frowned and looked at the younger man with some indecision. "Well, I look at it as just a temporary interruption." He hesitated. "Alright, I'll give you the short version if you like." He waited as Bronco scooted his chair to a better angle and sat back.

"I first felt the calling when I was fifteen years old." Preacher said. "I can remember details of that night like no other before or since. We were outside enjoying the evening. I was catching fireflies. The dogs were chasing me and each other. An old mare was lingering close by the gate. It was late June, and the hot day had cooled to velvet. It was just after dark, and the moon was in its first quarter. The stars appeared like a blanket full of lights in the night sky. The cows were milked, and the eggs were gathered. My mother and father were sitting on the front porch, watching me and the dogs.

Preacher closed his eyes and hugged the book against his chest. "It was one of those perfect evenings. Everyone was well and strong. My parents were happy. I remember looking around and thinking, "how could it be any more perfect?"

Bronco listened intently. He, too, had been an only child. He wondered what it was like to have both parents.

Preacher smiled. "John Wesley was a preacher. He described his calling by saying that he 'felt strangely warmed.' It was kind of like that for me too. I think he was praying when he got his calling. But, for me, it was standing under the dome of the sky, catching fireflies and feeling the wholeness of God's creation around me."

Bronco nodded. He also enjoyed those moments of peace but had never connected a religious meaning to them.

"I just felt His presence, and once I felt it that way, I kept feeling it as I got older. So, I started reading the Bible and examining the gist of the hymns and sermons. Every step seemed to be leading me toward a life in the church."

"Don't you have to go to special schools?" Bronco sat forward.

"Well, there are special schools. They are called seminaries. I had no money to get a formal education. I just paid attention. I got to know the local Baptist preacher pretty well. He let me read the scripture at church on Sunday, and I sang in the choir. I was an eager learner."

"So, did you ever have a church?" Bronco sensed belatedly that the question could put Preacher on the spot. He looked away after he asked it.

"Well, I kind of inherited one. The minister at our church got called away to tend to his elderly parents for a few months. That short time turned into a long time. At first, I was just a fill-in. Eventually, we realized that Reverend Dickson would not be able to return. So, I became permanent. Many sermons are published in books, and preachers often use them in whole or part for their services. I remember Reverend Dickson giving me one of those publications when he left and telling me to use it as a guide, so I did that. A lot of preaching is in the delivery. I learned that you couldn't hold people's attention if you just got up and read it out of the sermon book." Preacher laughed. "I learned that the hard way."

Bronco's eyes had closed. Preacher smiled and kicked the young man's foot before standing up. "Enough for tonight. Let's get some shut-eye."

Bronco hauled himself up, a little embarrassed. He hadn't intended to doze off and offered a subdued apology as they clambered up the stairs. Opening the door, they found Sarge stretched out on the smaller bed. He was already asleep.

<h1 style="text-align:center">25</h1>

Sarge awoke early from a fitful sleep. Sometime during the night, he relived one of his outfit's long marches, followed by a smoke-filled vista of dying men and horses amid the noise of battle. Somehow the dream included his brother standing in front of a firing squad. In the dream, Sarge was unable to intervene.

Sarge dressed quickly and quietly so as not to wake the other men. He walked to the livery stable, saddled his horse, and rode toward the farm. One thought settled in his mind. *So far, there has never been a thorough investigation.* They found the guard's body and searched the room until they found the moving bookcase. The investigation ended there. From that point, the question of guilt centered on Tom. The secret door was the total extent of the evidence. They had arrested Tom. End of story. There had to be more.

It was Sunday. Sarge presented himself in front of the company clerk at nine A.M and requested to see the major.

"The major always arrives at nine-thirty on Sunday." Corporal Yates said. The clerk, freshly shaven, mustache newly waxed, the big man sorted papers on his desk. Aside from his size and weight, he appeared to be a man of good habits. Sarge wondered if he dared to test this man's good intentions?

"Maybe you can help me," Sarge said.

The corporal stopped his sorting and waited for further explanation. "Yes?"

"I'd like access to the library."

"Why?"

"I don't know exactly." Sarge searched for words. "It's just that my brother is accused of a crime I know he is incapable of committing. I need to see how this ridiculous situation could have happened. Can you let me in?"

The corporal frowned and glanced back toward the major's door out of habit. He seemed to be weighing the need to involve his superior officer. Sarge waited. He had been in similar situations. As a non-commissioned officer, a corporal must try not to overstep his authority. Some commissioned officers were keen to hold all the reins; others less so. Finally, after a moment, Yates' eyes came back to Sarge. "I can't see that it could do any harm." He stood, and Sarge followed him to the library door. The corporal turned his heft to the side to reach the knob with his right hand. He turned it, pushed the door ajar, and stepped back.

"One requirement. Whatever you find is shared with me?"

Sarge nodded. The corporal gave the door another shove. "Help yourself." His voice seemed to indicate disinterest. He turned and walked back toward his desk.

Sarge pushed through the door. It was very dark in the room. He remembered the two large windows with heavy curtains allowing only a tiny amount of defused light around the edges.

The light behind him cast his shadow from the doorway. First, his legs elongated across the floor; his lower torso on the front of the desk; a more massive shadow of arms, chest, and head against the shelves of books and drawn drapes on the far wall.

Sarge crossed the room and spread the curtains wide, but the porch's overhang limited the light. He still wasn't satisfied. He walked back toward the door to the oil lamp and lit it. The room grew a little lighter. Not enough. Sarge walked to the desk and lit a second lamp. Suddenly, in a fit of impatience, he hurried to another table and lit the third lamp. Now the room had reached an unnatural brightness. For Sarge, standing in the library was like going back in time. There were the familiar knickknacks, apparently unmoved during his nine years of absence. The brown leather-covered chairs, the single sofa, and the massive desk remained in place. Sarge was sure it was still the most complete library in the county. Bound volumes of the writings of Jefferson, Hamilton, and other founders occupied the same spaces as they had when he was a boy. A framed copy of the Georgia Constitution's first page adorned the wall beside the door he had just entered. Hundreds of books on farming, animal husbandry, and novels by English and American writers filled their own bookcase. He pulled Hawthorn's volume, opened and closed it, and slid it back in its place.

Sarge threw himself into the oversized swivel desk chair. He swung it right and left and remembered that even the chair's design had historical connotations. Thomas Jefferson had invented it! What was there to find here to explain this incredible dilemma? The desk was large at eight feet wide and five feet deep, with an enclosed kneehole and a wide, shallow center drawer. On either side, there were two deep drawers. He opened the right top drawer, and his eyes took in odds and ends cluttering the bottom. He moved to the bottom drawer and then the center. He knew he was clutching at straws. Undoubtedly, the army's search had included searching the desk. To settle the matter, he looked in the rest of the drawers as well. He slammed the left bottom drawer shut in frustration. The one-of-a-kind desk, and the stylish shelves that circled the room, were all built of the same dense burled walnut, the handiwork of a local black freeman. All of it was created before Sarge was even born. For a moment, he just sat and admired the craftsmanship. After two score years, there were a few scratches and blemishes. Yet, the room in total radiated a kind of eternal quality.

He could remember a thousand days and evenings of his youth spent reading in this room. He could still hear the laughter of men from surrounding farms who met here from time to time to discuss politics and local affairs. More recent and vivid was Sarge's memory of arguments with his brother in this room. One in particular again flooded his mind, his dispute with Tom concerning the sale of the farm's only slave. It was evident that it was a purely economic decision for Tom, but that fact did more to fuel his anger. Finally, amid their argument, Sarge realized that Tom considered his opinion of no value. Ultimately Tom held all the cards. Sarge remembered again how fed up he was when he stalked from the room. Sarge had abandoned the house, saddled two horses, and with Brownie quizzing him about where they were going and why they rode away. For many years he considered his last glimpse back at the gate that evening as his last.

Sarge pushed the thoughts away. That was a different time and another problem. He stood and began to examine the perimeter of the room. Starting in one corner, Sarge slowly moved around the wall. Was there another entrance or hidey-hole that neither he nor Tom knew of? A secret closet? It didn't seem possible, and it hardly seemed to matter. Wasn't one such entrance known to no one in the building other than his brother sufficient? Still, he had to start somewhere. He moved from one section of bookcases to the next. He pushed against them, trying to detect any instability. Could there be a large safe or hidey-hole behind the books where someone could hide a strongbox? Only when he pushed against the bookcase behind which he knew an entry into the next room existed did he sense any movement. Even that wasn't easy to detect. He pulled it open and shut it again. How about the floor? Was there a hidden hiding place there? He pulled back the corner of a square of wool carpet in front of the desk. The protected oak flooring was smooth and unmarred. He walked from the entry into the room and rolled back the rug. Nothing! Somehow a box weighing over a hundred-and-fifty pounds empty was gone, vanished, and he felt no closer to knowing how that could happen now than he did two days before. He straightened up and swung toward the door as it opened.

26

"Making yourself at home, I see!" Major Rogers smiled at his little joke and stepped into the room, appraising its contents. "Imposing room. Good library. I have availed myself of it on several occasions." He walked to the desk and sat on the corner. "Your brother, of course, has been recovering from his wound."

Sarge said nothing for a moment. "I have recently learned that he lost his arm at the elbow." Sarge watched the major's reaction.

"Yes, he was in poor shape when we arrived. Overall, he has appeared slow to make progress." The major stood up. He had a bit of lamp oil from the desk on his hip. Sarge walked toward him and pointed at it.

"Something is on your pants." He ran his fingers across the desk's surface. He felt a trace of an oily texture as he rubbed his thumb and fingers together. Leaning down, he could barely see that something had spilled over the edge. His eyes followed the indistinct trail to the floor.

Major Rogers fingered the mark on his pants. "Damn, I forgot about that. They say the lamp was overturned and spilled oil in the scuffle between the guard and your brother. It's good that it wasn't lit, or we'd have probably lost the house." He frowned and swiped at his pants. "I hope it comes out in the wash."

"You mean the guard's attacker. My brother is innocent until proven guilty." Sarge looked for something to wipe down the desk. He remembered a dust cloth in one of the side drawers. He pulled it out and wiped the top and side of the desk, looking carefully for surface damage. There was little to see; a minor dent in the floor along the desk's length and a crack along the bottom edge. Sarge straightened up.

"Tell me, major, how much does the payroll strongbox weigh approximately?"

"About a hundred-and-fifty pounds empty would be my guess." The major moved around and sat in the chair. "It is armored, with the lid held shut with a pair of padlocks."

"That's what I estimated too. How could my brother, with one arm in poor condition, move such a weight, let alone carry it off the premises?"

Major Rogers swung the chair from side to side as he considered. "Interesting question." He frowned. "You think he had accomplices?" He looked thoughtful. "You may be right, and he must have anticipated that the guards would take the blame."

"Wouldn't that be too obvious?"

"What do you mean?"

"If the most likely accomplices were the guards. And if the guards would be the natural suspects, wouldn't that be an obvious obstacle for one or more of them to agree to assist him?"

"Ahh. I see what you mean. But, on the other hand, being such obvious suspects would encourage the man to run after the theft and killing, would it not? In this case, none of them did."

Sarge was ready with his retort. "So, you're suggesting that when an obvious suspect fails to run, it eliminates him as a suspect?" Sarge frowned. The major seemed rather blasé about the whole matter.

"What we know suggests that since your brother thought he was above suspicion, he would believe that the guards would be the primary suspects if they ran or not."

"Who else would be available to consider as a suspect?" Sarge wondered out loud.

"Well, there were two guards; one stationed in here with the box, the other outside the door. Of secondary suspicion would be any of several office personnel, the four guards outside the building, two front and back, the corporal, Captain Rumpole, and even myself." The major laughed at the thought. "Have you ever read Edger Allen Poe? I think there is an edition here some-where." The major swept his hand toward the fiction section of the library.

"You're referring to the mystery stories?" Sarge asked.

"Yes." Rogers pursed his lips. "I can see while believing in your brother's innocence, you would think yourself in a similar quandary." The major stroked his jaw. "On the other hand, as you have pointed out, I am in a similar situation. I should be looking for the accomplice as well."

Sarge's pulse quickened. That's what he needed! If the major would consider other suspects, there was a chance to throw some suspicion somewhere besides his brother. The major walked briskly out the door. Sarge was baffled at his sudden departure. In a moment, Rogers returned with the two guards from the front entrance.

"Madison Jones, you are under arrest for the theft of the strongbox and the murder of Private Thomas."

"Hold on, Major!" Sarge held up his hand. "That's crazy! I wasn't even in town when the strongbox was taken!"

"So, you say." The major motioned for the guards to take Sarge's revolver. They moved forward.

Sarge felt sweat form on his brow, and his mind raced. Then he smiled. "Whoa, again." Sarge stepped back a pace. "I have proof."

"Proof?" The officer held up his hand, stilling the guards. "How is that?"

"My discharge papers. The army discharged my friends and me four days ago. I was over sixty miles away the day someone stole the strongbox." Sarge reached into his inside coat pocket and produced his papers. He unfolded them before handing them over.

Major Rogers accepted the document and looked at it thoroughly. He smiled gamely.

"Nice try, sergeant. These papers were signed by your regimental commander and dated all right. But the date filled in is today's date." He held the papers aloft.

Sarge stepped forward and grabbed the pages. His eyes traced down the page to the bottom. There it was. He had never looked at them closely. The discharge document was duly signed but dated the last day of April. Today's date! For a moment, he refused to believe his eyes. "This isn't right! The army discharged us four days ago!" He waved the paper. "I don't understand it. They discharged us on April 26." He looked helplessly from the documents to the major and back again.

"I know you were discharged before today. You were in my office yesterday. No doubt the regimental commander signed the document before the date affixed to it, anticipating a delay in its delivery. Still, the question remains, what date were you sixty miles away? How easy would it be for you to receive a discharge earlier than you claim? You may have had plenty of time to travel and participate in the robbery. Therefore, Sergeant, I am placing you under arrest. You will be remanded to the local jail."

Sarge backed away. *No!* The closest guard reached him as Sarge reflexively reached for his gun. Sarge lashed out, fending off the private. The soldier staggered and grabbed Sarge's gun arm to regain his balance interrupting Sarge's draw. The second guard reached Sarge, grabbed his other arm, and twisted it behind him. Sarge cried out in frustration.

"So, this is how you exhibit your innocence?" The major picked up and refolded the dropped discharge papers and tucked them in his pocket. "Evidence." He motioned to the guards. "I'll have Corporal Yates arrange for your escort to the local jail." There was a look of satisfaction on his face as he left the room.

27

Preacher and Bronco roused slowly, well after Sarge's departure. It took them a few seconds to realize that he was gone. Bronco looked from the empty bed to Preacher, who shrugged.

"Maybe he wanted another visit with Tom. I wonder if the sheriff will oblige him again."

"Should we wait for him?" Bronco said.

"Yes, but let's wait for him next door at the tavern. I'm ready for breakfast."

"Good idea." Bronco grabbed his cap and hitched up his pants. "By the way, Preacher, I'm sorry I dozed off on you last night. I was pretty tired. Maybe you can finish the story over breakfast?"

"Don't worry about it. I was tired too. Preacher opened the door, and they clattered down the stairs, into the boarding house lobby, and through the doorway into the eating area. Mrs. Jordon looked at them and nodded toward the back of the room as she handed a red-headed man his plate of pancakes.

Leaning back in his chair against the far wall sat John Coates. Bronco, in the lead, reached for his gun. Preacher stayed his hand. "Let's see what his play is," he counseled as they approached the man, each at the ready. Coates saw them coming and grinned

"Well, here we are again with the blue bellies." John sneered. Men at other tables looked around. A few of them were wearing Union uniforms.

Preacher and Bronco pulled back chairs and moved to sit down without invitation. "How'd you get out of jail?" Bronco loomed over him for a minute before he sat down. Coates was sitting with both elbows on the table, so Bronco did the same. Preacher sat to Coates' right so he could keep an eye on his gun hand. Preacher spotted an old revolver in the holster.

"Well, the sheriff could only keep me twenty-four hours on the disturbing the peace charge, and he decided he'd let me out to eat on my own dime."

"You weren't just disturbing the peace, and you know it. You had every intention of killing me." Bronco growled.

"True, but the sheriff couldn't charge me for intentions on just your say-so. We gnawed around on that bone for a while, but what with me being a local and you being a heathen Yankee from up north and carrying no votes in the next election, he came up with the right decision." John took a sip of his coffee.

Miss Emmy approached the table with menus but kept them in hand. Both men ordered their usual bacon, eggs, and coffee, while Coates accepted a cup of coffee.

Bronco knew his purse was getting lighter every day, but he didn't want to acknowledge that in front of Coates, who made no move to add food items to his order of black coffee.

"I got the whole story about Jones while I was over at the jail. He has always been so uppity toward the rest of the folks around here. Serves him right to get his comeuppance." He grinned his satisfaction at using the long word.

"Funny, the Sheriff doesn't seem to agree with you, according to Sarge," Bronco said.

"Nor anyone else, according to the locals I've spoken to," Preacher added.

"Maybe or maybe not. It don't matter, given that the major out at Jones' farm is calling the shots. Maybe he just wants to move in out there permanent?"

"You don't even know Tom Jones, do you?" Preacher took a sip of his coffee.

"Well, that is true. And I understand his brother, the one you call Sarge, has been away for a long time. My kin moved here about five years ago. I came later. Not sure how long I'll be here. Not sure there is much in the way of opportunity in these parts," he smirked.

Sarah came out carrying two plates of food. Since Bronco was sitting with his back to the room to keep an eye on Coates, the other man spotted her first. He grinned and gave her a wink. "Purdiest girl in the county."

Bronco twisted around. "Miss Sarah! I was hoping you were working today!"

"She ain't 'Miss Sarah,' Yankee. She is Mrs. Jimmy Jordon. She is a married woman whose man is off to war, and as I said yesterday, I think it highly unproper for you to be panting after her." Coates guffawed a bit at his self-righteousness, but his eyes were full of venom.

Eager to defend her honor even at his own expense, Bronco said, "she has good reason to believe that her husband is a casualty of war. She would never do anything wrong." His hand moved toward his hip. Preacher kicked him under the table. Sarah's eyes betrayed annoyance with Coates. She spoke only to the other two men.

"I hope you enjoy your breakfast." She smiled a little. Bronco grinned back. Then he looked at John and glared. Sarah put down the plates and moved away.

Coates seemed to take no pleasure in watching them eat. He finished his coffee, and after a few more disparaging remarks about Yankees in general, he grabbed a piece of bacon from Bronco's plate and stabbed it into his mouth. John half backed away, grinning. Bronco and Preacher kept their gun hands ready until he was out the door. Bronco switched chairs and took over Coates' side of the table.

"I don't trust him any more than I would a rattler."

Preacher ignored Bronco's true reason for changing places, a better vantage point to watch Sarah. "That would be the safest course. Coates seems to have taken a proprietary interest in Mrs. Jordon." Preacher said.

"I wonder what is holding up, Sarge." Bronco looked toward the door again.

28

Sarge was shaking with anger. *How could I have let this happen?* He was manacled to a wagon seat, his horse trailing behind, heading back to town with two guards. The corporal holding the reins kept looking at him as if he would pull a gun any minute. He churned inside. The major's last words just went through him.

"Well, you wanted to see your brother. So now you are getting your wish."

Sarge tried to form a plan as they passed the barren fields. He remembered that only an hour before, he had bristled at the lack of a new cotton crop, the lack of gardens started, and no animals eating the green grass that was now shin-high. He had spent so much time on such minor concerns while Tom was practically in front of a firing squad. Sarge remembered wondering how things could get any worse.

Sarge turned and stared straight ahead as he carefully tested his bindings. It seemed the only way out was an escape. He pretended to follow the approach of a wagon bearing two red-headed men, but he didn't fool the guard. As he tried to slip his relaxed hand out of the manacles, he stiffened as he felt the end of a rifle barrel nudge him in his kidneys.

"I don't want to do it, Sergeant, but if you work your hands free, I will have to plug you."

Sarge relaxed his struggle. The group arrived at the sheriff's office a few minutes later. The corporal with the rifle handed the surprised sheriff an order from the major.

Sheriff Beckett was stunned. He looked at Sarge and shook his head.

"I don't believe this for a minute, Madison." But he shrugged in a 'what can I do' motion, took Sarge by the arm, and led him, still under the guard's watchful eye, back to the cell adjacent to Tom's.

John Coates hurried out of the tavern. A new plan began to form. His original intention to find a way to gain access to Tom Jones' gold had not panned out. The information regarding Tom Jones' robbery charge and imprisonment had nagged at him since he had heard the news in jail. The Union troops at the farm and Tom Jones sitting in a jail cell were two obstacles not easily overcome. With the man indisposed, John needed to hatch a new money-making scheme. His time in a cell next to the sick man had focused his thoughts as no other situation could.

Then as he sat in the Star, he observed how sparse the customers were. It looked wrong until it dawned on him that the reason for the reduced number of customers during his last several visits was that the troops hadn't been paid. With the payroll theft, the troops had gone two months without pay. He bet many disgruntled boys in blue were eager to wet their whistles. The still, John's family ran out at Rufus' farm had been a reliable source of cash from Rebel forces when the soldiers had any money. The odds were pretty good that business in that trade was pretty slack now. Once the Union boys got paid, they could be potential customers also.

It wasn't the moonshine that occupied his thoughts, though. It was the fact that the army, somewhere, somehow, was probably hustling to replace the stolen payroll. John's brain churned as he paid to retrieve his mount at the livery stable. Maybe his uncle's lack of income and the certainty that a double payroll would head their way offered an even better opportunity. Maybe there was a safer, more profitable way to get rich than attacking the Union forces head-on at the Jones' farm. He just needed to use his knowledge and persuasiveness to motivate his uncle and remaining cousins to take action. But, of course, that would take some jawing with Uncle Rufus.

Preacher and Bronco emerged from the Lucky Star into the bright mid-morning sunlight, Sarge's absence still a mystery. They had lingered at the table longer than usual, much to Bronco's delight, while Preacher debated checking their room. But it didn't seem reasonable that Sarge would go there without checking the tavern first.

"Bronco, why don't you check and see if Sarge is with his brother at the jail. I'll check with the livery stable for his horse. I suppose he might have gone out to the farm to see the major again."

Bronco nodded and crossed the street, headed west toward the jail.

Preacher followed along until they reached the stable. He was concerned. Sarge was usually pretty good at keeping everyone up to date. He felt a chill go down his spine as he remembered Coates' sneer as he left the Lucky Star. Preacher entered the livery and relaxed a bit when he found Sarge's horse missing. He retraced his steps and, after passing the tavern, headed toward the jail expecting to meet Bronco along the way. Instead, he saw Sarge's horse tied up outside and a wagon accompanied by two mounted Union soldiers reining around and heading out of town at a cantor as he approached. Preacher reached the entrance and opened the door. He found the office empty, but there were voices in the back. He picked up Sarge's angry retorts and even more confusing words from Bronco.

"Sheriff, this is ridiculous! You should let us all out of here right now!" As Preacher waited, the door opened behind him. A white-haired man entered with a leather case. He nodded at Preacher and stood at the desk. The sheriff came in through the door at the back of the office.

"Hello, Anthony!" The sheriff shook hands with the man.

"I'd like to see my client, Ben. I want to go over events at his farm again."

"Well, that's okay, John, except you now have three clients; Tom Jones, Madison Jones, and a young Union private named Brumley."

"What!" The white-haired man slumped and propped his hands on the edge of the desk. The sheriff shook his head in disbelief. "I'm about to run out of cells."

The sheriff turned his gaze toward Preacher. "What can I do for you?"

Preacher took a step toward the door. "I just wanted to check in, but I see you are tied up. I'll come back later." He skedaddled out the door as quickly as he could, hoping not to raise suspicion. Preacher stepped off the porch, stood next to Sarge's horse, and scratched his head, thankful that he had never crossed paths with the sheriff before. A murder trial in two days, and somehow Sarge and Bronco had managed to get themselves in the same predicament as Tom.

29

Sheriff Ben Beckett listened to the murmur of voices back in the cells and shook his head as if to rid recent events from his consciousness. No sooner did Madison show up with his army escort than Bronco wandered in. The major's order to put Madison in a cell as an accomplice to his brother's robbery and murder troubled him immensely. Since Bronco had already admitted his association with Madison in the Coates' matter, the lawman saw no option but to put the young man in with him. None of this made sense to him. He was capable of adding two and two, and this didn't add up. Tom was unlikely to be guilty of anything. Sheriff Beckett had not seen Madison in almost ten years, and he had arrived in town several days after the murder. As for Brumley, Beckett had only seen him once when he and Pappy Jordon ran Coates in for attempted murder. Of course, there wasn't adequate evidence for that charge, so he had kept Coates overnight for disturbing the peace. The sheriff sat down at his desk. Now he had close to a packed house, and from his perspective, every one of his prisoners was innocent!

There was pandemonium back in the cell block. Anthony Dulles sat in a cell with his client, Tom Jones, who was barely coherent from the overdose of laudanum he had just ingested before breakfast. Dulles shook his head in disbelief and looked at his two new clients through the bars. Sarge had thrown himself down on his bunk and crossed his wrists over his eyes. Bronco ran his hands over his bars, still wrestling with the reality of jail.

Coates rode back to his uncle's farm. Like all the other farms in Georgia, it bore signs of neglect though John knew the condition had nothing to do with the war. The fields were barren. The split rail fences sagged or were missing, and the gate stood ajar. The layers of whitewash the previous owner had applied many years before peeled from the wooden structures. He reminded himself that people in the western part of the state were well off compared with the central and east, where General Sherman's "scorched earth" strategy had turned everything to ashes for hundreds of miles. John Coates had seen the devastation along Sherman's route, and, like most Georgians, he was determined to avenge the destruction. His anger wasn't so much out of empathy but a general sense that all Yankees deserved to die someday somehow just for being Yankees. John was not opposed to destruction per se, but since the hated Yankees were responsible, he took everything personally. But before he addressed that grievance, there was the more pressing matter of relieving the army of a double payroll.

He dismounted and knocked on the door. While he waited, a couple of hounds sniffed at his trousers. When the older man opened the door, another hound came out and tentatively sniffed his leg up to his crotch. Coates laughed. "Old Andy will never change."

The old man eyed him sourly. "What are you doing back here, John? I told you to make yourself scarce." He had put on a black armband since John's last visit to commemorate his sons' passing.

"I know, Uncle, but I've just thought of a plan that will not only avenge my poor cousins' murders but put this place back on its feet. Heck, it will do more than that. Let's sit for a spell, and I'll tell you about it."

"Sit? I don't even want you in my house. The last time you came up with one of your schemes, you got two of my boys' kilt. Get off my porch before I bring out the shotgun." Rufus spit a stream of tobacco juice that splashed on John's snakeskin boot.

"Now, Uncle." John's voice went up an octave as he fawned over the old man and lamented the loss of his sons. "Didn't I rush home as fast as I could so Schooley and Barney could take the wagon back for the bodies? Didn't I tell you straight out that it was all Captain Owen's fault for heatin' up the situation? I'm telling you, we was almost home when he got drunk on some moonshine we took off a farmer over in Alabama. If he had just let sleeping dogs lie, pardon to your dogs, uncle, your boys, my beloved cousins, would still be safe and sound."

"Owens!" The old man's eyes were fierce with aggravation. "The most useless old coot I ever knew. He was worthless when we was in grade school over in Washington County. How he ever got captain's bars, I'll never understand."

"He stole them, Uncle."

"Say what?"

"He stole them." Remember when Captain Oats got shot over in Atlanta? Well, Owens was there, and he took off Oats' coat and put it on his own self." Coates looked earnestly into his uncle's eyes. "That's why he rode with his own outfit and not the regulars."

"How do you know that?" The old man looked at him suspiciously.

"He told me. That is how he said it happened. The night before our boys was kilt, Owens was so drunk he fell out of the saddle and tore his sleeve. He was upset about it and told me it was his only coat since he had taken it off, Captain Oats."

Old man Coates sank in a chair and absently caressed one of the dog's heads. It seemed to cheer him some as the other hounds gathered 'round to be petted. "What have you got for me, John?" He sounded resigned.

John Coates smiled, sat down at the man's feet with the dogs, and told him his plan.

Major Rogers sat at his desk, contemplating the document in his hands. It posed a bit of a dilemma. The date written on the discharge could support Madison Jones's involvement in the robbery and murder, but also the possibility the Sergeant told the truth. But then again, Tom Jones was the only viable suspect. Of all the people in the house, Jones alone knew of the secret entrance at the time of the robbery. Sergeant Jones had asked about other possible suspects. The obvious men were the guards themselves. Major Rogers had read somewhere that almost all payroll robberies were inside jobs. But if the outside guard had taken the payroll, why did he hang around? Without knowing about the secret door, the guard had to see that he would be the prime suspect. If he had taken off, the man could have had as much as a four-hour head start before his duty ended, and he and the other guard were relieved. That much head start would have afforded an excellent chance to escape. Major Rogers shook his head. It added up for the payroll to have been stolen by Tom Jones. The other options were so barely plausible that he satisfied himself that he had captured the right man. Still!

Rogers pulled a sheet of paper out of his desk. He dipped the pen in the inkwell and looked into space. He could inquire about the actual release date at the command where Madison and Brumley served. But, of course, there was no way to get that information promptly.

He wrote 30 April 1865 on the paper. He paused. He needed justice for his men. And he needed it to be timely. Rogers' pen poised over the paper. It could be weeks before this letter could find the proper recipient. *Damn it! This business was an inside job, an inside job by Tom Jones, and likely aided and abetted by his brother. My job is to present the evidence. The jury will decide guilt or innocence.* Major Rogers pushed the paper to one side and called out to Corporal Yates. He had other matters requiring his attention.

30

Preacher needed to think! He headed back to the room and threw himself on his bed. Quickly he reviewed the situation. Sarge and Bronco, along with Sarge's brother, were now in jail on murder charges. Coates was on the prowl looking for a way to kill the pack of them. The sheriff was under the thumb of a major aiming to protect his rank and reputation. The trial was now two days away. There was meager evidence to support Jones's guilt. The local civilians would likely acquit Tom Jones because a local jury would require more than circumstantial evidence to come up with a guilty verdict. But Union military personnel could go either way. Had he missed anything? He heard a knock at the door. Deep in thought, Preacher jumped up and threw the door open. John Coates and a shorter man stood in the doorway with guns drawn. "Please give me an excuse to shoot you right now," Coates said.

Preacher stepped back. He couldn't keep the disdainful grin off his face." I was just thinking about you, Coates."

Coates relieved Preacher of his gun and looked around the room. "Where are your friends?"

Preacher still had his wits. He lied. "Don't know." He pointed toward the table. "How about a friendly hand of cards while we wait for them?"

Coates dismissed the idea out of hand. "Catching you alone is a good thing." He pointed toward the door. "Let's go. I'll deal with your friends later." Coates marched Preacher down the stairs and out to the back alley, where three horses waited. Once mounted, he ordered Preacher to the front, and they turned onto Main Street and headed north out of town.

Curious, Preacher resisted the temptation to spur his horse and take his chances of catching a bullet. How could Coates think it benefited him to make him hostage? He and Sarge had played briefly with the idea that Coates' cohorts could be involved with the payroll robbery, but he and those of his breed, like them, had been miles away when it happened.

As they rode past the jail, Preacher spotted Sarge's horse at the railing. He wondered if Coates would recognize it. It had filled out over the last week of reduced miles and better grazing. Maybe not. He spurred his horse a bit to keep Coates' attention on himself, and they continued down the street without comment from either man.

Sarah repeatedly looked out the front window of the Lucky Star. For the past two days, Bronco had shown up precisely at twelve-thirty. Now it was well after one-thirty and still no sign. Finally, she turned and found her Aunt Emmy's eyes on her. The old lady motioned her back to a corner of the kitchen.

"Sarah, it is not seemly for you to be flirting with that young man."

"Flirting?"

"You know what I'm talking about."

Sarah turned away. "He is very nice," she said.

"That may be. But you are a married woman."

"I know that, Aunt Emmy! I have reminded Mister Brumley of that several times." She turned back to her aunt. "He is very polite. He is from Ohio, you know."

"I didn't know, and where he is from hardly makes a difference." Aunt Emmy pressed her lips together. "Do you want to explain him to Jimmy when he gets home?"

Sarah dropped into a chair and looked around the kitchen. She cupped her hands in her lap. "I'm afraid Jimmy isn't coming home." She bent her head down and studied her open hands. "I've prayed for just a letter. I've gotten nothing. Even his friends say they think he's not coming home." Aunt Emmy's face softened, and she put a consoling hand on her wrist.

The young woman stood and resolutely pulled back her shoulders. "That evil John Coates has threatened all three of those men. As a friend, I will do what I can to help them." She walked back to the dining area to look for them. Still no sign. She remembered her dream about John Coates the night before. In her mind, he had become a constant threat to the young man with steely blue eyes. Bronco was a Yankee, but she had satisfied herself, not an ordinary one. She didn't know of many places to look. Surely, he wasn't up in his room at this late hour. She couldn't recognize his horse to check for it at the livery stable. Did he have any reason to visit the sheriff? She couldn't think of any, but for lack of an alternative, she walked out the front door without explanation to her aunt. It would only take a minute. She strode to the sheriff's office and opened the door. The graying lawman was at his desk, eating lunch from home. Sheriff Beckett stood when she entered. He wiped his hands on his trousers.

"Can I help you, Mrs. Jordon?"

"Sheriff, I'm concerned about Mister Brumley. He and Mister Jones and Mister Gracey are friends of mine. Have they been by here?"

"Well, I don't know who this Mister Gracey is, but the other two are in cells out back." The sheriff looked a bit hang dogged.

"So, you're letting Mister Jones visit his brother now?" Sarah's face brightened.

"No, as I said, they are in cells. Cells of their own. Major Rogers ordered their arrest for the robbery and murder at the Jones' farm a week ago."

Sarah felt her legs go weak beneath her. She sat down. "Sheriff, how could you do that?" She popped back to her feet. "Sheriff, you and everyone else in this town know Major Tom Jones would not rob anyone. As for Mister Jones and Mister Brumley, that is crazy."

"I'm sorry to say that what any of us knows is not important at this point," Beckett said apologetically. "Who is this Mister Gracey, you mentioned?"

"Never mind! I want to see Mister Brumley."

The sheriff pursed his lips. Technically, he had no instructions about visitors for Madison and Bronco. He nodded. "Alright, but just for a minute." He motioned for her to follow and opened the door to the cells.

"I've never been back here before," Sarah remarked. She looked around quickly, recognizing Tom Jones lying on his bunk, apparently asleep. Sarge, too, was on his bed. He sat up for a moment to see who was coming in, acknowledged her presence, then lay back down. In the left-hand cell next to Sarge, Bronco peered out the window. He turned, and delight registered on his face.

"Miss Sarah!" He crossed the cell in two strides. She stepped back to remain at arm's length to avoid his reaching hands, so he grasped the bars.

"Oh, Mister Brumley! How could this happen?"

"Thanks for coming, Miss Sarah." Bronco devoured her with his eyes, and his long arms reached out between the bars further than she had anticipated and touched her shoulders despite her attempt to avoid physical contact. "I came to check on Sarge, and the next thing I knew, I was locked up too."

"This is crazy, Sheriff!" Sarah stamped her foot with impatience.

"I can't deny that." The sheriff nodded and held up the key. "I can give you about ten minutes. Then I'll come back to collect you."

Sarah nodded and looked at Bronco with soulful eyes. "Why?"

"Well, the major says that Tom robbed the payroll, and we helped. But we were in Alabama then. Sarge is sure Tom didn't do anything; we know we didn't. It just gets crazier every minute."

"Oh, Bronco! I lov..." Sarah stopped and clamped her mouth shut. She instantly regretted those fateful words. She had not only slipped into dubious territory using his first name but also added a forbidden endearment. Her color rose. She looked away. "I'm going to track down Pappy and see if he can do anything."

"Love me?" His eyes widened. "Well, I love you too! But, talk to Pappy, and it'll all work out."

Sarah turned away in her distress. Then, rather than wait for the sheriff, she hurried to the door back into the office and, giving the lawman only an angry nod, went off to find Pappy.

Bronco watched her hurry away. Her distress was evident. Ordinarily, such passion for his well-being would have been cherished. But now, the enjoyment was marred by circumstances. He realized that he might have misled her with his optimism. For the life of him, he couldn't see any way out of jail.

31

John Coates relieved Preacher of his scarf, coat, and Union cap and shoved him roughly into the root cellar behind his uncle's farmhouse. He was already plotting the capture of Sarge, Bronco, and Tom Jones. Coates wanted them for his plan as well. He teased himself with the prospect of pistol-whipping the man as revenge for his still-healing head. Partly rejecting that, he used his forty-four to give Preacher a single vicious blow to the side of his head. Preacher reeled in surprise and stumbled down the steps into the darkness. Coates could have followed up with more blows but reminded himself that he had many irons in the fire right now and didn't have time to get sidetracked with amusements. Besides, he wanted to keep Preacher mobile.

"Dooley, I will shoot you cold if he gets out." He looked at the older, heavily bearded cousin hotly. "I'm warning you. Keep an eye out, and don't open that door for any reason. Clear?"

Dooley nodded. He knew that John could be dangerous when lathered up. He wasn't afraid of his cousin, especially, but he had orders from his old man to cooperate. Still, the blood rushed up his neck. So instead of responding to the

Coates went around the back corner of the house and knocked on the front door. The old uncle came out and took his chair on the porch. "Did you round them up?"

"No, I found one, but the others were not around. I think I saw one of their horses at the sheriff's office. How about Zac in Winston?"

"He will be back here as soon as he knows anything. And as we planned, he will stay at his post until he has something to report." The old man frowned. "I'm warning you, John. If this goes sidewise like your other schemes, I'll skin you alive!"

Coates smiled callously to himself. *Your threats used to scare me to death, you old coot. Now, you are just a weak old man with missing teeth. Be careful, or I'll skin you.* Given the lack of hospitality, John mounted and rode back to town.

Sarah left the sheriff's office in a fury. Bronco and Sarge's arrest outraged her, and her expressions of affection toward Bronco embarrassed her. She dismissed her personal discomfort for the moment. For this perfectly good boy to be locked away was more than she could stand. She knew her Aunt Emmy would be waiting with her sharp tongue at the Lucky Star. There seemed to be no one for her to turn to except Pappy. The sheriff seemed good for nothing but empty apologies, and she hadn't seen Preacher since breakfast.

Meanwhile, this Major Ruggers or Rogers, or whatever, sat out at the farm, pulling all the strings and drumming up a trial that could cost these people their lives. She thought Pappy might have an idea, but he wasn't at his table when she returned to the Lucky Star. Then, a few minutes later, Sarah noticed John Coates stride in and take his usual seat against the back wall. As she poured coffee, it splashed into his cup so abruptly that some ran off the table's edge.

"What have you done with Mister Gracey?" Anger distorted her beautiful face.

"Huh?" Coates was taken aback. Her apparent knowledge raised alarms. "Whoa, Mrs. Jordon. What are you talking about?" Astonished, John played for time, his mind racing. He made a big production of using his napkin to absorb the liquid as he brushed it toward the edge of the table.

"Well, Mister Brumley and both Jones brothers are locked up in jail, and Mister Gracey is missing. Of course, he could be hiding out, but I've got a feeling you are responsible somehow." Sarah crossed her arms.

"What?" Coates' face registered surprise. "Why is that crew in jail?" He motioned for Sarah to take a chair, but she ignored him.

"Mister Madison Jones and Mister Brumley are in jail for the same reason Major Tom Jones is; the major thinks they helped Major Jones take the payroll and kill the guard." She stamped her foot. "So, you're saying you have nothing to do with this?"

"Ma'am, please explain how I could get the major to arrest those boys. As for the one they call Preacher, I haven't seen him and don't want to see him." Coates gulped his coffee and immediately regretted it." Whoa, that is hot!" Sarah smiled to witness his discomfort and savored it triumphantly as she turned on her heel and moved back to the kitchen.

Coates' watched her move away. He frowned, for there was no charm in her bearing today. The arrest of Bronco and Sarge was an unforeseen complication.

Sarge watched as Bronco fiddled with the cell door. First, he tried to slide his body between them. It had been close, but no matter what contortions Bronco managed with his limber frame, his head made no progress. So next, he shook, pushed, and pulled at the window bars. If their situation had not been so dire, Sarge would have found his efforts funny.

The lawyer, Anthony Dulles, had gone. He had not been successful in getting any more information out of Tom. Sarge realized now that it wasn't just because Tom was demoralized or because he had drugged himself. It was because he had no memory to draw on. There were no actual events that involved him. Tom couldn't rob or kill. He wasn't even in enough possession of his faculties to make something up!

Sarge also noticed that despite Beckett's convictions, as the day of the trial became more imminent, the sheriff became more security-minded. In his turbulent state, he started to mumble to himself. Beckett repeatedly reminded the three men that time was running out. He ceased wearing his gun when he returned to the cells, and the keys that usually hung on his belt now stayed in front. Sarge saw that he understood that the closer they came to trial, the more desperate they could become to escape.

Major Rogers sat at his desk when Corporal Yates knocked and entered. His girth filled the doorway as he made his announcement. "Sir, Captain Knight has arrived."

"Captain Knight?" Rogers looked up.

"Yes, Sir. With the Judge Advocates Corp." Corporal Yates hesitated for a moment, undecided.

"Oh, yes! Send him in."

The big corporal moved aside and allowed a medium-height man into the office, followed by a short second lieutenant. The two men stood at attention and saluted leisurely. Major Rogers returned the salute, and they all sat down.

Major Rogers leaned back in his chair. "Have you read the report, Captain?"

"I read the report before we left Command." Captain Knight pulled a document from his briefcase and laid the papers on the desk.

"You're a couple of days early, Captain." I wasn't expecting you until 3 May." Major Rogers sounded a little irked. He had more than enough to do without babysitting paper pushers.

"Yes, sir." Captain Knight glanced at his companion, and a smirk lurked at the edge of his mouth. He had anticipated precisely that reaction. There were more surprises to come. He loved it when these command types got put in their place.

Major Rogers caught the look and frowned. "I understand from Corporal Yates that the defendants just got civilian legal representation the day before yesterday. Therefore, I have given them the date to prepare for the trial."

"I'm sorry to show up early, Major, but events dictated our early arrival."

Major Rogers was flummoxed.

"Events? What events?" He eyed both the captain and the lieutenant. They seemed to know something he did not.

"Two reasons, sir. I understand that the replacement payroll will arrive here in two days."

"That is a week before I expected it, but what does that have to do with the trial?"

The captain reached into his briefcase a second time and retrieved another envelope of the type used to deliver orders. "Since I was coming here anyway, Command sent these along with me, sir." He handed the envelope across the desk.

Major Rogers unsealed the envelope in silence and peered at the contents. His eyebrows arched. "We are ordered to move our headquarters to Clarksville in three days?" He dropped the papers on his desk and looked at the two officers with astonishment.

"Yes, sir. The regimental command orders are that there is to be a general redistribution of resources all over Georgia."

"But this is absurd!" Major Rogers slammed his hand down on the desk. "Did anyone consider the organizational tangle created by simultaneously moving my whole command while attempting to get the payroll organized and hold a trial?"

Captain Knight raised his hands in a sign of helplessness. "I'm sorry Major. I didn't make the orders. I just delivered the envelope."

"This is outrageous!" Without another word, Major Rogers went to the door. "Corporal! Show the captain and the lieutenant to rooms at the back of the house. Then get back here immediately. We have work to do!"

The corporal's eyes were wide when he appeared in the doorway. He had seldom seen the major so agitated. Something was indeed afoot. He led the officers to rooms and hurried back to Major Rogers' office. Listening to his instructions made him as unhappy as the major.

32

After Sarah left the jail, Sarge briefly stood on the end of his bunk and looked out the barred window. Bronco looked over and then did the same.

"Sarge, I've tried my bars a hundred times, but they're solid. How about yours'?"

"Are you thinking breakout, Bronco?" Sarge grabbed the bars and alternately pulled and pushed to humor the younger man. He could detect no give what-so-ever. Not much of a view; the jail backed up to an alley behind which lay a pasture dotted with large walnut trees. A series of outhouses lined the other side of the lane behind the jail and neighboring buildings. There were no cows in the field. He felt a sense of dislocation, knowing that while the hours crawled in the jail, time in the outside world rushed them headlong into a trial for murder and an eventual firing squad.

Sarge stepped down and looked over into Tom's cell. Tom was asleep. It seemed that Tom was always sleeping. The large bottle of laudanum was still on his side table. In frustration, Sarge stretched out his arm. He could just reach the edge of the table. Gingerly, Sarge gripped the corner and scooted the table closer. He brought the bottle through the bars and looked at it angrily. In his anger, Sarge seized on a thought. *Tom will be useless until he is alert.* He walked resolutely to his cell window and poured out the remaining laudanum. Then he followed it with the bottle.

Bronco watched Sarge, puzzled. How could pouring out the laudanum help anything? He shrugged and fell back on his bunk. Unless Pappy could come up with a miracle, it seemed things could only go downhill.

Corporal Yates came out of the major's office more agitated than the officer himself. There were a hundred things on his plate in preparation for the move of headquarters. The corporal sent a sentry to notify the officers of a meeting in the major's office in an hour. He never anticipated this development. Corporal Yates stalked around the area to work off steam before he approached the library and stood in the doorway for a moment. Another payroll lockbox would sit on the big desk in less than twenty-four hours. As before, there would be guards stationed inside and out. Because of the secret, now well-known door behind the bookshelves, an additional guard would have to be posted in the adjoining bedroom. He closed the door and returned to his desk. The payroll would arrive in the morning and then be disbursed to the troops.

More importantly, to him, the company would be decamping that same afternoon. He knew that the officer's meeting would result in a rash of new orders. Anticipating that, he began preparing those orders for everyone, including himself.

Preacher sat on a box of apples and listened. It was quiet in the root cellar. The glancing blow from Coates' gun against the side of his head had startled more than injured him, and there were no lasting effects. But the indiscriminate nature of Coates' lashing out was cause for concern. Through the many cracks in the cellar door, he could watch the Coates cousin easily. Dooley was older than the two who accompanied Coates with the Rebel captain. The man passed the time smoking and petting a mongrel dog. Then there were five dogs. Preacher guessed that old man Rufus had let the pack out of the house. After a while, the cousin looked furtively right and left and disappeared from Preacher's field of vision for a few minutes. When he reappeared, he carried a jug of corn liquor. It wasn't long before he was asleep.

Preacher was pretty sure that if old man Coates came back just then, he would not be amused. Preacher's kidnapping did not surprise him, as Coates had plenty of reason to wish him harm. He knew Coates as a violent man and probably as unhinged as Captain Owens. But unlike the captain, John's bloodthirst was not dependent on high alcohol intake. Preacher pondered the more important question; why was he still alive. The fact that he was still kicking suggested there was a bigger plan. With Bronco and Sarge in jail, there seemed little likelihood of rescue. They had problems of their own and little time to work things out.

Preacher casually examined the dank underground room. There were indeed plenty of things he could use as a weapon. There were a few canned goods. Searching in the darkness yielded old tools on a rickety shelf, including a rusty claw hammer. The faint smell of ancient spoiled vegetables tainted the air. His search along the back wall revealed a box of home-canned peaches. He held a jar up to a narrow stream of light. They were bad.

He examined the wobbly cellar door and decided he could break it open at will. He decided it would probably be best to attempt his escape from the drunken guard before John Coates returned with reinforcements. Preacher peered out, and satisfied that the man was asleep, he tested the door board by board. He wondered how much noise he could make without consequences. He kicked the door. The clatter brought no reaction from his guard and only a couple of lifted heads from the dogs. He found a strip of rusty steel that could just fit between two of the boards. He used the hammer's handle as a fulcrum and prized a loose board further from its neighbors. Once he had one end free, it was a simple matter to free the whole board and those adjacent to it. Still, the guard slept. *Bless daddy's corn mash.* In a few minutes, Preacher carefully climbed the steps to the outside. He was tempted a little to capture the cousin on principle but decided against it. He didn't need the extra baggage, and there might be some value in keeping Coates in the dark regarding his escape as long as possible. Preacher lay the three boards he had pried free back in place. It was necessary to look closely to discover that they were loose. He was about to enter the barn searching for a horse when he heard a raspy voice behind him.

"Don't move, Yankee."

Preacher's head spun to his right. A gimpy-looking older man with angry eyes stood ten feet away, holding a double-barreled shotgun. Surrounded by his dogs, Rufus looked more comical than threatening.

"Nice to have a good dog around, isn't it?" Preacher asked amicably. "But, it looks like you are pushing a good thing to the extreme."

Old man Coates rubbed the tallest mixed breed's ears and looked at his sleeping son. Then, he brought the stock down on the man's shoulder with as much force as he could muster.

Dooley jumped and looked up groggily. He started seeing the older man's face and rubbed his shoulder.

"This Yankee could have shot you, you dimwit. I have a good mind to shoot you myself." The old man looked from his son to Preacher and back again. "Stranger, I don't see why you didn't. I'd almost appreciate it, even if he's my own."

"He just looked so peaceful." Preacher smiled. "And I'm a peaceable man."

At that moment, a rider entered the yard, scattering chickens and dogs alike. Rufus looked up at him.

"What's the news, Zac?"

The rider leaned out of his saddle and took a deep breath. He eyed Preacher and his cringing cousin and smiled. "The army payroll just got into Winston two hours ago. I hung around for information. Word is they are expected in Titustown tomorrow morning."

"Alright, Zac, get your tail into town and find John. Bring him up to date. I told him I didn't want to see his face around here."

The rider nodded and spurred his horse, and the three men watched him thunder through the gate and disappear over a hump in the road.

"What have you got cooking here?" Preacher stared after the departing rider. "Oh, wait; now I see it. You're plotting a robbery of the payroll. As a matter of curiosity, is this the same bunch of squirrels responsible for the robbery and murder two weeks ago?"

"Hell, no!" Rufus spat in the dust. "We had nothing to do with that." He genuinely seemed to take offense at the suggestion of guilt for the earlier robbery while simultaneously plotting to do that very thing within the next twenty-four hours. Preacher just shook his head.

33

The major spread papers out before him. He was working on plans for moving headquarters. Several things would have to happen simultaneously, so the timing was crucial.

Corporal Yates knocked and entered the office. "Captain Rumpole informs me that guards for the payroll are assigned, and he has taken the liberty of adding a guard in the adjacent room, Sir. "

Major Rogers nodded. "Can't hurt, but with our disbursement of the pay the day it arrives, there will hardly be an opportunity for another robbery. Besides, with the Jones brothers in jail, we have our best suspects out of the way. The trial will be in the library immediately after the pay is disbursed. It's getting late. I'll go have supper."

"Yes, sir." Yates withdrew and resumed his place at his desk, where he sat wringing his hands. It annoyed him that strangers were overrunning his work area. First, there had been Rumpole and his second, and now Knight and his aid. They were continually coming and going or sitting around the area smoking and talking. Just their presence interfered with his already divided attention.

It was late Saturday evening when the sheriff made his rounds of the town, checking locked doors and looking in storefronts. Finally, he stopped by the Lucky Star. One of the troopers had trouble standing up. He wasn't dangerous but loud and obnoxious. Sheriff Beckett grabbed him by the arm and escorted him toward the door. He tried to ignore Mrs. Sarah Jordon's glare, but it bothered him. Ben Beckett had been sheriff for a long time, and her husband's people were influential in the community. He reflected on his knowledge of her contact with Bronco Brumley. That relationship could eventually be an embarrassment for her. A smart politician like himself would want to stay clear of a situation like that. He had also noted the disapproval registered on Miss Emmy's face when Bronco and Mrs. Sarah Jordon were publicly fraternizing.

In any event, he acknowledged to himself that it wasn't his business. He opened his office door and listened. Everything was quiet. The soldier was staggering and overly talkative. As Beckett led him to his last vacant cell to sleep it off, the private kept insisting he needed to get back to camp. He had over-heard the news that headquarters was moving to Clarksville: the sheriff pushed him into his cell. *Now that would be an unexpected blessing!*

Tom's gaze moved around his cell, searching for his bottle of laudanum. Maybe he put it under the bunk? He leaned over and put his weight on his good arm to look under the bed. His eyes swept the room. Did the sheriff take it? No, the sheriff was his friend. His brother was in the cell next door. Tom's eyes lighted on Sarge and then the area around him. No sign of the laudanum. Tom's headache had taken on the annoying edge he tried very hard to avoid. He usually grabbed the bottle of laudanum at the first twinge. Now the twinge was growing more severe by the moment into a full-blown explosion in his skull. He needed the laudanum right now! He banged the cup on the bars next to his bed.

"Madison!" Tom watched his brother's eyes shift to him. "Madison! My medicine is missing!" Sarge came to the dividing bars and looked in.

"What is the medicine for, Tom?" Tom waved his stump.

"For the pain in my arm." Sarge shook his head.

"Your arm is healed, Tom."

"For my head! I need it for my head!" Sarge again shook his head.

"The laudanum is why you have a headache, Tom."

"No, no! It makes the pain go away." Sarge crouched close to his brother's level.

"What you are feeling is withdrawal from the laudanum. I know it's bad, but the pain will go away in a couple of days, and you'll be yourself. Do you remember being yourself?"

"A couple of days? We'll all be dead in a couple of days! This whole business is crazy! Ben! Ben!"

After a few more cries, Sheriff Beckett returned to check on the problem. Tom explained about the medicine. The sheriff looked at Sarge, who nodded his head.

"I poured all of it out the window," he said, nodding toward his barred window. "He needs a couple of days for the effects to wear off. I've seen this before. In a few days, he'll be himself."

He looked from the sheriff to his brother. "I need him to be himself."

The sheriff looked from Sarge to Tom. He had no interest in jumping into a family dispute. He shrugged and went back to the office amid Tom's continued protestations. Sarge suspected the sheriff was thinking the same as his brother. In a couple of days, they'd both be dead. Then his thoughts were interrupted.

"Hey, Sarge! Look!" Bronco came to the bars separating their cells from one another and opened his hand. He was holding a walnut. There was still a little of its crumbling husk attached.

"Where did you get that?" Sarge asked, only mildly interested.

"A squirrel brought it to me. The little fella was there in my window. When I got up to look at him, he dropped it right in my cell." He scraped off the remaining husk down to the shell. "Have you got anything to break this open?"

Sarge glanced around the cell but saw nothing in the way of a tool. He started to reply in the negative and then had a thought. "Try picking up the corner of your bunk and putting the nut underneath the leg. Then drop it hard."

Bronco tried it. The walnut broke neatly in half. "Hey, it worked!"

Sarge turned away. He didn't want to be angry with Bronco, but didn't the young man realize they were about twenty-four hours away from a firing squad? He looked over at Tom, sitting up in his bunk, holding his head in his hands. Tom's mind seemed to be going in a circle. Sarge wondered if his brother had already forgotten what had happened to his laudanum? That thought also made him sour.

Bronco ate several bits of his walnut and then had a thought. He took a small chunk of the walnut meat to his window and laid it on the sill. A squirrel appeared almost immediately, ate the bit, and disappeared. A couple of minutes later, it reappeared with another whole nut. Bronco repeated the process several times: get a nut, break off the husk, put the nut under the bunk, break it open, eat most of the pieces, and save one piece for the squirrel; repeat. *It is clever. Under other circumstances, it would be amusing,* Sarge thought.

Eventually, the squirrel got its fill and quit coming back. Bronco started gathering the shells to throw out the window, but something jolted his memory. He saved three half-shells plus a small pea-size piece of a shell and started experimenting with the shell game they had watched back in camp. After a few minutes, he motioned to Sarge.

"Sarge, see if you can find the pea!" Bronco sat on the floor next to the bars separating their cells and randomly moved the shell halves in circles and figure eights. Sarge walked over. Bronco lifted a half-shell, showed him the tiny bit, and swiftly rearranged the shells. Sarge pointed to one with his toe. Bronco picked up the half-shell. There was the 'pea.' Bronco did it again, and Sarge correctly picked the shell with the pea. "How are you doing that?" Bronco was disappointed.

Sarge couldn't help but laugh. "Well, in this case, each of the three shells is a little different. See, this one has a crack in the edge. That one has a mark on the back. So, if you show me which shell the pea is under initially, I don't have to follow the movement as long as you don't secretly move the pea to another shell. If you put the pea under the cracked shell, it will still be under the cracked shell when you stop."

Bronco nodded. "So, I'd have to trick you by switching shells. Is that what the guy in camp did?"

"I don't know, Bronco. From a distance, his thimbles looked identical to me, so maybe it was just the movement that threw us off." Sarge turned away and checked on Tom again. He was distracted for a moment as the private in the other cell began muttering about needing to return to camp. Suddenly Sarge stared at the walnut, stiffened, and abruptly brought the palm of his hand to his forehead. He moved quickly to his cell door. "Sheriff! I think I know where the payroll box is! Sheriff! Sheriff, are you out there?"

34

It was eight in the evening. Coates sat on a bench outside the livery stable as his brother Zac thundered toward him.
The younger man dismounted and sat down on the bench next
to John.

"The payroll wagon will be here by ten in the morning."

"That's about when I figured," John said. Zac leaned in.
"When do we make our move?"

"Now!" Coates gave Zac a nudge. "Get their horses out of the
stable and tie them up behind the jail." John watched for any sign
of interest from others in the street. Retrieving the horses took
a little time. When Zac rejoined him, they crossed the street and
sauntered toward the jail. There were few people in sight. John
pulled out the scarf and Union cap he had taken from Preacher,
satisfied he had planned this operation as well as any general.

Coates looked up and down the street to assure himself that
no one approached. He tied Preacher's scarf across his face and
slapped the Union cap on his head. It was about two sizes too
large and rested on his eyebrows. He cracked the door. He heard
Sarge's voice from the rear of the jail.

"Sheriff! Sheriff! Are you out there?" He saw Sheriff Beckett grit his teeth, rise to his feet and start for the door to the cells. Coates moved swiftly inside and closed the door. The sheriff turned and found the masked man's forty-four aimed at his midsection.

"Hands up, Sheriff!" Beckett glanced about, then raised his hands.

"Now, turn around and face the wall." The sheriff complied. He had spotted the coat and union cap. *Yankees! But that didn't make sense.* Maybe Madison had friends he didn't know about? Then he heard Madison's voice from back in the cells.

"I know who stole the strongbox and where it is!"

"Is this a breakout? Don't do this." The sheriff spoke over his shoulder. "It's just going to make things worse for Tom and Madison." Then everything seemed to happen at once.

The sheriff barely managed to get the words out before the barrel of the forty-four came down on the back of his head, and he slumped to the floor.

Coates quickly pulled Beckett over behind the desk and tied his hands behind his back with a loop to his ankles. "You're going to have a dandy of a headache tomorrow. I know from experience," he murmured. John grabbed the keys from the desk and opened the front door. Zac darted into the room with his gun drawn. He looked down at the lawman.

"Alright, keep alert," John said. "These three may not be as easy as the sheriff." Coates opened the door and strode into the cells. "Alright, we're getting you out of here," he announced.

Bronco was off the bunk in a flash of excitement. "I'm ready! Is that you, Preacher?" He recognized the coat, scarf, and cap in the gloom, but the voice seemed off.

Sarge rose from his bunk. A closer look at the man told him that it was not Preacher. He was too tall and lean, and though the hat and coat were familiar, they were ill-fitting. Then he recognized the boots. *Coates!*

John unlocked the cell door and motioned with his gun for Sarge to turn around. The other man secured his hands behind his back. Coates continued to hold his gun on Sarge while Bronco was allowed to exit his cell. "Turn around. Hands behind your back!" Bronco looked at Sarge. "What's going on?"

"That's easy," Coates responded. "We're breaking you out of jail, and from what I hear, we're doing you a real favor." He turned to Tom's cell. The older man was still sitting on his bunk with confusion radiating from his face. "Let's go!" Coates grabbed him by his shirt collar and brought him upright.

Tom, though dazed, still knew something was off. He grabbed the bars. "No!"

"Yes!" Coates clubbed Tom's clinging hand with the barrel of his gun, and it dropped away from the bars. Tom, dull-eyed, rubbed his injured wrist on his stump. He sat down on the bunk again, and this time Coates brought his pistol down hard on Tom's head.

"Zac, check the alley, then haul his ass out of here." Zac used a length of cord to secure Tom's arms behind him, high above his elbows. Then, with much difficulty, he hauled the injured man toward the rear door. He checked out the alley again and then exited with Tom in tow. Zac propped the door open for

Coates, Sarge, and Bronco and finally, with some difficulty, threw Tom's lean frame over a horse like a sack of potatoes. Sarge and Bronco tried dragging their feet but could do little to resist with tied hands.

"What is this about, Coates? Where are you taking us? Why?" Sarge's questions came out in a torrent, but Coates shook his head.

"I'll answer all your questions later, Sergeant," his whiney voice promised. "We are rescuing you three from a sure parade before a firing squad. So keep that in mind and cooperate." He turned to Bronco, who was twisting against his bindings. He drove his fist into his midsection as hard as he could. Bronco gasped as the blow took the wind out of him. "You too, kid."

When they emerged from the back door, Sarge recognized the horses. Zac had taken the bay, the pinto, and a third horse from the stable. Sarge instantly realized that this was his last chance to escape. He rudely cut off Bronco, who was about to clamber up on the bay at Zac's insistence. Sarge jammed his foot into the stirrup and awkwardly made it into the saddle before Bronco could mount. Zac swore, then shoved Bronco toward the pinto and grabbed the reins. Sarge knew he had to get to the farm! He had to see the major!

With their prisoners aboard, Coates and Zac mounted and spurred their horses up the alley. Zac followed Coates with the reins to Bronco's and Tom's horses in hand. Sarge followed last. Miraculously in the darkness and confusion, no one had grabbed the bay's reins. Sarge took a deep breath and urged the horse up the alley, closely following the other horses. Sarge looked at Tom, who bounced precariously on his horse's back. He wished he could take him with him, but the man was in no condition, even if he had not been bound and unconscious. As they neared the corner, Coates and Zac began to rein their horses around the end of the building into the passage that would take them to Main Street. At that moment, a figure lurched out the back door of the jail.

"Halt!" A shot struck the edge of the building, sending debris flying. "Halt!" The sheriff fired again.

With his hands tied behind his back, Sarge had only limited control of his horse. He repeatedly nudged the bay with his right knee to avoid following the others. Luckily the bay was responsive. Sarge managed to spur the bay straight down the alley, separating from the pack at the last minute.

At that moment, Tom Jones regained some of his senses and stiffened. He was balanced, insecurely across the saddle. The half-unconscious man contorted his body, and his movement threw off the delicate balance. He swayed a bit, tumbling from the back of his horse. His head and shoulders bounced on the compacted earth, and he was still.

Zac, who still grasped his reins, started to pull up. The sheriff fired again, and more fragments flew close to John Coates' head.

"No!" he yelled. "Let him be!" He motioned Zac forward, and his brother jerked the reins of Bronco's horse, spurring his mount to keep apace.

The sheriff rushed forward to Tom's body and fired again at the riders out of frustration. But it was fruitless. Three of the men had rounded the corner, and the fourth disappeared down the alley in the gloom. He stumbled over to Tom, stopped, and squatted down. "I believed in you, Tom. I believed in you and Madison." Tom didn't respond. The sheriff gathered up his friend and dragged him toward the back door of the jail. He knew that the accusations against Tom and Madison still didn't add up, but the escape attempt did nothing to bolster their defense.

35

An hour later, the rain stopped as John Coates, his brother Zac, and their hostage rode up to Rufus' farmhouse. He spotted the old man on the porch with his son, Dooley, and Preacher. The shotgun lay across the old man's lap. Preacher sat on the porch's edge, his feet dangling, his hands tied behind him.

"What's he doing out here?" Coates swung off his horse.

"He had ideas of taking off." Rufus glanced from John to his son and shrugged. "The best way to keep him here is to keep an eye on him. I thought you were bringing three men?"

John ignored the question. He looked at his two captives and felt tempted to just shoot them. They would be a lot less trouble dead. For a moment, his original plan to implicate all four men in the coming robbery seemed less plausible. Still, when he recalculated, John decided he could accomplish his goal of throwing the law off his trail as easily with two dead men left at the holdup site as four. He still might be able to leave the area without a passel of troopers on his tail.

Coates spoke to Bronco. "All right, get off your horse."

He grabbed the shotgun from Rufus and pointed it at Preacher. "If you make a move, you're dead. It don't make no difference to me."

Bronco threw one knee over his saddle horn and slid to the ground. "Why are you doing this? It makes no sense."

Coates laughed. "Oh, it makes a lot of sense." He puffed himself up. He had finally gotten the upper hand on two of the men who had humiliated him. Though he didn't have the one who had cracked him on the head, he knew Rufus would be pleased to have the one who killed his two sons. Now he was clearly in charge. To top it all off, the prospect of the payroll coming into his hands made his headache less painful.

Preacher shook his head, bewildered. "Not to me. I think you are just loco."

"This boy has always been loco." The old man grumbled. "A regular Jonah. He was always scheming, even when he was a little child. He got whipped almost every day of his life. Always was just worthless."

Coates glared at Rufus and turned to Preacher.

"All right. I told you I'd explain. The two of you are going to steal the army's replacement payroll," he smirked. "The payroll wagon is due at the Jones Farm in the morning. When it reaches Carson's Junction, we will all be there to welcome it."

"You are crazy! Every payroll wagon I've ever seen has had a driver, a guard in the box, and four out-riders. So even if we were interested in participating, it is unlikely we'd be successful," Preacher said.

John grinned and turned toward the old man. "Uncle Rufus, what is Carson's Junction known for?"

The old man stirred. "Bog. You get off the main road to the low side with a wagon, and you will likely get stuck."

"Yep." Coates turned back toward Preacher. "All we have to do is detour the wagon off the main road at a place I have carefully selected, and they will all be sitting ducks."

"But why do you need us?" Bronco said.

"I'll let you know that later. But, right now, get over there with your friend."

Sheriff Beckett's shots drew a small crowd. He untied Tom's bonds, grabbed him under his arms, and dragged him back into the jail. He had just returned him to his cell and onto his bed when Deputy Shires showed up.

"Shires, see if you can locate the doctor." He motioned to a townsman who had heard the shots and followed Shires. "Jack, bring me some water from the office."

Tom inert, his breathing barely discernable, lay still. Beckett examined his head but found no open wound. Someone brought water, and the sheriff tried to get some down the man's throat but couldn't get it past the clenched teeth.

Beckett leaned back and considered the possibility that there might not need to be a trial. It was a fleeting thought. Even if Tom didn't make it, there would still be charges against Madison and Bronco. He slapped Tom's cheeks and spoke to him. "Come on, Tom!"

The doctor arrived with a great flurry of orders for people to let him through. The sheriff's cell block, crowded with citizens, was in chaos with people who had never entered it before in their lives.

Sheriff Beckett stood and allowed the doctor to take his place. He started down the hall and into his office to subdue the turmoil. Most cooperated as he shooed them back out the front door. One figure stood firm.

"Sheriff, is everyone all right?" Mrs. Sarah Jordon refused to back away.

"Mrs. Jordon, Madison, and Bronco have broken out of jail. They tried to take Tom, but he fell off his horse and is back in a cell." He leaned close. "And I'm not sure he will make it."

"Broken out?" Sarah gasped. "I heard shots. Was anyone hit?"

"I don't think so."

"You had better hope not, Sheriff. They are no more guilty than Tom." She wheeled about and stalked out the door.

The sheriff watched her leave and slowly massaged his forehead. The woman's fussing gave him a new headache to go with the one radiating from the top of his head where Coates had struck him. He turned and walked back toward the cells to check on Tom. Then, between waves of pain, he stopped dead in his tracks.

What had Madison said just before John Coates forty-four connected with his head? Sheriff Beckett pressed the heels of his hands against his throbbing forehead and tried to remember. "*I know who stole the payroll. I know where it is.*" Sheriff Beckett's hands hesitated. His mind was still a bit fogged from the blow and the events of the last half hour. Did he imagine that? No, Madison had yelled the words at him a moment before the man in the Union cap entered the office and struck him from behind. "*Sheriff, I think I know who stole the payroll!*" Sheriff Beckett stiffened his spine. The breakout was the last straw. He rebelled at being the major's toady. He was tired of people coming into his jail without his say-so. He noted that Madison had not ridden off with the others. Three of the men had turned between the buildings toward Main Street. Madison had ridden at breakneck speed straight down the alley. Beckett calculated the odds. If Madison thought he knew who stole the payroll, logically, he probably headed back to the farm where the theft and murder happened. He called to his deputy.

"Shires, keep an eye on Tom. I'm going to take a ride."

Deputy Shires turned around and watched Beckett's back disappear through the front door. He didn't have time to respond, so he shuffled over to slump into the Sheriff's chair. It was the most comfortable one in the jail.

Corporal Yates looked up from his desk. His work area had become the social center of the house. The newly arrived captains and lieutenants lounged in the chairs in the old parlor with the major's officers and entertained themselves with jokes and stories. The visitors were all headquarters-type personnel who had never tasted battle, and though Yates also fell into that category, he felt contempt for them. He omitted himself from his blanket condemnation on the premise that he might not have ever been in battle, but it fell to him to handle the aftermath; the reports, the official letters to next of kin, and the arrangements for bodies to be shipped home. So, in his mind, he was different, certainly morally superior in the military sense.

Occasionally one of the officers would wander into the extensive library and peruse the shelves. But the frivolity in the parlor always drew them back to join the group again. Yates wished they would all go away permanently, and then he reminded him-self that he was also going away. This thought brought a frown and some more hand wringing on his part. He had chores of his own to take care of and little time.

36

Mrs. Sarah Jordon sat in her swing, holding the letter. There were tears in her eyes, and her hands shook as she reread the lines. Sarah had never been so conflicted in her young life. She stared at the street, blind to the wagon, the horse and rider, or the children playing with a hoop. Finally, Sarah cut her eyes back to the letter and read it a third time. The letters were big and vertical, like soldiers marching across the page.

11 April 1865

Dearest Sarah,

I hope this letter finds you well. I am sorry I have been so long in writing. I was slightly wounded and captured at Fredericktown. After weeks near there, they moved us to West Virginia to a camp. My group was here a month before receiving news that the war was over. I got some shrapnel in my legs, but it is so minor I hesitate to mention it. I will be home in a few weeks, I think. I have missed you so much! Please pass this letter on to my folks. With everyone writing letters, paper is hard to come by right now. Sarah turned the paper over.

I can't wait to see you again. Remember our rides around the farm? It's spring, and the war is over! I'll be there as soon as I can. Some wagons are heading south, but I may end up walking. No matter. I hope to see you soon.

With much affection,

Jimmy

Sarah set the paper down on the swing beside her and pressed her handkerchief against her eyes. As she set out to find Pappy, she had stopped at the post office out of habit and found the letter waiting for her. Now she felt like a swimmer caught in a riptide. For months her hopes had been centered on Jimmy. Then with rumors of his death, she had worried in self-absorbed conjecture, waiting for news of any kind for closure. Finally, as weeks had passed, she began to accept what seemed inevitable. Now she felt she understood why she couldn't truly let go. Jimmy was alive! And according to his letter, he was all right and would be home soon. Going by the travel time he mentioned, he should have been home the previous week!

A new foreboding came over her. Could something have happened to Jimmy on his way? Then her train of thought moved on to Mister Brumley. Sweet Bronco! No! She had allowed her thoughts of him to become familiar again! Her heart hurt. Ironically, her present feelings for Jimmy seemed like a betrayal of Bronco. Bronco was so kind and good and courageous. She had watched through the window as the young man faced down that horrible John Coates. While Jimmy's self-deprecating stories of his experiences during the war had been related clumsily through letters and received long after the events, she had seen Bronco at the moment of danger. She had been a part of it. She had witnessed his bravery and felt his protective hand on her arm at the moment of peril.

She wondered where each man was now. Was Jimmy traveling toward her at this very moment? Would he arrive tomorrow? The next day? Today! And Bronco? Had he been rescued, or was John Coates involved? Was he riding away to freedom, or had that terrible outlaw captured or killed him with Preacher and Sarge? It was too much! She couldn't think! Sarah rose from her swing and walked swiftly toward the Lucky Star. She still needed to find Pappy. Maybe he could shed some light on things.

In a way, Preacher was pleased with the addition of Bronco to his captivity. It meant that he was out of range of a firing squad. When Bronco whispered that Sarge had escaped, Preacher chuckled. So, all three of them were safe from the major's justice, at least for the moment. That still left Tom. Preacher was ready to bet the farm that Sarge's escape had something to do with helping Tom. But what? Appealing to the major had not been successful in the past. It didn't seem logical to expect it to turn out differently now? He had spent enough time with Sarge to sense a plan afoot, but having a plan did not guarantee the desired result.

Preacher could see John hunched up close to old man Coates, talking in undertones trying to coax some concession out of him. The old man's son was still feeling the effect of the corn liquor and dozed as unobtrusively as possible. Zac was the only man fully alert. The sun had set well before the jailbreak. Now the nightfall had given way to impenetrable darkness. The arrival of a blustery wind from the north suggested more rain coming toward them.

Preacher leaned close to Bronco. "I think our little family get-together involves more plotting. So, let's keep an eye on Zac. If he gets distracted or sleepy, we'll make our move."

Bronco nodded. Some success with his bindings encouraged him. His wrists had been tied clumsily in a rush to leave the jail. With the arrival of total darkness, he could work on them more aggressively. He slid his index finger into the slack he had managed to create between two wraps of the cord. He worked the slack close to the knot and tried to pick at it to unravel it. He yearned desperately to jerk his wrists apart, but he knew that would be counter-productive. *Patience. Patience.*

Coates looked over from jawing with Rufus and caught Dooley asleep. He gave him a vicious kick in the ribs. Dooley awoke with a start and made to draw his gun, but Coates was quicker and placed the barrel of his forty-four against the man's neck; the threat was real. Coates felt sick of dealing with him. Rufus' shotgun swung toward John. After a momentary stalemate, Coates nodded and slipped his weapon back into his holster. The old man turned the gun away, and Dooley got up to stretch and yawn while looking mockingly at his cousin before sitting again and leaning back against the post.

Preacher watched and waited. Bronco moved his fingers methodically among his bindings. The temperature dropped, and the wind grew in velocity.

Old man Coates shivered. His bones were brittle, and the wind cut through him like a knife. He considered the options. He could invite the whole crowd into the house or point them toward the barn. He rose shakily to his feet.

"It's going to be raining soon. Take this bunch to the barn." He motioned weakly with the shotgun.

John Coates nodded. He didn't want to spend more time in close quarters with the old coot than he had to. The barn was fine. He nudged cousin Dooley and pulled his six-gun to signal the move for Preacher, Bronco, and Zac.

Dooley licked his lips. The barn promised more corn liquor, and Dooley was instantly thirsty. Stretching out in the hay was much more appealing than sitting on the porch. Preacher and Bronco stood. Zac grabbed the horses' reins and, walking abreast with Dooley, started leading them toward the barn.

Bronco finally unraveled the knot and felt his hands go free. Coates paced a step before him on the right. Zac and Dooley walked directly ahead, leading the horses. Approximately two hundred feet stretched between the group and the barn, and the doors were open. Bronco elbowed Preacher and sidled by him. He moved his near hand to his hip. Preacher could not see the freed hands in the darkness, but he caught enough of the motion to understand the message. He nodded. Preacher's bindings were still snug. Bronco nodded toward the bay, which plodded directly ahead of him. Then, thinking quickly, Preacher pretended to stumble. He grunted as he went down on his sore knees and pitched to the right out of the loose formation of horses and prisoners. Coates forty-four followed his movement. Preacher dropped the rest of the way with hands still bound, landing hard on his shoulder. He rolled as if trying to get his feet under him again. Each effort took him a few feet further to the right away from Bronco. Coates' gun tracked each floundering movement.

Suddenly Bronco made his move. Thankful for the darkness, he took two long strides and seemed to levitate high onto the bay's hindquarters. In an instant, his freed hands landed on the horse's rump, and he leap-frogged into the saddle. Then, without a wasted motion, he gave a blood-curdling yell and kicked hard against the bay's flanks.

For a moment, the animal experienced the most primal fear its kind can know. Its forelegs pawed the air. Then the hindquarters kicked in unison. The bay charged forward as if launched from a catapult. Zac and Dooley barely had time to look around before the horse and rider were on them, trampling them underfoot like rag dolls and galloping on toward the barn.

Coates forgot Preacher for a moment as he tried to track Bronco, whose head was on the bay's neck, urging him on. In the confusion that ensued, the other horses scattered. Two of them stumbled on the staggering Zac and inert Dooley. One horse veered toward Coates, distracting him from his attempt to fire into the dark toward Bronco.

Preacher rolled to his knees in time to see the shadowy figure of Bronco disappear through the doorway into the barn. As the deeper darkness of the interior enveloped the horse and rider, Preacher managed to regain his feet and put himself behind the horse that had strayed toward Coates.

With the disappearance of Bronco, Coates swung back toward Preacher's last location, but he was no longer there. Coates cursed. He swung his weapon right hand left, trying to find a target. His rage at the turn of events demanded a target. He was ready to fire at anything. Too late, he heard the thunder of Bronco's horse's hooves coming up fast from behind. The bay's massive chest crashed into him, and he went sprawling. As he hit the ground, his forty-four spun away into an abyss of blackness. Bronco pulled up, grabbed one of the loose horses' reins, and put his hand out to Preacher. He grasped him by the crook of his arm, giving him enough support to get a foot in the stirrup. Preacher swung aboard.

Hearing the commotion, Rufus came a few feet off the porch. He knew something was out of kilter, but his poor eyesight, combined with the darkness, and compromised hearing, left the entire affair a mystery. Rufus blindly stumbled forward and then, hearing hoofbeats, instantly regretted it. He held the shotgun at the ready with no idea what could happen next. The old man swore under his breath. He made out more hoofbeats coming closer. Rufus imagined horses galloping toward him and braced himself in fear before, as a last resort, he scampered back to the porch on arthritic legs.

"Hold on, Preacher!" Bronco tugged the reins and spurred the bay. In a moment, the barnyard was behind them. Preacher did his best to use his knees for purchase on the galloping horse. At last, they slowed well out of range of any gunfire. Bronco leaned over and worked on Preacher's bindings in the dark. Even with his hands free, it was difficult. Finally, he located a knife in his saddlebag and sliced at the rawhide. Preacher finished the job with a powerful hunch of his shoulders, and they sat in the dark, catching their breath for a moment while he removed the bindings.

"Now what?" Bronco broke the silence. "What do we do now?"

Preacher rubbed his skinned wrists. "No choice. We don't know where Carson's Junction is. We know the reception we will get in town. So the only choice left is the Jones farm!"

37

John Coates swore. He stumbled around the barnyard darkness, trying to make out the fallen figures of Dooley and Zac. Then he was on his knees, feeling around in the dirt for his six-gun. Everything was going to shit! He found the gun and stumbled over to Zac, who sat up where he had fallen. Coates shook his brother's shoulder and felt the sticky texture of blood. Zac wrenched his shoulder away with a yelp. He seemed to know he had a nasty gash, but not how bad it was. Dooley lay still, almost invisible a few feet away.

When the sound of Preacher and Bronco's horses faded, Uncle Rufus hurried closer through the darkness. The old man called out. "What's going on? John? Dooley? Zac?" John knew what would happen next. Once the old man figured out the disaster for what it was, he would hurl abuse at him like he always did. Then, out of the black, Rufus suddenly materialized at his elbow.

"What happened?" Rufus could not see well enough to make out his son's outline on the ground. But, once he identified John and Zac, he moved away and continued his search.

"Dooley?" Rufus stumbled further through the darkness. Then, "Dammit, dammit, dammit!" John knew he had found his son.

Zac felt around on himself and tested his extremities to determine how badly he was scrambled.

John stood and silently cursed the darkness. He mutely cursed Preacher, Bronco, Sarge, Tom, the sheriff, and the escape. Then Coates cursed another round out loud. He could feel himself coming unglued and welcomed it. Uncle Rufus sank beside his inert son. His voice rose in bitterness rather than mourning.

"You idiot! Johnny, you worthless idiot!" Rufus shouted the words toward his nephew over his shoulder. The old man's words calling him by his hated boyhood nickname brought back all the abuse he had suffered at the man's hands and pushed John closer to the edge.

"Everything you touch turns to shit." Rufus staggered to his feet and retraced his steps toward John. Rufus cocked the shotgun. John's anger flared into an inferno. He strode forward and met Rufus halfway. He felt the shotgun muzzle jab his ribs. John jerked the gun from his uncle's arthritic hands, flipped it around, and shoved the barrel into Rufus Coates' sunken chest. Then John grinned with pleasure as he pulled the trigger. In the flash of the muzzle, he saw surprise, fear, and death in an instant. The impact of the blast tossed the small shrunken body backward. The concussion sent a bruising concert of pain into John's shoulder. He flung the shotgun away and felt a rush of liberation wash over him. Then he heard Dooley moan. He wasn't dead! The dazed man was trying to sit up.

"Damnit!" Coates knew only one way to fix this. Once his worthless cousin saw the old man, he would be looking for his own revenge. Coates pulled his handgun and stepped toward the groaning man on the ground. He put the first slug in his gut. In the darkness, John could only imagine that the surprise on his cousin's face would match his old man's. Then, he shoved the barrel forward and found his favorite target. The second slug penetrated his cousin's forehead just below the hairline.

"You're welcome." Coates pivoted and stalked toward his horse, shivering up against the side of the barn. He grabbed the reins and walked back toward Zac.

"I've wanted to do that all my life, brother. Let's go back to the house." Zac griped his bloody shoulder in the dark and grunted in agreement.

Sarge slowed his horse after getting out of range of the sheriff's handgun. He let the animal catch its wind, then headed toward Tom's farm. Twenty minutes later, he rode up as close as he dared and dismounted behind a shed, a sensible distance from the house. Since there was as yet no payroll in the office to protect, there were no guards at the front door at night. However, that did not guarantee that there were none about the farm's perimeter. In the evening shadows, he moved silently to the side of the house and looked briefly in the front parlor window. The corporal still sat at his desk. He appeared to be working on a stack of papers. Sarge moved toward the rear of the house to the location of the major's office. Light still radiated out of that window as well. He looked in. The major also appeared busy. Sarge moved back to the front to watch the corporal.

Sarge was torn. He felt sure he knew the fate of the payroll box. It added up. The new information of the pending move from the farm, combined with Bronco's antics with the squirrel, somehow completed the puzzle he had gone over a hundred times. His insight went through him like a bolt of lightning. And as he pondered the equation, the more Sarge's ambitions grew from simply locating the box to proving who had taken it. If he was right, the thief might move the payroll tonight.

The knowledge that Coates held Bronco and possibly Preacher captive hung over Sarge like a cloud. He felt a nagging responsibility to rescue them if he could. Only one chain of events could prove all of them innocent of theft and murder. He hoped that proof, once obtained, would enable him to secure their safety. Ultimately, one thing seemed inevitable; if he was wrong and recaptured, there was a good chance he and Tom would go in front of a firing squad the next day. Everything rested on him.

Of paramount importance was the answer to the question, could he trust anyone? Was the major potentially a friend or foe? Given the man's attitude so far, Sarge had to assume the major was, at best, neutral. A few minutes later, Sarge watched the officer stick his head out of his office door and speak to Corporal Yates. Sarge surmised that he told the corporal he was turning in for the night. Yates nodded to acknowledge the officer and went back to work.

A few minutes later, he watched the corporal leave the house by the front door and walk toward the barn. Sarge hurried to the back bedroom window. The major appeared to be preparing for bed. This moment seemed like the most opportune time to act.

Quickly, Sarge moved back to the front of the house, stepped up on the front porch, and cracked the door. All was quiet inside. A moment later, he moved through the parlor and slipped into the library. Heavy draperies hung across the windows. Sarge stationed himself behind the curtains to one side of the windows and waited as an hour passed. Sarge prayed that he was right. Another thirty minutes passed. Another fifteen minutes. Another ten went by without a development. He prayed for something, almost anything, to happen.

Sarge felt his patience waning and pleaded with himself to hang on a little longer. His doubts assailed him. Maybe he was wrong. Perhaps in his anxiety, he had fabricated the whole scenario? He pictured the faceless killer peacefully asleep in his bed while he wasted his last night of freedom, standing in the dark in the empty library.

Then, with the rattle of a doorknob, everything changed. Sarge heard the sliding bolt and the click as it cleared the door jam. With the hallway dark, Sarge could barely make out the presence of another person, a shadow hidden in shadow. Sarge held his breath and prayed that the curtain would conceal him once a lamp lit the room. As Sarge waited, the shadowy arm reached its left and struck a match. The door closed almost silently, and the shadow became Corporal Yates. *Was I right?*

38

Bronco rode beside Preacher through the damp night air with a sense of dread. There had been so many dead ends over the last few days. Coates remained such a constant threat. It seemed that dealing with him now consumed them. Sarge couldn't seem to get untangled from the major out at the farm or the sheriff in town. They knew about a robbery attempt at Carson's Junction but didn't know where that was! Riding hard for Sarge's farm, the two men had no idea what awaited them there. He looked sidelong at the dark figure of Preacher beside him. Bronco's life of breaking horses in Ohio seemed tame by comparison. The only bright spot was Miss Sarah. Beautiful Miss Sarah! Just the thought of her raised his spirits.

Preacher slowed to a cantor, and he and Bronco looked ahead into the darkness surrounding the farm. They dismounted and walked their horses toward a shed east of the house. They tied their reins to a bush. They were about to walk away when a whinny alerted them. They walked around the shed and found Sarge's horse tied to a tree. Secured with it was another horse that neither recognized. Now, at least they knew Sarge was here! But who belonged to the other horse? A little light spilled from the front parlor window. Further back, another oil light flickered dimly in what could be a bedroom.

"What are we looking for?" Bronco whispered.

"I don't know." Preacher motioned forward, and they moved like ghosts across the yard. A look in the parlor window revealed the big corporal's empty desk. Then, peering around the casing in the back window, they discovered a figure in the bed, with the covers pulled up. Bronco looked at Preacher, who shrugged. Since Sarge wasn't outside, he must be inside?

Dressed in full uniform, Bronco seemed the best choice to enter the house first. When he opened the front door, he immediately heard angry voices and spied light from under a door down the hall to his left. Bronco half-turned and motioned to his friend. Preacher followed him into the parlor, and they moved a few steps toward the sliver of light. Then, the floor vibrated as a thunderous roll of sound enveloped them. They looked at each other in wonder.

Sarge held his position behind the curtain. A faint light emanated from the single lamp. Corporal Yates set down a long stout jimmy bar and stacked two short lengths of posts beside it. He picked up the oil lamp from the desk, set it beside the one on the table by the door, and lit it. Next, he moved one of two ladderback chairs from the front of the desk close around to the side and centered it. Then, without hesitation, he picked up the five-foot jimmy bar and, with a slight scraping sound, slid it along the floor hard enough to ram the sharp tip under the edge of the enormous desk.

Sarge watched this and remembered the tiny crack in the desk and dent in the floor he observed two days earlier. He cursed himself for being unable to make anything of those two marks at the time. The corporal lay one of the post lengths on its side as a fulcrum and levered down on the bar with his foot using his massive weight. The bottom of the desk rose an inch, then two, and then four, level with the post. With some difficulty, Corporal Yates bent down to nudge the other short post length under the edge of the desk. He released the bar and stood straight to relax his muscles.

Yates took a deep breath, then faced away from the desk. With his feet on each side of the short length of the post, the huge man squatted. He was able to grasp the bottom in his large hands. Yates brought his burden upward high enough to balance it on the opposite bottom edge. He temporally supported the weight against his shoulder while, with a free hand, he swept the chair into position so that about two inches of the seat were beneath the edge. Yates gently lowered the desk to sit on the chair with a great inhalation of breath and stood away. The big man panted for a moment, then went to his knees. He extended his left arm underneath the desk as if to reach something beneath it. In doing so, Yates turned his face away from Sarge and toward the door.

Unarmed, Sarge had but a moment to act. In three strides, he crossed the room, bent behind the big man, and tried to jerk the corporal's sidearm from its holster. But the man sensed Sarge's footsteps. He looked over his shoulder and reached back with astonishing swiftness to grasp Sarge's wrist, staying his attempt.

Sarge's hand was trapped. Hoping to ride Yates to the ground, Sarge threw his leg over the corporal's enormous back, but again, he underestimated the man's strength. With a heave, the big corporal shrugged Sarge off as if shedding a great cloak.

Still, without a weapon, Sarge found himself sprawled on the floor. The corporal rolled clumsily about, trying to get his bulk to a position on his back that would allow him to draw his gun. Sarge saw the man's dilemma and threw himself at him again, punching his face and body with his fists. It felt like beating a mattress. Yates' great bulk absorbed every blow with no effect. Finally, the big hands moved to Sarge's chest, lifted him like a child, and threw him to the side. Sarge gathered himself and attacked again. Both men panted with exertion. Suddenly Yates locked Sarge in a bear hug. The corporal heaved side to side, and Sarge realized he was trying to roll over and get under him. Sarge struggled to stay on top. But again, the unrelenting strength of the Yates stymied him. Staving off defeat, Sarge switched his strategy. He twisted and managed to get a hand on Yates' throat. He pushed down, using the corporal's effort to pull him toward him to his advantage.

After a moment, with his air cut off, Yates released the bear hug, and Sarge pulled away. Corporal Yates twisted to his right, panting. His left hand instinctively went to his throat. Then Yates threw his right arm carelessly away from his body. That movement brought the arm crashing into the chair supporting the desk. The impact was enough to shove the chair far enough to release the dense mass. The desk toppled awkwardly from the chair, with the front corner striking the floor first.

The shock wave sent a shudder throughout the house. Then in a scissoring movement, the remaining bottom edge descended and teetered on the edge of the four-by-four before slipping off. The big man's arm was injured but not crushed as he pulled it away just ahead of the desk's leading edge. The desk fell the final four inches to the floor. Only that momentary delay saved Corporal Yates' arm from amputation. But now, with the corporal's gun hand free, Sarge knew that time had run out.

Then suddenly, Sarge became aware of another figure in the room. He whirled to find Sheriff Beckett standing just behind him. The lawman stepped toward Yates with his gun drawn.

"Pull that gun, and you're dead!" He looked back at Sarge. "You alright? "Sarge wiped away the cold sweat that had formed on his forehead.

"Whew! I think I just wrestled away about ten years of my life!"

39

The thunderous vibration brought Preacher and Bronco to a standstill. An ominous silence followed the boom until they saw the major, still in his nightshirt, leave his bedroom and cross to the library door ahead. Unaware of the two men in the darkened room, the officer thrust the library door open. Then, as it closed behind him, they heard him yell, "What's going on here?"

Moving forward, they reached the door as two other men in nightshirts arrived. Bronco threw the door open.

They found Sarge, Sheriff Beckett, and Major Rogers standing over a big soldier with corporal stripes. He seemed to be nursing an injured arm.

"Here is your payroll robber, major!" Sarge panted, pointing toward the corporal. He pulled the man's revolver from its holster. "Your payroll is under the desk."

The big man lying on the floor was ashen in color, his arm already beginning to swell.

"What's going on?" One of the two night-shirted officers pushed Bronco and Preacher aside and forced his way into the room.

Sarge handed Yates' weapon to Major Rogers and sat heavily on the edge of the desk. The major addressed Yates. "What do you have to say, corporal?"

Sarge tapped the desk with his fingers. "He is probably the only man within a hundred miles stout enough to pick up this desk by himself. His motive is obvious, and he had the opportunity. And now we have proof."

Major Rogers rubbed his jaw. "You do if it's there, all right."

"Yes, he does." Sheriff Beckett faced the officer. Unable to contain himself, he barked, "This all looks like a piss-poor investigation on your part, major."

"I need to see a doctor. My arm is smashed." Corporal Yates interrupted the conversation regarding the merits of Roger's investigation.

"Tell us about the payroll box." The major ordered.

"I have nothing to say."

"Suit yourself, but if someone doesn't treat that arm in a hurry, you could lose it." The major inspected it from afar.

The big corporal looked down. He was kneading his bicep as if that would ease the pain. "Alright, I stole the box!"

The other two night-shirted men looked around. "What box?" One looked at the other behind him, who flung his hands out helplessly.

"Preacher, Bronco, help me roll the desk over," Sarge said. He eyed the group of officers.

The three men took positions on the near side of the desk, and with some grunting and swearing, they managed to set it over on its far side to reveal the strongbox.

"So, that's where it's been all this time?" asked Preacher.

"Yep, all the time, the major was accusing Tom and then us," Sarge smiled, "Hiding in plain sight like the pea in the shell game we watched over in Alabama."

"Then he must have killed the guard too." Bronco cut in.

"But, why kill the guard?" The major looked at the corporal, who turned away.

"I'm just guessing." Sarge said, "but maybe they schemed together, and the guard figured out belatedly that when the box went missing, he'd be the logical suspect. Since Yates couldn't have his cooperation, he killed him to keep him quiet. Or, maybe he just had to get rid of the only witness. There seem to be a lot of maybes."

The major looked thoughtful for a moment. Then the man's eyes brightened.

"Outhouse!" The major slapped his hands together. "Yates was the backup when one of the guards needed to go to the outhouse. Yates relieved the outside guard while he visited the outhouse and killed the inside guard!" He looked at Yates, who remained silent.

"What about the secret door?" Sheriff Beckett looked from the major to Sarge.

"I think the business with the door was just a lucky break for Yates. Its discovery put all the suspicion on Tom, so Yates' possible guilt was never seriously examined."

Rogers walked around the corporal and looked at the strongbox. It took only a small portion of the space enclosed by the desk in its original position. "A perfect hidey-hole. How did you figure this out, Jones?"

"The key was my realization that desk is just a big hollow box. With all the guards outside, Yates couldn't exit with the strongbox the night he killed the guard. I think that he expected to remove it when things cooled off. Just as I started putting things together, a private in the next jail cell started mumbling about you moving headquarters. That's when I decided to come out here and hide out, realizing that this might be the last chance the killer would have to take it out of hiding. But, of course, I still didn't know who the killer was for sure." Sarge shrugged. "If Corporal Yates had already retrieved it, I would have been out of luck on both counts. But it was Yates who ran out of time."

The major nodded. "Lieutenant, go roust some guards and a wagon. We need to get Yates to the doctor in town."

"Well, it all makes sense to me." Sheriff Beckett looked at the major as if defying contradiction. "Satisfied?"

"Yes, I am" The major ignored the sheriff's challenging tone and motioned to the lieutenant to get moving.

The following morning John Coates tied his horse to the back of Rufus' wagon and climbed into the box. Zac had already headed to a renegade Rebel camp five miles away to enlist additional riders. He would offer generous payment for assistance in dealing with the payroll detail coming from Winston. By shooting his cousin, Dooley, Coates had left himself seriously undermanned to take the Union soldiers in the best of situations. Now, it was suicidal for them to tackle this job without more guns.

On the other hand, John was confident that a cut of the double payroll would provide adequate incentive to attract the help he wanted. The escaped Preacher and Bronco were loose cannons, but who could they go to for help? Both the sheriff and military would probably lock them up on sight.

He clucked at the team and made a beeline for Carson's Junction, both exhausted and exhilarated. After dragging the bodies of Rufus and Dooley into the barn and unsaddling the horses, John had intended to enjoy a good night's sleep. But the rush of adrenalin did not subside and sleep evaded him. Despite the previous night's disaster, it did not take him very long to convert the catastrophe into a stroke of genius on his part. In his amended view, he got rid of the two troublemakers in one fell swoop and found a little cash in the old man's house. Despite the downside, the icing on the cake was killing his uncle Rufus in such a dramatic fashion. It was the fulfillment of a lifelong yearning. John shrugged off finishing cousin Dooley, for the man had always been worthless. They had both been expendable and filled with satisfaction. Expecting the payroll wagon to arrive at the junction in approximately an hour, he clucked at the team again.

John decided that he could still utilize his original plan. The intersection of the main road and two secondary trails formed the junction. For a wagon coming from Winston, the road on the right led to a farmhouse. The road to the left would take the wagon down to the bog. Time was now running short. When he arrived at the junction, he unloaded the large hand-made detour sign he had brought along. He dragged it to the center of the road. No one could miss it. Starting out, he had decided he would need the wagon to carry off the loot once he completed his scheme. After peering up the road in the direction from which the payroll wagon would be traveling, Coates carefully drove his horses and wagon down the incline. Then he moved them out of sight of the main road.

Coates smiled grimly to himself and rehearsed his plan in light of the features before him. This bog was at most four feet deep. The floating debris and the gelatin-like, semi-solid surface had fooled unwitting men in the past. When drivers came off the road and down the incline, they should always keep left at the bottom as he had just done. If they went straight, which most unwitting people were inclined to do, they would be axel deep before they knew it. The payroll wagon would be trapped while he and his men would be well prepared for the shoot-out. He carried the shotgun, a carbine, and two six-guns in the wagon. He smiled. If his plan succeeded, he would take out at least two of them before they knew what hit them.

Preacher's Yankee cap and scarf were still crammed into John's inside pocket. His plan to murder Preacher and Bronco at the scene had seemed foolproof. The bodies would have tricked the authorities into a wild goose chase looking for the third man of the trio. He had hoped that with them exposed as the robbers, he could make off with the loot while they took the blame. It irked him that they had escaped. Their freedom would rob him of the pleasure of personally shooting them, but with the three on the run, he would not have to worry about their future inter-ference. He consoled himself that sometimes sacrifices had to be made. John scanned the terrain and reaffirmed that his hiding position under the road would give him a clear field of fire. All he needed now was for Zac to arrive with additional gunmen before the payroll did. He could feel his anticipation burning like a hot cup of java. This little ambush was going to be good, real good!

40

In Winston, Colonel Smith, the Union regimental payroll officer, prepared to send another payroll to Major Rogers' command post near Titustown. He had learned long before the costs of taking unnecessary risks. That knowledge had served him well the entirety of the war. So, with a double payroll to deliver, he was as alert as usual as he descended the steps of the Regimental Headquarters office to meet with the officer in charge of the wagon preparing to leave.

"Captain Biggs!" The colonel approached the captain and the tall, lean, black sergeant from behind.

"Yes, sir?" The two men turned and saluted. The captain was experienced in handling payroll deliveries. Through much dedication, the black man had worked his way up to his elevated status in the payroll detail in only two years. The two men's eyes were alert, and their manner businesslike.

"I want you to keep an eye out more than ever on this trip. The last payroll mysteriously disappeared after delivery last month. So, I want you to be sure this one doesn't meet the same fate." The colonel scowled. "The war may be over, but let's keep in mind that we still are in enemy territory. Alright?"

"Yes, sir!" Captain Biggs responded. Sergeant Brown nodded and surveyed the preparations. There were four outriders, the captain, the driver, and himself riding shotgun. He had been delivering payrolls with Colonel Smith for over a year without incident and wasn't looking to allow one now.

"Alright, then. Let's get this wagon on its way."

"Murphy, you ready to go?" the sergeant looked up at the little black man holding the reins for the four-horse team.

"Ready, Sergeant."

"Bill, Fred, Mitch, Walt?" He sang out each outrider's name and noted their responses. Then, he swung his body up into the wagon and ensured the carbine was secured by his right leg.

Captain Biggs mounted his horse. Murphy waited for his nod, then gave the reins a shake to start the wagon forward.

Colonel Smith watched the wagon out of sight and returned to his office satisfied. Captain Biggs and Sergeant Brown were steady hands, and the other men were dependable. He was confident nothing would go awry.

After the previous night's rain, the horses and wagon kicked up little dust. Sergeant Brown watched the countryside pass. Occasionally, they saw a Rebel group of two or three men coming toward them. They were a shabby bunch, and most didn't even look up. The soldiers could read the fatigue and failure in their faces. However, when they encountered a group of freed slaves, they found themselves being cheered. Looking at the smiling black faces, Sergeant Brown wondered what their lives would amount to, starting with no money and few possessions.

The terrain was hilly and densely forested, with intermittent fields in many of the valleys. Sergeant Brown had participated in transports near Atlanta for a time. The area they were passing through had been one of the gathering places of men and equipment for Sherman's campaign six months earlier.

Brown had seen the destruction highlighted by some newspaper stories. Some applauded the actions taken by the Union general. The argument that he had shortened the war and saved lives on both sides was more acceptable in the north than in the south, particularly after Lee's surrender. And some felt he had abused his authority by taking the fight to the civilian population. Sergeant Brown had withheld judgment until he had observed the area around Atlanta firsthand.

The sergeant looked sideways at Corporal Murphy. The small black corporal had done his time in the trenches. Brown knew that he relished sitting up in the wagon with a team of four horses under his command. He smiled as he acknowledged that he, too, enjoyed a bright spring day rolling through the countryside. Since Appomattox, the Union army had both rejoiced in victory and seen its numbers drop rapidly as many men took their final pay and mustered out. He had heard that there were still outbreaks of southern resistance; Rebel firebrands were still carousing through the countryside, claiming to be defending the Confederacy. Sergeant Brown suspected that most of them were feeding other, more base impulses. Jefferson Davis was said to be in hiding in Virginia.

"Sarge, you going to stick it out in the army?" Corporal Murphy clucked at one of the lagging horses and looked sidewise at the sergeant.

"I haven't decided." The sergeant looked out on the countryside. He took a deep breath of fresh air. "How about you?"

"I sure miss Boston," Murphy said.

"I enjoyed Boston." The sergeant said. He reflected on his time there. But did he miss it? No, for him, it was merely another place .to hang his hat.

"But you have a family there." The sergeant nudged Murphy, who grinned. Sergeant Brown knew Murphy had a three-year-old baby girl.

Captain Biggs, just in front of the wagon, stiffened. His left front outrider rode rapidly toward him.

"Sir, we have a detour coming up."

"Detour?" Biggs frowned. Possible reasons for a detour flitted through Sergeant Brown's mind; washout? Tree across the road? Highwaymen? He fingered his rifle. "Can you see any reason for a detour, private?" Briggs pursed his lips.

"No, there's just a sign with an arrow."

"How far ahead?"

"Just around that bend, Sir."

Biggs peered ahead, then looked closely at the surrounding landscape. Finally, he wheeled his horse around and spoke directly with Sergeant Brown.

"Mitch says there is a detour sign ahead. You men stick with the wagon and keep your eyes peeled." Sergeant Brown nodded and motioned for Murphy to move forward. Murphy shook the reins, and the wagon lurched on. As they entered the slight downgrade, the woods seemed to descend closer to the road. The air was almost chilly, and bright shafts of light gave the dappled ground a heightened three-dimensional quality.

When they reached the detour sign, Sergeant Brown stepped down from the wagon with the rifle, and Captain Biggs dismounted. Bill looked back at them and shrugged. His horse's ears perked, and both men noted its foreleg pawing the ground.

"Something's not right here, sir."

Captain Biggs nodded and examined the scene. The crudely painted detour sign was in the middle of the main road, which continued without apparent obstruction until it curved to the right out of sight a quarter of a mile ahead. To the right and left were secondary roads, one leading slightly uphill and the other down. The arrow pointed toward the downhill option.

"I guess either or both of them could rejoin the main road up ahead," Bill said. "But Samson is suspicious." He patted his nervous horse's neck. "I don't like it when Samson is suspicious."

"Bill, ride ahead until you can see around that bend." Sergeant Brown ordered.

Bill reined his horse around the sign, galloped up the road, and disappeared. A few minutes later, he came back into sight. He rode up fast. "Sergeant, Sir, I can see for another quarter mile around that bend. There's nothing up there to hinder our wagon that I can see."

The sergeant looked at Mitch and Murphy. "What do you think about this?"

"You got me." The private rubbed his jaw. "I guess if there is a road problem up ahead, we can always turn around."

"That's what I'm thinking," said Murphy.

41

Sarah found Pappy at his usual table at the Lucky Star. He stared at his coffee until she approached. She guessed from Pappy's expression that he was pondering the state of his health as he was inclined to do of late. However, he brightened when she sat down.

"Well, good morning, Sunshine," he said with a smile. "I was just sitting here, wondering what would hit us next. I hear our three friends are fresh out of jail, but Tom is still in there. Any chance the boys visited you since they escaped?" He looked at her quizzically.

"Pappy, I don't know what happened to them. I hoped you might have an idea. The Sheriff said that the leader of the bunch that broke them out wore a Union cap and a scarf like I remember seeing Preacher wear. But I can't see them taking off and leaving Major Tom Jones behind. Besides, if they tried to take him, I doubt he'd go. Everything important to him is out at his farm."

Pappy nodded. "I couldn't prove it, but John Coates seems to have his hand in every kind of devilment. From what Bronco told me, it seems his main reason to get them out of jail would be a chance for revenge."

Sarah took an envelope out of her dress pocket. "This came this morning. I wonder if you could share the news with Cal and Wanda?" She handed it to Pappy and watched his expression as he opened the envelope and read the letter.

Pappy brought it almost to the tip of his nose, skipped the endearments, and absorbed the gist of it in little more than a glance. "Well, bless his soul." He grinned at Sarah. "This is mighty good news! Cal and Wanda and the girls will be celebrating for sure." He looked at Sarah from under his eyebrows. "Might this letter complicate things a bit for you?" He handed her the paper and took a sip of his cold coffee. He made a face. "Do you have any important decisions to make? That young Bronco has seemed pretty serious here of late."

"Mister Brumley." Sarah seemed to be testing the name as she stared at the letter. She wanted to reread it. "I don't know, Pappy." Her eyes were noncommittal. "I am so glad Jimmy's all right that I can't focus on anything else right now."

"Tell you what, Darlin. You do some thinking, and I'll ride out to Cal and Wanda's and give them the news. This letter will be the answer to a lot of prayers." He patted her hand. "As far as those three boys are concerned, I don't have any ideas worth saying out loud. Let's just be happy with the news we have and not spend a lot of time on the news we don't."

Preacher, Sarge, Bronco, and Sheriff Beckett stood and watched the guards escort Corporal Yates to a wagon for his trip into town. Sarge remembered his brother.

"Ben, I saw Tom fall off his horse when Coates broke us out. Is he all right?"

The sheriff shook his head. "He was hurt bad, Madison. When I left him with Doc, he was still unconscious."

Sarge looked toward town. It was early morning, well before full daylight, and all of their eyelids drooped. The four men followed Major Rogers into his office and waited while he pulled out pen and paper. They watched while he started preparing written instructions for the sheriff regarding the release of Tom Jones and the incarceration of Corporal Yates until arrangements could be made to move him to another prison facility.

Sarge interrupted. "Sir, Tom was hurt pretty bad when Coates tried to break us out, according to Sheriff Beckett. So, assuming he recovers, if it's all the same to your Sir, I'd like my brother to continue his time in the jail for a while longer." He looked from the sheriff to the major. Bronco and Preacher exchanged glances.

"Oh?" The major looked at him, bewildered. Sheriff Beckett cocked an eyebrow.

"Yes, Sir. I am worried that he has become addicted to laudanum. I'm afraid that if he gets out of jail too soon and gains access to the drug again, he may be unable to break his addiction. So I'd appreciate it if you'd just leave the release date open so that Tom will continue his time in his cell until I come for him."

"I would generally refuse such a request as it hints of illegal incarceration," the major said. "But as it seems in your brother's best interest, I'll do as you request. I will be out of this area before the end of the day, so I'll leave the matter between you and Sheriff Beckett."

Beckett nodded. He rolled his eyes, reacting to the major's sudden concern about illegal incarceration. "I'm agreeable, Madison. I'd like to see Tom get back to himself as much as you."

Preacher stepped forward and interrupted their conversation. "Major, are you familiar with a man named Coates, John Coates?" He asked.

Major Rogers shook his head. "I don't think so."

Sarge's eyes were instantly alert as they shifted to his friend. He had just been arguing with himself about whether to go into town, though he couldn't do anything for Tom or jump into bed and catch up on his sleep. Now, the dreaded name caught his attention as few could.

"He is going to rob the payroll wagon this morning." Preacher glanced toward Bronco. "He is planning to intercept the shipment between here and Winston. He mentioned a place called Carson's Junction. Bronco and I don't know where that is. Do you, Sarge?"

Sarge thought for a moment. "Well, it's been a long time for me. It does seem, as you say, that it is on the road between here and Winston."

"Yes." Sheriff Beckett said. "I know where that is. I'd say it's about halfway. Just over the county line."

"Intercept?" Major Rogers finished his note for the sheriff and handed it to him.

"Without knowing where this Carson's junction is or the payroll wagon's schedule, it's pretty hard to estimate when a hijack attempt might occur," Preacher said.

"Do you know any more? The scheduled payroll should arrive here this morning," Major Rogers said.

"He plans for an ambush as far as we can tell. He, his brother, and a cousin planned to use Sarge and me in some way. He said that was why he broke us out," Bronco said.

"He mentioned a bog." Preacher added.

"I've hunted that swampy area," Sarge said. "But it's been a long time."

"I'd better put together a detail to meet and escort the payroll wagon immediately." The major left the office to speak to a new enlisted man sitting at Corporal Yates' old desk.

Sheriff Beckett said his goodbyes. He mounted his horse and, with the wagon and army escort, headed off toward Titustown with Yates in custody.

Thirty minutes later, Sarge, Preacher, and Bronco mounted up and joined a detail of six men led by First Lieutenant David Scott. They couldn't help but notice the beautiful smoky black horse he was riding. Major Rogers addressed the lieutenant.

"We expect the payroll wagon before noon this morning, so you may run into them anywhere between here and Winston. That means you could come across this man Coates before you reach the payroll detail. Be alert."

"From our experience, John Coates is loco and very dangerous," Sarge said.

The lieutenant saluted the major. "Yes, sir." He turned to Sarge. "I'd like the three of you to ride in front with me."

Sarge nodded and glanced at Preacher and Bronco, who looked anything but alert given their lack of sleep the previous night. He shared their exhaustion and preferred to go into town with Corporal Yates and Sheriff Beckett and check on Tom and get some shut-eye. But since it involved John Coates, he knew both men wanted to stay the course.

The lieutenant gave the signal to move out, and the big kladruber horse he was riding snorted and pranced forward, headed toward the junction outside of Titustown, where they would pick up the road to Winston.

Sarge looked the troopers over. They seemed reasonably fresh. He keenly felt the need for urgency. Coates was dangerous, and doubly so when money was involved. As sick as he was of death, he could feel the raw emotion boil in the pit of his stomach. He sensed that another encounter with Coates could leave someone dead.

42

The lieutenant's detail rode away from the farm at a gallop. With only fragmentary information, Lieutenant Scott did not want to waste time. He was eager to locate the place called Carson's Junction. It seemed apparent that it would be better to get there before the payroll wagon came under attack. But doing so could jeopardize his men if they stumbled into a rat's nest of outlaws already in place for an ambush. With the payroll wagon coming from the other direction, they could be riding up on the Rebels' rear. His tactical training had taught him that approaching an enemy position from the rear could be advantageous, but that only held if they did so on purpose.

The three tired men had already shared all they knew, and the pace did not encourage conversation. The road led through heavy timber in places. Lieutenant Scott remained alert to the danger they were riding into with so much cover available for enemy forces along their route. Then he spotted a lone rider ahead. It appeared to be an older man. He rubbed his lower back as they overtook him, and he seemed unaware of them until they were on him. He looked back just as they were almost abreast. He frowned at the sight of the lieutenant and troops but brightened when he recognized Bronco, Preacher, and Sarge.

"Well, bless my soul! How are you boys doing?" He stuck his hand toward the closest and shook with the other two when they reached him. He seemed apprehensive until he noticed all three were armed.

"Pappy, I can't tell you how happy we are to see you," Sarge answered. This officer is Lieutenant Scott. We're heading for a place called Carson's Junction, and all we know is it's somewhere along this road."

Pappy smiled. "Last I heard, you boys was busted out of jail. But after thinking on it, I decided that maybe John Coates had something to do with that. Glad to see you're okay." He paused. "I'll be damned if I can understand how you went from being prisoners to riding with these damned Yankees." Then, seeming to realize what he had just said in front of the lieutenant, he reached over and patted Bronco's shoulder.

"I have to say I'm right fond of all of you despite you being Yankees."

"Well, Coates did take us out of jail, but it was against our will, and we got away," Bronco said. "Fortunately, Sarge caught the real killer right under the major's nose." Bronco grinned. "It's a long story, but that's it in a nutshell."

Lieutenant Scott frowned at this bit of news. It seemed his loyalty to the major made such gossip unwelcome.

"Sounds like quite a tale, young fella." Pappy scratched his head and hesitated as if prepared to say more on the subject but remembered Sarge's implied inquiry.

"Carson's Junction is about five miles ahead by this road. You can recognize the place pretty easy. Two lanes branch off. One goes over the hill to the left toward the Carson farm. The other goes down and winds around what we call a bog."

"A bog!" Bronco said. "Coates is planning to ambush the payroll wagon at the bog, right, Preacher?"

"Preacher nodded. "That's the plan he pitched at us."

"Well, I'm headed for my nephew's place just a few miles ahead. I'll ride along if you don't mind." He avoided looking at the lieutenant, who he still considered the enemy, and directed his words to the three men he knew. Then, seeing the lieutenant's frown, Sarge jumped in.

"I think that's a good idea, Pappy. The more you can tell us about this bog, the better, right Lieutenant?"

Lieutenant Scott pursed his lips for a second and nodded. "Not a bad idea, Sergeant. We can use all the intelligence we can get. Tell me, Sir, are there several ways to approach this bog?"

"Well, boys, usually you'd just follow the lane down from the junction. But, past the deepest part of the bog, that little lane wanders for a mile or so and peters out at a hay meadow. But I can tell you where you can take off cross-country and hit the lane and follow it toward the junction from the near side."

Lieutenant Scott looked at Sarge. "That would be helpful, sir." Sarge nodded his head and made another suggestion.

"Lieutenant, we aren't adding much to this operation riding with you. We could cut across and go in that back way. Then if Coates has set up for an ambush, we'd be well behind him."

"That seems like a good strategy, Sergeant. Let's consider that until we get to Mister Jordon's turnoff." They continued in silence down the road. After a while, Bronco rode closer to Pappy and looked around to see if anyone was listening.

"Pappy, have you seen Miss Sarah in the last couple of days?"

Pappy smiled. "I saw her at breakfast this morning. She's as pretty as a picture as usual." He grinned at Bronco. "She had me kind of worried about you boys. I am happy you're alright. He started to say more but thought better of it and flicked his reins so that his horse caught up with Sarge.

"This is my turnoff," Pappy said. "Follow the road about another mile, and you'll come to a large walnut tree on the right side. Cut straight south, and I reckon you will come on the track in about half a mile. Go left on it, and be careful. The land through there is pretty swampy in places as you go toward the junction." Pappy leaned out to shake hands all around and turned off the road, and then rode off up the lane. Lieutenant Scott motioned, and the riders moved forward again. Soon they came on the big walnut tree Pappy had mentioned.

"Lieutenant, it sounds like with the cut we are making off the road, it could take about twenty extra minutes to reach the junction. So I'd suggest you hold with your men for a little bit and let us get a good start before you go on." Sarge said. "We still don't know when the payroll wagon will get there, but it seems like it would be good for us all to get there before the shooting starts."

"You've got fifteen minutes, Sergeant." Lieutenant Scott pulled out his watch and noted the time. Then, he ordered his men to dismount. "I feel that the sooner we get there, the better." Preacher and Bronco waited while Sarge and Lieutenant Scott finished their planning, and then the three men hightailed it east across a field and into a wood that would take them to the little-used track leading to Carson's Junction.

Coates was encouraged when Zac arrived with four riders. He recognized two of them as hardcase deserters from the Confederate forces who had ridden for a time with Captain Owens. From their appearance, Coates guessed that the other two would fall into the same category. He was pleased but also cautious. John knew such men could turn on him once the holdup was successful. He would have to keep an eye on them. He pulled Zac aside and made him aware of his concerns. His brother nodded his understanding. Zac chose his place near the bog on the hillside down the wooded slope from the road. Coates moved off to his left about ten paces to take up his position.

It was only a few minutes before Coates and his men, hidden below the road, could hear the payroll wagon approach and slow. First, there was a "whoa" command from the driver, followed by muffled voices, then the rapid hoofbeats of a horse galloping past on the road just above them. Silence followed for a few minutes, and the horse and rider returned. After that, it was quiet again for a long time. Coates imagined the men up above, scratching their heads and trying to make a decision. It was taking them much too long. For the first time, John started to question his plan.

Get your asses down here!

Coates looked around him. If the payroll wagon kept to the main road, he was screwed! The road was a hundred feet up the wooded hillside. Suddenly in a panic to get things back on track, John abandoned his position and started to climb through the pines up the steep incline. He slipped and struggled in wet leaves and pine straw as he pushed himself from tree to tree one-handed. Sweat poured from under his hat. His heart pounded. His plan!

He had to get that wagon and guards down into the bog! There was still no sound from the group of men on the road. Panting, he emerged from the woods sixty feet from the detour sign. One of the men was starting to drag it to the side.

"*No!*" Coates, reckless with urgency, fired his forty-four at the horse and rider. The team of horses panicked. They found the road to their right blocked by a horse and two men on foot. The road ahead still had the sign and a man in the way. The team veered to the left and started down the only available option.

43

The lane that Preacher, Sarge, and Bronco followed from the meadow wandered a bit, and they carefully avoided boggy places along the way. Suddenly, they heard a series of shots fired up on the hill above and to their left of their position. An uproar ensued, and they watched in astonishment as a wagon and four horses careened down the mountain on the far side of the boggy area. The driver pulled on the reins and used his brake to no avail. The panicked team hit the shallows sending a low swell of muck across the bog that lapped thickly against the nearby bank. The downhill momentum carried the horses and the wagon into the deeper peat in a moment.

Instantly, the chaos of horses neighing and the driver cursing filled the air. The little driver feared his wagon would submerge in the sludge. Preacher realized that neither they nor the driver or horses had any idea of the depth of the bog. They only knew the wagon was sinking. The driver held on to the edge of his seat in panic.

Someone on their left bank fired a shot at the driver. The pill hit the seat close to the little black man's right hand, and he drew back in alarm. In an instant, he scanned his surroundings and picked out two riflemen who didn't bother to take cover. The driver dropped the reins and scrambled to the back of the wagon to get as close to shore as possible. His attempted broad leap was short but put him close to the shoreline. He landed in the muck on all fours just as a couple of shots sent splinters flying across the side of the wagon bed.

Bronco knew the man was doomed unless he could attract the attention of the shooters. So, in an instant, he aimed at one of the exposed men and got off his first shot. Then Bronco wheeled in the saddle and caught another gunman aiming his weapon toward the driver, who tried valiantly to wade to shore through the thick muck sucking at his feet. Bronco jumped from the saddle and slapped his horse's flank. Then, he fired again at a third shooter even before the animal could take flight. He missed, but the man ducked away and failed to get off a shot.

Sarge and Preacher had their guns drawn when they jumped from their horses. Bronco's volleys had been successful, as the men's desire for self-preservation now trumped their interest in target practice at the driver. Sarge and Preacher ducked behind two large oak trees and fired at a man directly across the pond. He disappeared with a cry. Sarge tried to determine how many men they were up against. He did not recognize any of the gang he had glimpsed so far. If Coates had recruited more men, the situation was infinitely more dangerous than he had anticipated. So, where was Coates?

From the perspective of the payroll detail, the tall, skinny man standing in the center of the road seemed to appear from nowhere. As the man fired his first shot Captain Biggs, closest to the road's edge, ducked to the right behind a tree. Sergeant Brown seeing the man with his gun in hand shoved two of his men right toward the captain on the road's uphill side and brought his rifle to his shoulder. A bullet whispered past his right ear. The man, his eyes wild, did not attempt to aim while firing two more shots. Then, he leaped back into the bushes.

The initial shot from John's revolver nicked one of the lead horses in the wagon's team. It screamed in fear, and fear is contagious. Two of the three escape routes were blocked by either the detour sign or the payroll guards. All of the horses looked for an escape, and the majority started for the lane down the hill. In a heartbeat, they were in full flight down the slope. Sergeant Brown heard the explosive impact of the horses and the wagon hitting a body of water. Almost instantly, a rifle fired, and then another.

At the sound of shots, Sergeant Brown looked for his outriders. Mitch and Walt pulled rifles from their scabbards upon arrival fifteen yards to the wagon's rear. Now they seemed undecided about following the wagon down the incline. Brown made an emphatic downward motion for them to dismount. As they did, he turned his attention back down the road past the detour sign.

The tall, lanky man had disappeared, and since his initial shots, there seemed no threat from that direction. Nevertheless, Sergeant Brown kept his eyes trained on the shooter's former position and waved to Bill and Fred to follow him. They ran to the edge of the lane to their left, leading downward toward where the wagon had disappeared.

The captain caught up with Brown. "Sir, I suggest we work our way down slowly until we can see what's happening. Murphy is alone, but I don't want us to walk into anything."

Captain Biggs nodded and motioned for two of the four outriders to fan out on both sides of the lane. The men inched forward until they were in sight of the bog. The wagon was buried up past its axels, and the horses continued to struggle in their panic. But to Sergeant Brown's surprise, the gunfire seemed directed toward the opposite bank at men in the dense trees on the other side of the bog.

"Sergeant, those men on the other side are wearing Union uniforms."

"Yes, sir! Sergeant Brown drew a bead on one of the Rebels and fired. The other men followed his lead. The ambushers ringing the pond tried to fire back, but the crossfire from the two groups of uniformed Union men was withering.

Captain Biggs fired his handgun toward two Rebels hidden behind one of the giant oaks. His bullet sent debris flying.

44

John Coates had never felt more naked. He fired his gun twice more at the riders standing around his detour sign. John saw them reach for their weapons and was suddenly conscious of the foolhardiness of standing on the road alone in a gunfight with six men. He got off two more shots in their general direction and dived sideways back into the brush toward the downhill slope from which he had emerged. His rapid breathing was coming in painful gulps. He rolled downhill a short distance until he came to rest against a large pine tree.

John scrambled to his feet. He leaned against a tree trunk and tried to make sense of the sounds coming from above and below. His men were in a semicircle around the deepest part of the bog, where Coates had planned for the wagon to come to rest. He anticipated that the soldiers in the wagon escort would arrive at the bottom of the hill with the wagon. Now that plan was spoiled. At least six men had been at the sign when he spooked the wagon's team. He couldn't tell, looking through the dense foliage, whether the wagon had ended up deep in the bog or not. He knew the six riders would not follow the wagon into the marsh at this point. That put his men at the bottom of the slope in jeopardy. He could foresee their destruction at the hands of the trained troops holding such a superior position.

45

Coates' chest heaved as he braced himself behind a tree and tried to assess the situation. His shots had successfully spooked the payroll wagon's team. He was shaking from the adrenalin set loose by his momentary exposure on the road. Gunfire had broken out below him after he heard the wagon hit the water, but he couldn't account for so many shots fired. From his vantage point, the man driving the wagon seemed the only possible target. The soldiers he had just abandoned standing in the road had not had time to engage his men around the pond. So, who were his men shooting at so enthusiastically? John skidded as quickly as possible down the steep incline. Finally, he reached a spot with a clear view of the area around the pond. His first glance told John that his brother, Zack, lay dead twenty feet below where he crouched. Blood pooled from the younger man's temple. On the opposite side, the little wagon driver slogged as quickly as he could across an open area to crouch behind a tree. Shock ran through John. How could so much have happened in the few minutes since he charged recklessly up the hill?

There were hoofbeats up on the road. Coates recognized the sound of troopers arriving from the direction of Titustown. He looked through a space in the leaves directly across the pond. He spotted Bronco Brumley taking his weapon from his shoulder. *Brumley!* He had to suppress saying the hated name out loud. He knew Preacher and Sarge must be nearby as well. Rage surged through him. For a moment, he fought the impulse to charge down the hill. Then he shivered as the first surge of fear caught up with him. His brief feeling of reckless immortality up on the road abandoned him. Now fop sweat covered him. He wanted those three men dead. He could taste his hatred. But suddenly, his overriding emotion was pure fear. He had to get away!

Only one option remained. John knew the only way out of this mess was back up the hill. Cautiously he worked his way around the way he had come. Coates carefully placed his feet to avoid tripping. He stopped several times to listen to the activity above. Finally, mounting the top of the hill, he halted just inside the tree line. The new arrivals had tied their reins to limbs on each side of the road. A stout black stallion with a Roman nose moved restlessly directly above him. John knew only one way to survive.

He craned his neck to peer to his right and watched as the men assembled by the detour sign. They then moved down the lane, following the same route as the payroll guards. Coates stepped from the bushes and untied the reins of the stallion. Then, very slowly, he started leading it down the road. Every clop of its hooves sounded like detonations to his ears. He was thankful that everyone's attention was directed toward the bog where bullets were still flying. John expected at any moment to hear a shout followed by a bullet with his name on it. But he made it to the curve in the road unobserved and finally took a full breath. John Coates lept on the horse and kicked it in the ribs as he cleared the curve. He was away and at that moment he didn't have any idea where he was going.

Sarge, Bronco, and Preacher brought up the rear behind the surrendering gang members. Three men were dead, and Sarge ordered the men still standing to drag their remains along with them.

"That's Zac!" Bronco exclaimed. He did not let his gaze linger on the familiar still, gray face. Bronco had sensed that Zac was perhaps the most humane of the Coates clan during their captivity. As in times past, it seemed to him that there was a sad humiliation in lying dead under the casual perusal of strangers. His eyes scanned the surrounding woods. He knew that Coates had to be somewhere in the area. His eyes searched again among the men ahead but still did not see John's skinny form among them.

Preacher looked around. They were all standing in the clear now and easy targets for the crazed outlaw. He saw nothing of the man. Then, finally, he caught up with an outlaw pulling Zac by his shirt collar, asking after John Coates. The man cursed and shrugged. He looked up the hillside, but nothing caught his eye. He said he only knew where Coates had planted himself before the shooting started. Preacher guessed from his demeanor that the captive was hopeful that Coates was somewhere on that hillside dead. The slim possibility that Coates might get away gnawed at Preacher as well.

Sarge followed the others toward the Union troops gathered at the bottom of the slope. The fact that the enlisted men with the wagon were all black caught his attention. His mind flashed back to when blacks weren't welcome in the Union army. He made out a white Captain facing in his direction, talking to three Union soldiers and gesturing toward the wagon. The little wagon driver stood apart. He had slime on his trunk up to his chest. Sarge judged the little man lucky to be alive.

The captain looked over Sergeant Brown's shoulder, saw the three men approaching, and stepped forward to welcome the new arrivals.

"Gentlemen, I don't know where you came from, but I'm deeply thankful you are here." He extended his hand. Preacher and Bronco shook as Sarge joined them.

"Madison?"

Hearing the voice, Sarge released the handshake, and his eyes swept past the captain. The black sergeant stood frozen in place. Sarge's mouth fell open. He staggered a step to one side. He recovered in time to return the embrace of the big black man who arrived in a rush. Their arms encircled each other, and they stood rocking back and forth for a moment, slapping each other on the back, stepping away, and returning to embrace again.

Preacher and Bronco exchanged glances with the surprised captain. The latter's astonishment grew in intensity with the second round of hugs.

Finally, the men stood apart. There were tears in both men's eyes.

"Brownie, I thought I'd never see you again," Sarge said.

"Same here." Sergeant Brown replied. He wiped his eyes with the back of his gloved hand.

"I take it you two know each other?" The captain smiled cautiously. He looked at Bronco and Preacher, and his smile spread into a grin. "I'd guess you two either don't know Sergeant Brown or are much less demonstrative."

The festivities were interrupted by the arrival of Lieutenant Scott and his men. He saluted the captain and surveyed the area.

"We seem to be late for the action, Sir!" His eyes took in the seated Rebels, the three dead bodies, the wagon and horses in the pond, and the three men he had sent via the shortcut. He acknowledged Sarge, Preacher, and Bronco. He looked at the captain, "I sent these men via a shortcut that seems to have been shorter than expected."

"Yes, Sir. I guess Pappy miscalculated our distance for us, didn't he?" Bronco grinned.

"Well, it turned out just the way God intended." Preacher said, looking around at the group with the expression of a wise old owl. "It always does."

That brought another laugh. "It appears so." the lieutenant agreed.

"Sir, I guess it's time to get that wagon back on solid ground." Sergeant Brown said. The captain nodded, and the sergeant went over to speak with Murphy.

After arranging Corporal Yates' installment in a cell and treatment by the doctor, Sheriff Beckett sat at his desk briefly until startled by the all too familiar racket of a cup rattling against the bars. He quickly rose to his feet and hurried to Tom

Jones' cell. The man was standing at the cell door, ashen, but he was standing.

"Sheriff, I'm out of water."

Beckett shushed Tom and looked over his shoulder at the massive figure occupying the bunk in an adjacent cell. Corporal Yates' arm was in a sling, and he lay with it resting against his chest. The revelation of the hidden strongbox justified the sheriff's initial opinion of Major Jones' innocence, and Beckett had not been timid in pointing that out. "I knew they didn't do it all along," he announced to the folks who gathered around when the sheriff and his captive arrived back in town.

Beckett looked at Tom with a sense of relief. Twelve hours before, he wouldn't have given the man much chance of surviving. The doctor had checked on the unconscious major many times and could not determine anything except that he was still breathing. But it was shallow breathing, and the doctor told the Sheriff that each breath could easily be his last.

"Tom, I'm happy to see you on your feet!" He took the cup to stop the clatter on the bars. "I'll get you some water."

"Thanks. I think I'm halfway myself. What's Corporal Yates doing in that cell?" Tom nodded toward the other cell.

"Well, Tom, Yates is the man who stole the strongbox and killed the guard." Tom's question reminded Beckett that the officer had been unconscious when they brought the man in. "Madison figured it out last night. So you're set to get out of here soon."

Tom tried to absorb the information. Once he sifted out the meaning of Beckett's words, his reaction was immediate, and he grabbed the barred door and tested it.

"Why not now?"

"I'm sorry, Tom. Remember, Madison poured out the laudanum and said he didn't want you to have any more. He wants you to be completely off that stuff before you're released. He's to let me know when you are well enough to get out. I'll get your water." Beckett pulled away and took a step back out of reach. He turned to go back to the office.

"I don't care what Madison wants. I'm ready to get out right now." Tom stumbled back and just made it to the bed, laying back and pulling the pillow to his chest.

"I'll get you the water," Beckett repeated from the door. He was gone for a couple of minutes. When he returned to find Tom asleep, the sheriff set the cup on the table and quietly slipped back into his office. He was happy to see improvement in Tom's condition. His two injured prisoners made his jail feel a lot like a hospital.

46

At first, John Coates just rode like a bat out of hell. He had stolen a fast horse and let it have its head. After a mile or so, he slowed and gave the animal a little breather. At a stream, they both took advantage of the cooling water. Coates splashed his face and neck. A little refreshed, his calculating brain quickly went over recent events and his options.

First, killing Uncle Rufus and Cousin Dooley would surely come back to bite him. At the time, he had been high on blood lust. The prospect of taking the payroll, going far away, and living like a king had affected his judgment. John thought at first that maybe he could put those killings off on Bronco, Sarge, and Preacher, but he knew now that at least one of the crew he had just abandoned would name him as the ringleader for this robbery attempt. His word was worthless with the local law. New Orleans had been at the forefront of destination possibilities. It was very far away, and he had heard of a lawless element there, so he knew he could fit in.

He marveled that such a good plan could have gone so wrong so fast. Letting Bronco and Preacher live had been the root of the problem. His instinct had been to put them out of their misery when he had the chance, but he had listened to his clever self and thought he could finesse not only stealing the payroll but putting the law on their tails simultaneously.

Coates caught sight of a rider ahead. He thought he recognized how the man listed a little to the left in the saddle. He was sure when the old man reached behind to rub his back. It was Pappy Jordon. Coates wondered for a moment what he was doing out of Titustown but remembered the old man's nephew lived out this way. A few minutes later, he pulled up even.

Pappy looked a little confused when he recognized John. Coates noted that Pappy's eyes slipped past him to look back toward the rear horizon. He wondered if someone had already found the bodies of Rufus and Dooley. Was the law looking for him in connection with that already?

Pappy's gaze went back to Coates' face, and he grinned. "Great day for a ride, ain't it?"

"So it is." Coates agreed. "You been out for a visit with the family?"

"Exactly that." Pappy hooked his thumb back and to the left. "Hadn't seen them for a while except for Sarah, of course." He ran his finger over his mustache and laughed. "Her marrying Jimmy was kind of a family miracle."

Coates grunted. Without knowing it, the old man had raised one of his peeves. The reminder of a Yankee breathing the same air as the prettiest female in the county raised his hackles, and that it was Bronco brought his blood to a boil again.

Pappy had no love for Coates, and knowing the varmint had no appreciation for someone else's good news, Pappy figured what he said next would irk him for sure. Of course, he could have held back, but it was just too much of a temptation.

"We got the news that Jimmy is okay and will be coming home in the next few days," Pappy said, interrupting John's internal conversation. "That's why I rode out to my nephew Cal's place. They were mighty happy to hear about that. The whole family broke out, rejoicing. Let me tell you. The tears were flowing."

"That's good news for sure." Coates jerked his horse's reins and sat in place for a beat and a half. Although Pappy correctly anticipated his lack of appetite for anyone else's good fortune, this news trumped his usual sour attitude and sent a thrill through him. This was news sure to upset Bronco's apple cart. John's appreciation of that easily outweighed his disdain for family joy. The only drawback was he couldn't be there to see the expression on that idiot Bronco's face when she told him. Then a new idea clicked in his head. *Who says I can't be there? That* new thought struck him so forcefully that he spurred his horse and rode off without another word, neglecting to put a bullet in Pappy.

Sergeant Brown had the little driver wade back out in the muck and unhitch the horses. Murphy slowly walked the animals around the wagon to dry land and used a rope to connect the traces to the wagon's back axle. With the abundance of additional horsepower available, it took but half an hour to have the wagon ready to resume its journey.

With some amusement, Preacher imagined that with two wagons filled with prisoners and two payroll boxes, a seven-man payroll team, and a half dozen extra Union soldiers plus the three of them, they could make for an event in the small town.

Biggs pulled out his pocket watch. "Time to roll. Somehow, we will only be two hours late getting this payroll delivered. But, first, we'll stop in town and unload these prisoners."

Mrs. Sarah Jordon sat in her porch swing and let her mind wander over the preceding four days. She refolded the letter from Jimmy and slid it back into her pocket. Sarah was weary of the whole matter. She repeated the same conversation she kept having with herself. Sarah admitted that flirting with Bronco had been a mistake. She was a married woman! Had she forgotten that? Well, not forgotten; she had just been so tired of being worried. With his easy ways and good humor, Bronco had been the distraction she needed. At first, an absence of mail from Jimmy had not alarmed her. A week or so would often elapse with no word, and then one day, letters written several days apart would arrive together! By turn, she resented the poor mail service while acknowledging having mail at all during wartime was kind of an achievement.

But this time, it had been different. This time four full weeks passed without a word before one of the returning boys that Sarah had known since grade school came home with a gaping wound in his thigh. According to the report, he told his family that he heard that Jimmy had died in exploding cannon fire. He said it had landed right on top of a bunch of boys, and he thought Jimmy was in the middle of them. His family had passed the terrible news along.

Sarah remembered how she felt getting that third-hand news. As horrible as the words of death were, they were worse because they were not definitive. The boy only heard that Jimmy was killed. Over the weeks that followed, with no more information, she imagined it would be easier to know than to wonder. She decided it would be possible to heal if she knew. Living instead in limbo was uncertainty piled on uncertainty.

After a few weeks, she went to visit the boy. Brent was a few years older than Jimmy. He seemed to be healing up. He showed her the ugly stitches, done too quickly in a room full of the dead and dying. It seemed she had known him all her life. He had always been around. He had gone away with Jimmy and other boys many months before. Now he was home, still a bit ornery but sweet in his near-apology that he had made it back and Jimmy had not. He had seen things he would not talk about. Things that made him seem older than his years.

Sarah had put her hand on his arm and, in an awkward moment, had tried to console him for surviving. Then, as the wagon took her back to town, she resolved to accept Jimmy's passing. But she couldn't quite manage to do it. A small part of her still held out for the possibility of Jimmy returning, but talking to Brent and seeing firsthand how fragile a man's flesh could be, dealt a severe blow to her hopes.

Bronco! When Bronco appeared, she wondered after a few days of his evident devotion if he was a sign from God that Jimmy would not return. Maybe God was giving her someone else to care for to make up for losing Jimmy?

Now, everything had switched again. Once more, the girl's primary identity was Sarah Jordon, a married woman! Her life and Jimmy's were again intertwined. Suddenly, because of a few short paragraphs in a letter written over a month before, in a prison camp far to the north, Bronco had become redundant. He was part of an uncomfortable situation that she would have to find a way to resolve.

What would Jimmy think of her when he found out what she had done? She had always thought of herself as a respectable girl. Would he look at her differently? Would he forgive her?

Mrs. Sarah Jordon hugged herself in her distress. She reminded herself that she was not without defense. After all, nothing scandalous had happened. Bronco had been respectful toward her, and they had done nothing out of the public eye. She looked out at the street and watched the people walking past. Occasionally someone she knew would notice her and wave. But, no, she and Bronco had been but friends. Their hearts may have come too close, but their brief interludes had been respectable.

Except. Except? She felt a wave of guilt wash over her. No, not entirely respectable. She remembered standing in the jail in the presence of all those other men saying words that had seemed so poetic when uttered, then suppressed. But now, with the changed circumstances, they seemed almost lurid. She had spoken aloud in her fear and affection the simple words meant to bind them together.

"I love you." Oh! Her heart had raced when he repeated them back to her. She had been both embarrassed in front of the audience and a little gleeful for the acknowledged feelings. But even then, the perfection of it was marred by her anger that he was a prisoner and innocent. Now, she had no idea what had become of him. But then, she realized the horrible truth. Things had changed more than she realized until this moment. Now, with Jimmy coming home, she felt a prisoner of her divided affections.

47

John Coates slowed as he approached the junction just out of town. He could go into Titustown or back to his uncle's farm. Both the town and the countryside seemed iffy. All the patrols on the lookout for him and Bronco and friends hanging out in the town made capture seem assured. Maybe it would be wise to go to Rufus' farm and dispose of the two bodies from the night before. It wasn't that his uncle had a lot of friends. But if troops got paid today, visitors might be looking for cheap liquor.

He could bury the bodies in the barn. Then, there could be a little time before the law would get around to looking for him.

One thought gnawed at John. He knew that regret would hound him if he didn't get another shot at Bronco. It was almost noon. John felt tired and hungry. Both of those conditions had heightened his desire for revenge. But, for the moment, it was settled. He reined his newly acquired mount west toward his uncle Rufus' farm.

Forty minutes later, John unsaddled the horse in the barn and looked around. He saw the bodies where he had left them. Aside from the dogs, who were thrilled to see him, there was no sign of life. Inside the house, he found some food. He ate quickly and returned to the barn to dig a hole for both bodies.

Once he got the bodies into a single shallow hole, he did a second search of the house to find more valuables but was unsuccessful. The Coates clan had never had much of value. He had hoped to change that, but Bronco Brumley and the Union troops had spoiled his brilliant plan. He put the horse in the barn and threw the blanket over a mound of hay. Coates thought it more likely he'd be alerted by any new arrivals out there than in the house. He remembered the moonshine and took a couple of swigs before settling in. Sleep came as the five dogs nestled down around him.

Pappy watched John Coates retreating figure as the man galloped ahead toward Titustown. He recognized that Coates rode a Union horse. Somehow, the man had managed to avoid capture at Carson's Junction. Nevertheless, Pappy still felt confident that his gang of cousins and other ruffians had been unsuccessful in wresting the payroll away from the army.

Pappy rubbed his back and rode on at his own pace. He thought about how wonderful it had been to bear good news to his kinfolk for a change. They were reliable people who were willing to work for what they wanted. And now, with Jimmy returning home, their most crucial concern had suddenly vanished.

Pappy licked his lips, pulled his canteen, and took a deep drink. There were still several unknowns. When would Jimmy arrive? Would Tom be well enough in the head to get out of jail? How would Sarah handle the situation with Bronco? He thought on that last question, then nodded to himself. He was confident that she would do the right thing.

Half an hour later, Pappy left his horse at the watering trough in front of the Lucky Star and took possession of his favorite table. It was close enough to the window that he could keep up with the latest doings in the street. He ordered coffee and felt disappointed when Aunt Emmy delivered it instead of Sarah.

"Where is Sarah? She was here earlier."

"She was feeling poorly, Pappy. She is taking some time away." The old lady shook her head. "For a girl who just received such wonderful news, she seems downright sulky." Her eyebrows rose quizzically. "Of course, we wouldn't know why that would be, would we."

"Your tone is not very sympathetic to your only niece," Pappy said. "I expect she just has some adjusting to do. She'll be alright."

The little woman huffed and retreated to the kitchen. Forty-five minutes later, Pappy heard the commotion outside and walked out on the porch. The Union payroll wagon with guards, plus an extra wagon accompanied by the additional troops he had encountered on the road, seemed none the worse for wear. He was pleased to see Preacher, Sarge, and Bronco bringing up the rear with a tall black sergeant. The black man seemed vaguely familiar. There was something about the way he sat his saddle. The jawline was lean. The eyes were stern. Finally, Pappy looked away. Though the man seemed familiar, he couldn't quite place him. Pappy strolled down the sidewalk and arrived as the three prisoners left the wagon and marched into the jail.

He didn't have to be inside the jail to know what Sheriff Ben Becketts' reaction would be to more prisoners. Pappy grinned to himself. Bronco looked over, and Pappy waved and motioned toward the Lucky Star. Bronco nodded and peeled off from the group. Preacher noticed and followed him. They all assembled at Pappy's table. When they ordered, Pappy could see that Bronco was eager for the food to come. His face fell in disappointment when Aunt Emmy carried the plates out.

"I wonder where Miss Sarah is." He said after the old lady departed.

"Well, I wondered that myself," Pappy said. "I asked earlier, and apparently, she wasn't feeling well and is staying home for the rest of the day."

Bronco immediately lost interest in his food and made a move to rise. Pappy put his hand on his arm. "Sometimes, Bronco, when a lady is feeling poorly, it's a good idea to give them time to feel better before you interfere."

"Oh." Bronco frowned but sat back down. Then he looked at his food with renewed interest and dug in.

Sarge dismounted and found a place for his horse at the hitching post close to the jail. He was not an official member of the payroll detail or the troopers that Major Rogers had sent out from Tom's farm. He felt a trace of regret, but he quickly shook it off. That part of his life was behind him. The three prisoners marched in to take the cells he and Bronco had inhabited just hours before. He could hear Sheriff Beckett raising hell inside. In a moment, Deputy Shires came out in a hurry and took over the Coates wagon, and Sarge guessed he was going to take it over to

Doc's office. The men lying on the floor didn't need treatment, but Doc was also the undertaker. He walked over to the payroll wagon and spoke with Brownie.

"Where do you go after the payroll is delivered today?"

"Well, we head back to Winston. The war ending has kind of put a squeeze on the whole process. So many boys are anxious to head home, and Colonel Smith has had to delegate some of the deliveries rather than oversee them all himself." Brownie pulled off his bandana and wiped his eyes. "I haven't decided what to do about staying in or getting out myself. You reckon I should go in and see Tom?"

Sarge grimaced. "I don't know. He was glad to see me when he thought I'd get him out of jail. It might be best if we go in together for a minute."

"That's about as long as I can stay. I imagine Major Rogers is about to have kittens out at the farm." Brownie said. The two men entered the front office and waited for the sheriff and a couple of soldiers to clear out of the back.

"Sheriff, you may remember Brownie?" Beckett threw his head back and looked again at the vaguely familiar figure standing tall before him.

"Well, I do. Union Army, I see. That seems to have suddenly become a popular occupation around here." He did not offer his hand. He turned toward Sarge.

"Madison, Tom has come to. "Sarge's eyes widened with relief.

"Can we go back and see him?"

"Might as well. Everyone else seems to come and go whenever they want to." He looked at Brown again. "So, Sergeant, do you know how long these hoot owls will be here?"

"Sorry, Sheriff, I'm with the payroll detail," Brownie said. "I don't know what Major Rogers will want to do about this bunch."

Sarge opened the door leading back to the cells, and Brownie followed him through the crowded room. Three sullen men sat on a bunk in a cell on the left end of the row of cells. The big corporal was immobile in the middle cell. Sarge surmised that they were all contemplating their futures. On the right, Tom stood at his barred door. His eyes were clearer than they had been when last Sarge saw him, but they still had a desperate appearance that grew with intensity as they approached him.

"Madison! You've got to get me out of here!" He searched his brother's face for confirmation. Then his eyes lit on Sergeant Brown. "I'll be damned." For a moment, there seemed to be an internal struggle. "Brownie!" He stuck out his good left arm and offered an upside-down left-handed handshake. "Good to see you!"

Brownie smiled. "Good to see you, Tom." He glanced at Sarge and back at Tom. "So much water under the bridge. Reckon we'll ever get that water back?"

"Probably not," Sarge said. He was relieved that Tom looked so much better, almost normal. Maybe his brother had not been addicted but just under the temporary influence of the laudanum.

Brownie straightened and stepped back. "Well, gents, I'd like to stay longer, but I suspect Captain Briggs is getting antsy out front." He shook Tom's hand again and put a hand on Sarge's shoulder. "Are you staying here or heading on, Madison?"

"I'm pretty sure I'll be headed west at least as far as New Orleans," Sarge said. "I don't know after that. My friends think they want to end up in San Francisco."

"Good luck." Brownie slapped his shoulder, turned, and walked back to the front.

"Madison. I'm a lot better." Tom said.

"You do look a lot better. So what say, I have the Doc come to take another look at you and maybe get you out of here in the morning?"

"How about now. This place gets on my nerves."

"Just one more night, Tom." The army will be clearing out of the farm this afternoon. Then Tomorrow, you can go back to a normal life again." Sarge said this with such finality that Tom backed off.

"All right, I'll look for you in the morning," he agreed. However, Tom's disappointment was still evident.

Sarge stopped and visited Sheriff Beckett for a minute on the way out and confirmed that he'd probably fetch Tom the following day. He was worn out. He correctly guessed that his friends would be at the Lucky Star. Sarge led his horse to the hitching post with theirs, entered, and joined everyone at Pappy's table. Miss Emmy took his order. When she also delivered his food, he looked questioningly at Pappy, who gave a quick negative shake of his head.

"Pappy says that he saw John Coates riding this way on his way back to town from his nephew's farm this morning." Preacher said.

"You're kidding! I knew that roach was hiding under a rock somewhere out there." Sarge frowned.

"He was hell-bent for leather and riding a fine army broom tail when he caught me. He was coming from the direction of Carson's Junction, all right." Pappy said.

"The man is crazy. We'll have to guard our backsides all the time as long as we are in town," Preacher said.

"You're right. What say we give up our room at the boarding house and head out to the farm?" Sarge said. He pulled out his watch. "They will probably finish with the payroll by the time we get there, and with no trial this afternoon, it should be pretty quiet," he smiled.

"Pappy says Miss Sarah is feeling poorly, so maybe I shouldn't go check on her," Bronco said. "What do you think, Sarge?"

Sarge glanced around the table and got another negative signal from Pappy. His eyebrows went up. "Well, Pappy probably knows much more about women than the rest of us. So what say we buy some provisions and head out? I bet you boys can use some shut-eye as much as I can. I am about whipped."

"I'm with you," Preacher said. He pushed back from his empty plate. "I'll go get our stuff out of the room."

"Okay, I'll go with you," Bronco said. "But I'm coming back to town tomorrow for sure."

"I'll be ready to leave for the farm by the time you get back." Sarge ducked his head and started devouring the first food he had eaten in twenty-four hours.

Bronco held the door for a pretty little blond lady on his way out but didn't give her a second glance.

48

Bronco, Sarge, and Preacher met a column of army wagons on their way to the farm. After a quick tour of the house, they found that the army had left the kitchen bare and the rooms a mess. With Preacher and Bronco's help, Sarge settled the massive desk back in its proper location. They unsaddled, brushed, fed, and watered the horses, and the men's tails were dragging when they finished and ate a light supper.

"Boys, it's early, but I'm going to bed," Sarge said. "Tomorrow is our gold-digging day. Let's sleep until we wake up. You boys pick out rooms for yourselves."

Preacher and Bronco nodded and headed down the hall. Sarge automatically went to his childhood room. It had been ten long years, but it still carried many memories of his time there. He closed the drapes to shut out the afternoon light and took off his boots. A little light seeped around the folds of cloth and gave the room a dusky half-darkness. He lay back and, for a moment, looked up at the crack in the ceiling plaster that had appeared close to his seventh birthday. He knew that, most likely, the house's settling caused it. At the time, he had thought it looked like a horse's head. Now it just seemed like an ordinary crack in the plaster. He rose and undressed and fell back into bed. He was asleep before his head hit the pillow.

Bronco lay on another foreign bed far from Ohio and thought about the future treasure hunt. It had seemed pretty exciting when they started from camp, and the promise of actually digging up real gold still fascinated him. He had never had a lot of money at one time. When his grandfather died, he had left Bronco almost a hundred dollars. The money had made him feel wealthy for the first time since his father had given him that dime. He thought hard about what to do with his inheritance. Finally, in a surge of enthusiasm, he bought the Henry rifle, and later, with the horse trader's encouragement, he joined the Union army. The weapon was a prize that he held dear. Thinking back to their escape from the thicket in Alabama, he wondered how many times it had saved his life. He thought about Sarah and promised himself he'd see her the next day. The moment to retrieve the hidden gold they had traveled so far to find was upon them. Bronco wondered if he'd ever go to sleep. Then he did.

Preacher returned from the outhouse and opened the door into a small bedroom. His big head had started to ache a little. He guessed he could track the pain back to the whack John Coates had given him in the fruit cellar. Or, maybe he was just tired. It seemed they had been bombarded continuously with twists and turns since leaving the army.

Preacher wondered if he should have tried to stay in the army but dismissed it immediately. He had another vocation waiting for him somewhere, somehow. Everything he had experienced supported his belief in the invisible hand of God in men's lives. Events had undoubtedly provided evidence of the unpredictability of those plans. He sometimes wondered how other men seemed to go about their lives in blind obedience to nature's laws while failing to perceive the hand that touched their daily decisions and fortunes. He confessed that he fought impatience at times. He closed his eyes and dreamed of a church down a distant road where he might explore all the questions looming in men's lives with a flock of his own.

49

Sarge awoke well after daylight. After so many hours of wakefulness, his sleep left him groggy, but he felt much better. He thought over the events of the last week. He was much heartened by Tom's appearance. Maybe things would be all right now. Perhaps they could part on better terms this time than they had many years ago. Then he smiled. It was time to go prospecting. The whole purpose of their journey, to find his inheritance, had been obscured and delayed by events. How many times had they had to defend themselves? How many people had died? Somehow, the count of the dead did not include him or his friends. The gold they had started on their recovery journey had gotten lost in the rush of events. Well, now it was front and center of his attention!

Sarge swung his legs off the bed and dressed. He found Preacher and Bronco in the kitchen. They had already started breakfast from the supplies bought in town. After washing up, Sarge sat down and bit off a hunk of bread.

"Boys, this is the day."

"What day?" Bronco looked over, still a little groggy, himself. Upon awaking, he had immediately thought of Sarah.

"The day we go treasure hunting," Sarge said, gulping down some coffee. "I don't know about you boys, but I'm ready to do what we came here for."

Preacher nodded. He smiled, for he, too, had awakened with his thoughts elsewhere.

"Dang! I kind of got off track." Bronco laughed. He looked at his friends and straightened up. "So, today is the day!" He forked the rest of his breakfast into his mouth. "Let's get started!"

A fence, built from four by four rough-cedar posts with three rough-sawn plank stringers running between them, surrounded the big house. The lumber had been sawn at Sarge's father's saw-mill more than twenty years before. Bronco and Preacher rode just behind Sarge as he began his circuit at the sagging front gate. Many of the posts leaned in and out of line. Looking ahead, they could see a number of the cross-pieces had come loose. Sarge examined a post and rode on to the next. The sun and rain and the freeze and thaw of more than a dozen summers and winters turned all of it gray and splintery. Knots had contracted on themselves and fallen away, leaving silver dollar-sized holes. The cross pieces were just as bad and pulled awry. It looked lonesome and abandoned at the edge of the farmyard. But Sarge knew it was special.

"That's one, I think." Sarge pointed.

"How can you tell?" Bronco was excited. Now, with Sarge's words, the men dismounted. Bronco wiggled the post. "How can you tell?" He asked again.

"Well, there's the gate." Sarge pointed. If you count three posts down, you come to this one." He motioned for the men to look closer. "See these four nails on the inside of the post making four corners of a square?" He pointed. Preacher leaned closer. He noted to himself that his eyes weren't what they once were.

"Well, I'll be. Four nails in a square, sure enough." His finger traced the place as if tactile verification was needed.

"So, do we just pull out the post?" Bronco pushed it back and forth again, testing its stability.

"Looks pretty rotted, so I doubt we could get the whole thing," Sarge said. "Let's get the shovel and dig down beside it. That way, we won't tear up Tom's fence, such as it is." He walked over to his horse, unlashed a shovel they had rescued from the barn, and returned.

"Who wants to get us started?" He looked expectantly at Bronco.

"Heck yeah." Bronco took the shovel and stomped the working end into the rocky, northwest Georgia soil with his big shoe. The blade penetrated only a couple of inches. He was undaunted and started wide and narrowed the hole as he got deeper. The hold revealed nothing yet. He widened the gap some more and gained some room to get the shovel ever deeper. As he worked his way inch by inch, Bronco levered back against the side of the hole, scraping the end of the blade up the side of the post. At two feet, the outer layers of the wood started shredding away. A few inches more and chunks of the rotted post crumbled and came up with each shovel-load. "How deep is this anyway?" Bronco was starting to break a sweat.

"Here, let me take a turn." Preacher patted his friend on the shoulder. Bronco passed the handle over. "Any idea of how deep we are going?" Preacher widened the top of the hole even more, anticipating a long dig.

"No. My father didn't say anything about depth," Sarge smiled.

Preacher emptied the shovel and pushed the blade in again. They were now approaching the bottom of the post. With no dirt supporting it on that side of the hole, it leaned a little toward them, but the loose post and attached stringers were still partially supported by the posts on either side. Bronco pushed the top of the post back to vertical out of the way of the shovel.

Preacher kicked the shovel past a pocket of tightly packed rocks, and then it glided a bit. "I think we may be on to something." He grunted and expanded the bottom of the hole. He spotted one side of what looked like a ceramic jar. "I think we're there. This being your inheritance, I think you should do the honors." He straightened up and stepped to one side.

Sarge sighed as he went to his knees. He had to lay on his side to get his shoulder into the top of the hole and his arm deep enough to work his fingers around the squatty object. Sarge was glad to be wearing leather gloves as a rough or broken edge could easily slice into his hand. He worked the dirt loose around one side and then the other. Sarge could feel the hardness of the container's outline against his palm. He pulled it free and did a one-handed pushup to extract himself from the hole. He grunted as he rolled away, clutching the small object against his chest.

"Well, boys. The moment of truth." Sarge sat up and retrieved his knife. He worked the sharp edge through the sealing wax and carefully prized open the lid. He could see the glitter. "No point in wasting any."

Bronco and Preacher got down on their knees and leaned toward the jar. "Dang!" Bronco said. "Is that real gold?"

"Looks like it to me." Preacher leaned in further to see better and extended his finger to stir the contents, mostly pea-sized pebbles, but when his finger came out, so did a bit of glitter.

"Dang!" Bronco said again. "I used to shoot marbles when I was a kid. Do you know what I just thought of, Sarge? Wouldn't it be great to have a shooter marble made out of gold like this?" Then he laughed at himself. "Probably too heavy to shoot!"

Leaving the container on the ground, Sarge picked himself up and searched his saddlebags. He pulled out several new pigskin pouches. "I've been carrying these since Sweetwater." He replaced the cap, slipped the jar into the new pouch, and pulled the drawstrings tight. He looked at Bronco and Sarge. "Well, men. There are three more to go. Are you game?"

"Just a minute." Preacher grabbed the shovel and quickly refilled the hole. He stomped the dirt and wiped his brow. "Now we're ready! Lead on!"

They found the second and third jars quickly enough. The fourth was harder to extract since the maple tree's roots had surrounded the fence post over the twenty years since the gold was buried. That ring of roots made digging hellish, with the blade of the shovel ricocheting away in random directions. Bronco found a small ax in his saddlebag that helped a little, but the deeper they got, the less room there was to swing it.

"Whew!" Sarge straightened up and grabbed his back. "I'm ready to let this one go!"

"We need a different system here." Preacher said. "How about we remove the post and work our way straight down the existing hole?"

"Wish we had an auger," Bronco said. "It would be easier to get the rotted wood out."

"Best we have is this hoof nipper," Sarge said, pulling the tool out of his bag.

"I'm game," Bronco said.

They knocked off the loosened planks and worked the post slowly, trying to get it to break off at the deepest place possible. The tree roots hindered even that effort. Finally, with all three men pulling together, they got almost two and a half feet of buried post out of the hole pretty much intact. Bronco lay down and carefully reached deep into the hole. There were long fragments of solid wood like stalagmites to be dealt with, as the post had not rotted uniformly. He was thankful for his glove. He worked the solid pieces back and forth and pulled up chunks of rot with the hoof nipper, using the tool like tweezers. He was about to hand the device over to Sarge when he felt something hard. He fingered it, then applied the hoof nipper and pulled a rusted bucket out of the hole with a whoop of joy.

"Look, it's twice as big as any others." Bronco hefted the bucket gingerly in both hands and handed it to Preacher, who passed it to Sarge.

"This is probably the first one my father buried. Over time the gold in the area got harder to find, and he had other things to do."

After replacing the post and reattaching the planks, they returned to the house. "Let's get cleaned up and go into town," Sarge said.

50

Mrs. Sarah Jordon was startled awake after a restless night. By turns, her thoughts had alternated between Jimmy and Bronco. She had excused herself and condemned herself for her actions and emotions over the last week. She had fretted over what action she should take now. Jimmy was coming! How would Jimmy react if she told him, or worse, someone else told him she had sashayed around town with another man? A Yankee, to boot? How would Bronco react if she told him she couldn't see him anymore? Questions! She had lots of questions, but she could come to no conclusions in her restless, often interrupted sleep. By the time she awoke, she ached for resolution.

Still at odds with herself, Sarah dressed and made the short walk to work. Her Aunt Emmy, as usual, had risen earlier and arrived before her. Sarah hardly heard her words when Emmy greeted her; she was so deep in thought. Sarah busied herself with her daily chores. She forced herself to put her most pressing questions on the back burner.

Without fully realizing it, she began to avoid revisiting them. But there was one reality that she could not prevent. Her eyes went to the door from the rooming house lobby often. Would Bronco be coming through that door this morning? She had half expected him to show up at the house the day before when she went home early and had been both puzzled and relieved to reach the end of the day without encountering him.

She welcomed Pappy when he came in. Unlike her aunt, he seemed to have some empathy for her plight. "Was Bronco in yesterday?" she asked as she refilled his cup.

"He was. He was right disappointed that you wasn't here." The old man took a sip and put the cup down. "He was about to light out and check on you, but I discouraged him," Pappy said. "I figured that if you wanted to see him, you'd of been here. So, I guess you are ready now?"

Sarah stiffened. "I don't know if I am or not, Pappy. I'm here now because I couldn't let Aunt Emmy down again. I guess I don't rightly know the answer to many things." She went back to the kitchen.

John Coates awoke with the chickens. A big hen pecked at his boots until he kicked her away. His dreams had not been pleasant. He thrashed in the hay for a minute, trying to get his bearings. All night he had relived his first encounter with the Yankees and then all that followed. His nightmares included being trussed up helplessly with his bloody aching head and then his uncles' contempt. The worst was his brilliant plan gone awry, his foolish dead cousins, his standing in the road with his forty-four revolver naked of defenses, his dead brother, and his ride away from the Yankees at Carson's Junction with fear roiling in his gut.

When John had finished one dream sequence, he'd picked up a piece of the dream and run the different segments out of order. But on waking, John relived uncle Rufus' beautiful death. It soothed him for a moment. But then he relapsed and couldn't keep the events out of his head. When viewed together, the depth of abuses against him over the last two weeks burned like coals in his belly

Coates dusted the hay out of his shirt and pants legs, peered around the corner of the barn door, surveyed the surrounding landscape for visitors, and walked across a barnyard still scarred by the hooves of panicked horses. His horse was secure in the barn. Two other animals were grazing through the open gate in the pasture. One was still saddled; its owner buried a few feet deep in the barn. John wondered how long it would be before the law would come looking for him. Not before noon for sure, he told himself. So many things were going on with the Sheriff and the Union soldiers at the moment. It could be as long as a couple of days before they'd get organized and come for him. But given his recent misjudgments, he still needed to be wary.

As he foraged for breakfast, he reflected on all the places he could not show up. Chief among them was the Lucky Star. He could picture the three Yankees huddled around the table with Pappy. He derided himself a bit for not shooting that old man when he had the chance. He could picture Mrs. Sarah Jordon serving them coffee and flirting with young Bronco as if her husband was totally out of the picture. He wouldn't give a plug nickel for Jimmy Jordon. He was a tongue-tied hopeless idiot, but it was the principle of the thing!

This vision started the new round of scheming, for Coates needed a salve for his wounds. He needed revenge for his bad luck. He needed a plan to take down the three Yankees and, barring that, a plan to take down Bronco Brumley and the unfaithful Mrs. Sarah Jordon. Though he had no religious foundation, John was confident that their sin should not go unpunished. When he finished eating, he went out and sat on the porch and looked off at the horizon to reassure himself that a posse wasn't at hand. Finally, a plan did indeed come to him. He reloaded his forty-four and concluded that the fact he was still alive was a sign from the Almighty. With that thought, he assured himself that his mission of vengeance was a sanctified one if any task ever was.

Bronco was the first man back on the porch. He seated himself in a rocking chair, hefted the double fist-size pouch of gold nuggets, and smiled. Sarge had divvied the contents of three the modest jars and a gallon bucket in four roughly equal shares. The new pouches strained at the seams. Sarge handed one each to the other men and tucked two into his saddlebag. "One for each of us and one for Tom," he said. Sarge paused when he caught their questioning looks. "These probably will assay at a value of several thousand dollars each. Since we are headed for New Orleans via Birmingham, we can have it assayed there. We each have more than enough to get us where we're going. Tom needs some seed money. This place is a shamble. He will need to buy cottonseed, building materials, and livestock."

"Of course. It's your call." Preacher hefted his bulging pouch and dropped it in his saddlebag. "I think you are more than generous to both of us. Given that Tom will end up with not only the farm but part of your inheritance, you are very generous with him."

"In some strange way, I also owe him for Brownie," Sarge said.

"There is that." Preacher nodded just to be agreeable.

Bronco put his pouch away and caressed his saddlebag. He had more wealth at this moment than he had ever dreamed. He looked at his companions expectantly.

"So, I guess we're ready to head for town." He grinned. "Now that I have some seed money of my own, I'm going to talk with Miss Sarah about maybe getting married."

"Married!" both of the other men said in unison. "Married?" repeated Preacher. He stared at Bronco, astonished. Sarge shook his head. Bronco's grin broadened.

"Bronco, have you really thought about this?" Sarge asked.

"That's all I think about," Bronco said truthfully.

"I mean the actual married part, not just the pretty girl part," Sarge said.

"You've only known the girl a week, Bronco," Preacher said, looking dismayed.

"I knew I wanted to marry her the first time I saw her," Bronco said. It seemed entirely reasonable to him.

"Bronco, I don't want to pee on your campfire, but do you think she will be able to say yes even if she wants to? She is already married. She may think your courtship has been a little short," Sarge said.

"I've thought of all of that." Bronco looked with a trace of annoyance at the two men. "First, Jimmy is not coming back.

Second, she feels the same way as I do about her. Sarge, you were there when she said she loves me. I know we can't get married right away. I'll have to wait a while longer for her to be sure about Jimmy. I don't know what you have to do about getting married when your husband disappears. Maybe we'll have to wait a while longer for that. I've thought that you men can head on west, and once she and I get everything out of the way here, we'll start that way too. Miss Sarah told me she has a brother in San Francisco. I bet she would love San Francisco."

"We could be talking about months." Preacher said. "There is no telling where Sarge and I will be a week from now, let alone a month."

"Don't forget, Bronco, that pouch is valuable, but it won't last forever. It is possible you could run through it before you're even ready to leave town," Sarge said.

"Oh, I'll have a job," Bronco said confidently.

"Oh?" Sarge said. Preacher's eyebrows went up.

"Sure. With the war over and seed ready for planting, I bet farmers will be bringing wild horses in here by the hundreds just like they did back in Ohio during the war. I'll break broncs for a fee for each one. So I'll be able to make lots of money and even save some to go with the gold. I'm going to be fine!" The two other men eyed each other again.

"So, just to be clear. Preacher and I are heading out to-morrow for New Orleans and on west, and you're going to stay in Titustown?"

Bronco nodded his head. "Well, I didn't know you were leaving tomorrow, but yeah."

"We talked about that at breakfast," Preacher said.

"We did?" Bronco shrugged. "I guess I wasn't listening."

"You're okay with that?" Sarge asked.

"Sure," Bronco said. "I guess so. There's no reason for you two to stick around here."

"Well, let's saddle up and head for town," Sarge said.

They made the short ride to Titustown in relative silence. Once they reached Main Street, Preacher spoke up. "I think I'll go to the church for a few minutes, boys. I'll meet you at the Lucky Star in a little while."

"I'll go by the jail and get Tom out," Sarge said.

51

John Coates saddled his horse. He looked around his uncle's dilapidated farm. He recalled the two cousins who had taken off for Alabama to collect the bodies John had left there. He wondered which of two would end up with the farm. The old man and his five sons had put more effort into building the corn liquor business than making a go of the farm and not a lot of energy at that. Coates had no interest in it himself. He preferred the social life of saloons and the danger of raiding parties, which had brought him and Zac to join his kin in Harlan County, to begin with, three years before.

Now his life in Harlon County would be ending. He had heard that saloons and loose women were abundant in New Orleans. Without Zac, he would be traveling light. It had been agreeable to have someone around who looked up to him, but Zac hadn't provided a lot of companionship in the carousing department.

He had been thinking about where he could hole up until he got his shot at Brumley. Of course, he would have preferred to drill Brumley's two friends as well, but it seemed unlikely he'd be able to arrange a showdown where he could successfully take on all three.

They knew him at the livery stable. He couldn't hang out at the Lucky Star or anywhere else on Main Street, for that matter. But then he thought of the perfect place where no one would look for him, a place where Brumley was guaranteed to show up eventually. Half an hour later, Coates entered the town on a side street. He walked his horse through an alley and tied the animal to a sapling behind the house occupied by old Miss Emmy and Mrs. Sarah Jordon.

He looked around and knocked on the rear door of Miss Emmy's house. As he expected, there was no response. He tried the knob. The unlocked door made entry easy. John walked inside and inspected the interior.

Word around town indicated the house had belonged to the middle-aged spinster a good while before Sarah and her brother moved in as young orphans after their parents died. He parted the curtain a bit to see out into the street. Satisfied, all he had to do was wait, confident that sooner or later, Bronco Brumley would show up.

John entered the first of two bedrooms. It had a stand-up wardrobe and a dresser for clothes and other personal items. He could tell the room belonged to Mrs. Sarah Jordon because there was a small tintype of a young Jimmy Jordon on the dresser. A folded sheet of paper lay beside the photo. He casually picked it up and scanned the surprisingly neat handwriting.

John was barely literate, but this appeared to be a letter from Jimmy, dated many weeks earlier. Coates studied the words. Some of them evaded him, but what he could follow suggested that Jimmy Jordon was coming home. The letter undoubtedly was the origin of Pappy's news shared the day before on the road.

"Well, welcome home Jimmy!" He said to himself. John wondered if Mrs. Sarah Jordon had bothered to tell Brumley yet. It spoke to her lack of character if she knew her husband was returning and was just leading Brumley on. But, on the other hand, if she had told Brumley, and he now knew of Jimmy's return and was still pursuing her, it was a sign of his willful defilement of southern womanhood. Coates had learned about judging others from his Pa and Uncle Rufus. His disgust grew each time he read what words he could of the letter. It was apparent to him that both Bronco and Sarah deserved to die. John returned to the parlor and propped himself up in a chair facing the front porch. It was overly warm in the house, even with the windows open, but he did not dare crack the door for additional ventilation because an open door could spook the girl when she returned. He loosened the top buttons of his shirt and waited.

Preacher rode the two blocks over to the Baptist Church. He hoped to find the friendly Miss Maggie playing the piano there again. He dismounted and listened, but he couldn't hear any music. Preacher found the door unlocked, so he walked inside and looked around. He was alone. He breathed in the stuffy scent of old hymnals and dusty corners. The lid of the piano had been closed over the keys. He walked to the front and sat on the first row of pews close to the keyboard. He noticed a hymnal lying on the seat nearby. He picked it up and fanned through the pages. The names of familiar hymns somehow comforted him, though he did not realize he needed comforting. He had an extensive repertoire of hymns in his memory. He didn't need the book, but he held it open anyway. He hummed the first verse of a song and then the first verse of the hymn on the next page. He closed his eyes, then opened them and looked up at the pulpit. He wondered if he would ever stand behind one again.

Preacher believed that his thanks were the most important of all the things he could say to his Lord. So, he sat in silence and went over recent events. Preacher said thanks for each step of their trip from Alabama to Titustown, Georgia. He was thankful for his friends, and he was grateful for the journey to come. Who knew what new adventures they might have? He thought of Bronco, who was about to ask the presumed widow to marry him. Who knew how that would turn out? He thought of Sarge and his brother Tom. The older brother might or might not be addicted to laudanum. Who knew if he was or not? Preacher smiled. He was certain who knew, and he thanked Him for all that had happened and all that was to come. Then he stood and walked to the door of the church. He greeted the sunshine on the porch with a big inhalation of breath. Preacher's eyes traveled around the churchyard one last time before he mounted his horse and rode the short distance to the Lucky Star.

Returning Confederate veteran Jimmy Dale Jordon didn't hesitate when he got to Carson's Junction. He knew the road to the right led over a rise to the Carson farmhouse and would have tempted him on another day. He and Billy Ray Carson had spent many hours together squirrel hunting in their youth. They went off together to war for the Confederacy but were separated early on. Neither had any inkling of the other's doings since.

Nor was he interested in the lane to the left, leading down into and around the bog. Raccoons and possums could be found in abundance there. Many an evening had been spent in that lowland following the barking dogs. Jimmy could remember getting their shoes mucked up and occasionally falling into the muck while navigating through the inlets, trying to keep up with the dogs in the darkness. Of course, there had been some illicit drinking and much hilarity during those evenings. There had often been coons treed and prizes taken home.

Today, there was only one road of interest to Jimmy Jordon. It was the curving road that led between the two lessor lanes. The road led Jimmy over a primitively painted detour sign that someone had pulled half out of the road to lie flat on the ground. The marked boards now bore damage from being trodden by horses and wagons. All had taken a toll on its crudely painted letters and arrow marking. Jimmy noticed it. He knew no reason for a detour sign at the junction and instinctively dismissed it.

Jimmy Jordon was a practical man, and he liked to build things. In a different time, with more education, he could have been an engineer. He was comfortable working alone. His conversations were usually short and to the point. As he walked over the detour sign, Jimmy was but two miles from home. His tattered uniform hung loosely from his swinging arms. His shoes were hardly more than coverings for his bruised and blistered feet. He had layered an abandoned newspaper in the bottoms of his shoes that morning. It was wadded and worn through after half a day's walk.

In his practical mind, Jimmy Jordon had but one goal. He aimed to walk the two remaining miles to his father's house. He intended to hug his parents and sisters and take a bath. Jimmy aimed to shave his neglected face, put on clean clothes, and ride proudly into Titustown to surprise his beautiful wife. Jimmy fleetingly wondered where she would be. Would he find her at the Lucky Star or her Aunt Emmys? It didn't matter. He would find her wherever she was! The sight of her beautiful face and her gentle touch was all that mattered.

Jimmy stumbled a little from time to time. But, as he rounded each curve in the road, he targeted the next one a quarter of a mile away as his next goal. Jimmy had pushed himself, tricked himself, and promised himself, in just this way, to keep walking for over four weeks. Now in his home county, Jimmy knew for the first time that he wasn't just kidding himself. He was going to make it. This was the day. No, this was the hour when he would return to his father's house!

Bronco mounted the steps and entered the Lucky Star just as Sarah moved toward the kitchen from the far corner table. They met abruptly in the center of the room. For Bronco, it seemed that everything else around him dissolved. Sarah looked suddenly glued to the spot. It appeared that her legs wouldn't work, and her face couldn't form any expression. Finally, she looked at Bronco and mutely pointed toward his favorite table by the window.

Bronco's smile faded a little as they parted, she for the kitchen, and he for the table she had indicated. Did her lack of expression mean something? He didn't know. He felt a strange sensation down his spine. Bronco looked toward the window at the passing shadows. People passing outside on the walk brightly backlit at this hour had no discernable features. The bright sunlight brought no warmth to his heart. He waited for Sarah to return, smile at him, and blush at his compliments. She didn't.

The elderly Miss Emmy stopped by for his order. Bronco briefly asked for coffee and a ham sandwich, and Miss Emmy poured the coffee without comment while he looked around the half-empty room. There were no Union soldiers anymore. They had moved on to their next post, and it was too early for Pappy. The old man came for breakfast most mornings and then went to the stores to visit his old cronies before showing up for dinner.

Aunt Emmy brought his sandwich. He was about to ask after Sarah when Sarge and Tom came in, causing a stir from the few other customers in attendance. Tom stuck out his hand, and Bronco shook it. Even Miss Emmy was animated enough to tell the major that his lunch was on the house. Bronco watched the old lady disappear back into the kitchen. Tom looked remarkedly improved since Bronco had last seen him in jail. His color was better, and he strode rather than staggered across the floor. He carried himself taller, and his smile was broad and relaxed. Bronco noticed it was almost a duplicate of Sarge's standing next to him.

Bronco took a bite of his sandwich. It wasn't as tasty as he remembered ham sandwiches to be. Then through the window, he saw the outline of Preacher dismounting and tying his reins at the hitching rail. He came in looking in good humor. He shook Tom's hand and congratulated him on his recovery and jail release. Tom thanked them all for clearing him of the army's charges. Bronco took another bite and waited to see if Sarah would bring the other men's orders.

52

Pappy left the Pepper Street bakery shop and returned to his rented room via a path between two houses. He walked around the back corner and reached to open the door when he noticed the horse tied one building south behind Miss Emmy's house. He entered his room, placed his baked goods under a bowl to keep out any critters, and then backed out to the porch. There was no mistaking this horse. He had seen a black Kladruber only once before in his entire life. There was no missing the horse's Roman nose, army rig, or the recent Union army issue saddle. The last time he had seen it, John Coates had been sitting astride, twitching like he had fleas! Pappy reentered his room and fetched his forty-four.

Sheriff Beckett watched Tom and Madison walk out of his jail with relief. He was thrilled on two fronts. First, his friend, Tom Jones, was out of jail and a free man. Second, the sheriff declared to himself and anyone else who would listen that freedom should have been the case all along. "Leopards don't change their spots!" he had told Tom. "I knew you were innocent all along, but that blasted major made me hold you anyway. So it is sure good to open this door."

On another front, he was glad to be down to only three prisoners. The major had promised to send a wagon and guards to pick up Corporal Yates and the two men from the outlaw bunch who tried to rob the payroll wagon. It seemed to the lawman that the three could have been in any of the dozen wagons that had already left the area.

The sheriff tilted back in his chair on the front porch, congratulating himself on having an empty jail in a few days, when two men in a wagon stopped out front. They looked like the Yocum boys who had a small shack north of town.

"Sheriff, we got two bodies in the back," Booger, the oldest, announced. "They have been dead a couple of days, by my guess. They was shot. The older one is only about half there. It looks like he was blasted with a shotgun."

"You don't say." Sheriff Beckett stood and took a step toward the wagon. He could see the rough outline of the bodies covered by a tarp. "So, who are they?"

"Well, one is old man Rufus Coates, and the other is his son, Dooley."

"I'll be. Just yesterday, Zac Coates turned up dead out of Carson's Junction. He was part of a gang that tried to hold up the Union payroll. The two fellas inside say John Coates was the ringleader. I wonder if he is responsible for these two. If so, he's probably out of the county by now. Where did you find them?"

"They was buried out in Rufus' barn. We stopped by to buy some of the old man's moonshine. Nobody came out when we hollered, so we checked in the barn. All the old man's dogs were gathered around a hole they had dug in there."

"You don't say." Beckett took off his hat and rubbed his scalp

"So, Sheriff, what do we do with these?"

"Take them down to Doc's. He'll take them if you tell him I sent you."

Jimmy Jordon's mother, Wanda, passed out when Jimmy opened the kitchen door and appeared at her elbow, silent and haggard-looking. His two younger sisters were in school. He hurriedly fetched a wet rag, gently touched her brow, and brought her back. When Wanda awakened, she gazed up and touched his face gently before she gathered herself and ran to the porch to ring the dinner bell. Jimmy's father, Cal, out riding the fence line, heard the alarm. He came galloping toward the house, ready for trouble. When she returned, Wanda pulled her son's head to her bosom and stroked his dirty hair, and kissed his dirty face. The tears streamed down her pale cheeks, and she almost fainted again.

Then Cal Jordon burst in, saw who it was, and thrust his gun back in his holster. He grabbed his boy from behind and swung him around in a circle. Then, he turned his son around, and the parents silently checked him for two arms and two legs and cried when they were all there. His mother started pumping water from the well until the big galvanized washtub was half full. She heated every pan she could get on the stove at one time and finished filling the tub with the steaming water. Then she shooed her husband out, so Jimmy could wash up and shave and become part of civilized society again.

Jimmy didn't luxuriate too long. He had completed only half of his mission. He was so thin that his best clothes hung limply on his body. But he was home! Cal had the wagon hitched and ready when Jimmy arrived on the porch. His mother promised that she'd have him fattened up in no time. Or wouldn't that be Sarah's job? They all laughed and hugged him and sent their love to Sarah. He whistled at the white-blazed horse, Moon, and started off briskly toward town.

Mrs. Sarah Jordon watched her Aunt Emmy return to the kitchen. The old lady had solemnly delivered Bronco's sandwich and then been sidetracked to warmly greeted Tom and Madison Jones. Emmy was still smiling when she turned away from them, but her eyes drilled right through Sarah when she entered the kitchen. Her lips pressed together to show she didn't trust herself to speak. Sarah didn't trust herself, either. She felt in her pocket for the letter from Jimmy. It was missing. She had intended to let Bronco read it rather than explain its contents to him. She checked her bosom as a last resort before she remembered she had left the letter on the vanity in her bedroom. The idea of denying her feelings for Bronco or Jimmy hurt her heart. She hated indecision in herself and others. One of the things that both Jimmy and Bronco exhibited was decisiveness. Now she disparaged herself for this additional moral shortcoming.

Sarah wrote a short note for Bronco on an order pad. She folded it and handed it to Aunt Emmy. "I'm going home for a bit. Would you give this to Bronco when he is through eating?"

Aunt Emmy took the note like it was a dead mouse. But then, she pressed her lips tighter together and nodded.

Sarah started for the dining room, then thought better of it and went out the back door into the alley. She needed to get to Jimmy's letter and time to compose what she would say!

Sarah walked two blocks down the alley and was surprised to see Pappy standing behind Aunt Emmy's house with his gun in hand. He saw her coming and silenced her with a finger to his lips. He led her away from the back door toward the corner of the house.

"I think John Coates is in there," he said. "That's the horse I saw him riding yesterday."

Sarah looked at the revolver and up into Pappy's eyes. "I'll go get help."

"That's a good idea." Pappy ran his finger over his mustache. "I'll see that he doesn't get away." Then the back door swung open.

Bronco finished his sandwich and drank the last of his coffee. Sarge, Preacher, and Tom were hashing over the events at Carson's Junction. He waited. Sarah did not reappear in the dining area. Bronco stared out the window at the sunny street. He was about to rise and head for the kitchen when Miss Emmy appeared and handed him a folded piece of paper. He opened it hurriedly and read the words with relief. The message was short.

Mister Brumley, can you meet me on the porch?

Bronco grinned. His eyes glanced around the table. He refolded the paper and put it in his pocket. Then, he rose, and the conversation stopped. The other men looked at him expectantly.

"I've got to go see Miss Sarah," he said.

"You sure?" Sarge's face was expressionless.

"We're headed out to the farm in a minute," Preacher added.

"Yep!" Bronco shoved back his chair." You go ahead." He walked to the door, donned his cap, looked right and left, and headed down the street. The light shimmered from the noonday sun. He didn't notice a woman crossing the street bearing a basket on her arm nor the redheaded man who shouldered around him on the walk. He did not pay any attention to two wagons moving at a good clip far down the street on his right. Bronco didn't notice anything about the world around him. His heart was pounding.

53

"Hold it!" John Coates stepped out of the backdoor of Aunt Emmy's house. He had his gun trained on Sarah Jordon. "Put the gun down, old man, or I'll plug her where she stands." He motioned to Pappy, who had his gun trained on him. Coates pulled the hammer back. "I'm not joking."

Pappy looked at Sarah, then glanced around the alley for alternatives. At ten feet, Sarah was an excellent target. Pappy knew that even if he plugged Coates, the man might be able to follow through on his threat. Pappy did not doubt that the killer was serious. Nervously he bent and let the gun fall a few inches to the ground.

"Okay. Now you two march in here." Coates pushed the door open and waved them inside. Pappy looked at Sarah and grimaced.

Sarah preceded the two men, then stopped in the parlor and turned toward Coates. Her voice sounded shaky. "Why are you here?"

"We're here to celebrate the passing of Bronco Brumley," Coates said with a sneer.

"Bronco isn't here." Sarah waved her hands to encompass the interior of the house. She looked from Coates to Pappy.

"But he will be, won't he?" Coates said. "I've noticed he manages to show up anywhere you are."

Sarah looked at Pappy with an expression of dread. Coates had no idea of the truth of his prediction. Bronco was not only sure to show up eventually; he was sure to show up in the next ten minutes because she had invited him!

"Why are you doing this?" Sarah challenged the hostile motives of John Coates even though she already knew the answer.

Coates motioned them to take the two chairs. He holstered his gun but kept his hand at the ready. Once they were seated, he sat on the sofa facing them. Sarah sat facing the front door. Pappy had dropped to a chair to her left.

"I took a look at the letter you got from Jimmy," Coates said to make conversation.

"I didn't know you could read," Pappy mumbled.

"Yes, old man, I can read well enough to know Jimmy Jordon, this woman's legal husband is headed this way from North Carolina thinking she's waiting for him." He looked at Sarah and snarled. "But you aren't, are you!"

"I told you about Jimmy on the road," Pappy said. "You didn't have to read the letter."

Sarah looked down. Her face burned. To be lectured by this lowest of men was humiliating. Panic rose in her. Her fear was matched with an equal measure of resolve that Bronco would not die on her account.

"How is any of this any business of yours?" Pappy growled. He was itching to have his gun back. He pictured it lying in the dust outside the back door.

"It's not. My business is with Bronco and his two friends. They hit me in the head, killed my two cousins, and stole our horses. A few things on that list are hanging offenses, but they are parading around town like they own it." Coates' voice rose with self-righteousness.

Through the curtain, Sarah saw movement beyond the door. Her feeling of dread went up a notch. It was Bronco approaching. Coates saw her reaction and also looked out.

"Well, here's our boy now!" He pulled his weapon and waved at Sarah. "You go to the front door and invite him in. If you so much as look cross-eyed, I'll plug all three of you."

Sarah got unsteadily to her feet. She moved to the door and waited for the knock. Coates moved behind her and concealed himself on the left side of the door so she could open it unimpeded. They all heard Bronco's big shoes stomping on the porch. Then the knock. Sarah made a strangled sound with her intake of breath and turned the knob. Bronco grinned down at her, bright-eyed and eager. She saw his face, and his smile rushed straight to her heart. His voice was strong, clear, and sure.

"Miss Sarah!" He reached for the handle and began to pull the screen door toward himself. The girl had opened the door a crack. Her eyes closed for a second. Her throat contracted, her lips parted as if to speak, but no words came.

Instead, Sarah's shrill and overwhelming scream rocked Bronco back on his heels. Sarah shrieked with all the energy she could muster. She grabbed the door with both hands and swung it open, with all of her diminutive being behind it, battering John Coates' face and chest. Sarah knew that she could not let evil triumph. She could not watch this good man die right in front of her. No matter the cost, she would not allow it!

It was the scream that defeated John Coates. It was the scream of a wild, agonized animal in the dark, forbidding jungle. For two heartbeats, he stood paralyzed, unable to react. Frozen in place, he could neither move out of the way of the driven door nor could he slow it. His body slammed against the wall, driven by the door, his hat flew off, and his gun hand crashed against the wood trim of the adjacent doorway. With the painful impact, Coates' hand opened. The gun flew across the room and landed in front of Pappy Jordon.

Pappy was as frozen in place as Coates. He watched the gun tumble through the air. It hit the floor and spun clockwise as it slid and nestled at his feet. He looked at it dumbly. Pappy's eyes moved up to Sarah through his eyebrows. She was still pushing with all her strength against the door to hold Coates in captivity. Never had Pappy felt his age more keenly than when he bent to take possession of the firearm. It seemed to him that every muscle screamed, every joint rasped. He leaned down, grasped the gun, and straightened just as Coates recovered, and the door rebounded to shove Sarah backward as though she had suddenly become weightless.

Pappy held the gun in both hands and thumbed the hammer. Any pressure would send a bullet flying with lethal force into Coates' chest. Flinging the door away, John leaped toward Pappy. But seeing the six-gun, he did not complete his attack. Instead, he hung for an instant, motionless, straightening and rocking back on his heels. John realized midstride that he was too late. He lurched to a stop within inches of the end of the barrel, his hands high in the air like a great cat about to leap on its prey.

Pappy took his left hand away from the gun and used it to push himself off the chair. The force of the door threw Sarah to her knees. Bronco pushed the door open and grabbed her arm.

"Bronco, put your gun on this varmint," Pappy cried.

With Sarah clutching his left arm trying to stand, Bronco pulled his gun and stuck it in Coates' ribs. Pappy thrust Coates' gun under his belt. He hurriedly glanced around the room and grabbed an apron hanging on the back of a kitchen chair. Then, pulling his knife, he cut off the strings to make four turns around to tie Coates' wrists together behind his back.

"I'm taking this worthless shit to jail. Beg your pardon, Darlin." Pappy edged Coates around toward the back door. He meant to remove John Coates from the room as quickly as possible, for witnessing Coates' readiness to kill the two young people in cold blood repelled him to his core. Pappy opened the back door, followed Coates down the steps to the ground, and retrieved and holstered his gun. He pushed Coates into the alley and started their march toward the jail.

<h1 style="text-align:center">54</h1>

It was silent for a moment except for Sarah's labored breath after Pappy and John Coats passed through the back door. Sarah hugged her arms around herself. Bronco moved to try and assure her, but she evaded him and pushed open the screen to the front porch.

Bronco stepped to one side for her. There seemed to be lighting in the air. Sarah dropped into the swing, and Bronco followed. She knew what was coming would be momentous. Bronco, too, could feel the tension. He started to speak, but Sarah touched his chest to quiet him.

"Mister Brumley, I can't see you anymore." She looked into his eyes and then down the street and back. All the words of explanation she had contemplated added up to that one simple statement. She pressed her lips together and watched him absorb her words.

Bronco was silent. It took a couple of seconds for him to comprehend her meaning. He followed her gaze while those seconds ticked off. Then he felt like a bull steer was suddenly sitting on his chest. Sarah continued resolutely.

"I got a letter from my husband yesterday. He wrote it four weeks ago in North Carolina. He is coming home." There, she had said it. The facts lay there between them now. Bronco, though stunned, heard the pain in her voice and responded to that.

"But I love you. You said you love me." Bronco touched her hand. She pulled away gently, regretfully. Sarah looked into his eyes.

"When I said those words, I was upset that you were in jail. I thought a firing squad might shoot you. I thought Jimmy was dead."

"Did you mean it?"

She seemed to weaken a little. "Of course, I meant it when I said it, but I am married to Jimmy." Her tone was imploring as if willing him to understand.

"But do you love Jimmy?"

"Yes."

"And you love me?" He looked intently into her eyes.

"I thought so."

"Well, you are in a pickle, aren't you?" He waited while her eyes darted away and then returned. "Cause I only love you."

Without realizing it, her address to him became familiar. "Bronco, if I keep seeing you now that I know Jimmy is alive, I could end up leaving him. I'd break my marriage vows. I can't do that." Bronco brightened for a moment. She had called him Bronco only once before when she had said those cherished words in the jail. That moment again flashed before him before his eyes darkened.

"So, you're saying you love me enough to leave your husband if you keep seeing me, but you don't love me enough to want me to keep coming around?"

Her eyes averted again. "I guess so."

"You know this would be easier for both of us if you just told me outright that you love Jimmy and don't love me." He looked at her gravely, and she shrank back a little as the words hit home. "Cause I'm gone if you say you don't love me. I don't hang around if I'm not wanted."

"I never was any good at saying goodbye." The earnestness of her voice cut him like a knife. "Even when I was a little girl, I cried whenever company left. It just seemed so sad."

Bronco considered her words for a moment. "My grandpa always said, believe what people do, not what they say." He shifted away and swiped the moisture from his eyes. He stood, took two steps down from the porch, and looked at Sarah over his shoulder. The finality of the moment seemed to sweep over both of them.

"Well, you know the best part? The three of us are going west in the morning. So I guess your problem is solved."

Bronco took the last step down into the street. He walked toward the far corner to turn right up Main Street. He did not look back again.

A wagon with a young man about his age made the turn at that moment, going in the opposite direction. His suit hung on him like a potato sack. He flashed a grin when he spotted a pretty girl sitting on a porch.

Tom sat in the saddle, impatient to move on. Preacher filled his canteen while his horse drank. Sarge looked back toward the road they had just traveled.

"Expecting something?" Preacher asked.

"Well, kind of." Sarge pointed. "Isn't there a rider out in front of that dust back there?"

"Appears to be." Preacher followed the movement for a moment, then capped his canteen and took the second one from the saddle. He knelt, and water gurgled in for a moment. He stood and mounted.

"We didn't leave town owing anybody, did we?" Sarge said with a smile.

"Don't think so," Preacher grinned.

"Hellbent for leather. If the war wasn't over, I'd guess it was a leg case," Sarge said.

"That is so." Preacher hung the second canteen and leaned into the saddle.

"Damn, my hide. I think that's Bronco's Pinto!" Sarge said.

"If it is, that was one short engagement." Preacher shielded his eyes against the sun.

The rider arrived in a cloud of dust, jumped off his horse, and charged the stream. Off came the Union cap. Bronco dunked his head twice. Water splashed over his shoulders, and he shook the curly tousled hair.

Preacher looked at Sarge and raised his eyebrows. Sarge nodded, and they started to dismount.

As he surfaced, Bronco saw his friends' movement from the corner of his eye. He remembered the dunking he had received at their hands at the little stream outside Sweetwater. Before their boots touched the ground, Bronco quickly drew his forty-four and twisted around.

"Don't even think about it!" he growled. Bronco pushed to his feet. His ears burned. He was determined not to show his hurt and humiliation.

"Well?" Preacher laughed, slapping his leg.

"Women!" Bronco said. "That's all I'll say." He put his brogan in the stirrup, lifted himself into the saddle, and wiped the moisture from his face. "Let's go!"

THE END

About the Author

Charles Reed is the author of four other works. *Mission in Harlon County* (The second novel of The Pursuers Series), *Justice in Harlon County* (The third novel in the Pursuers Series), *Tracks to Harlon County, Twenty-One Tales of Life and Adventure,* an anthology of stories about the *Pursuers* characters' earlier days, and *The Long Caper,* a time travel adventure novel to the Harlon County of 1865.

Charles was born in Saint Louis, Missouri. Because of his father's occupation, he often moved throughout his early years. During that period, he attended twelve schools in four states. When not writing, Charles is an avid reader of biography, history, and historical fiction,

Charles has run three marathons, three half marathons, numerous *Tulsa Runs* and ridden his bicycle in the *Free-Wheel across Oklahoma* six times. In addition, Charles has traveled in Europe, the Orient, South America, the United States, and Canada. His first flight was to Southeast Asia, where he served in the infantry with the 101st Airborne Division. Finally, Charles is a "throw the seed down and see what happens" gardener.